## 'My life was devoted to my husband, my lord.'

'Come now, lady. Who would know if you were to share my lonely bed for a while? Send your man away on some pretext. No one pays any heed to the gossip of servants, as long as they cannot give the evidence of their own eyes. And I dare say that it wouldn't be the first time that you had spoiled yourself with a little idle pleasure...'

At that moment she became very conscious of her loneliness. The animal attraction of Emil Selest's warm, taut body had taunted her before, but this was the first time that Elena had admitted such a longing to herself. He had put her guilty fantasies into words and it brought deep shame.

'I have told you, my lord. My husband comes—came first and last with me.'

Born in Somerset, Polly Forrester has been writing for as long as she can remember.

Her working career began with twelve years as a humble office clerk. Escaping to combine her love of history and the countryside in a new career as a writer, her work is used by several national publications.

She now lives in the depths of rural Gloucestershire with a cat, a dog and a flock of very eccentric poultry.

Previous Title

KNIGHT'S PAWN

# JEWEL
# UNDER SIEGE

Polly Forrester

*First published in Great Britain 1990*
*by Mills & Boon Limited*

© Polly Forrester 1990

*Australian copyright 1990*
*Philippine copyright 1990*
*This edition 1990*

ISBN 0 263 77004 4

*Masquerade is a trademark published by*
*Mills & Boon Limited, Eton House,*
*18–24 Paradise Road, Richmond, Surrey, TW9 1SR.*

*Set in Times Roman 10 on 10¼ pt.*
04-9010-79611 C

*Made and printed in Great Britain*

# CHAPTER ONE

AT LEAST the rain had stopped. There was nothing worse than a wet Easter, but now the sky was clearing nicely. Elena swept a wrap about her shoulders and slipped out into the garden through the dining-room doors.

Ascony would murder her if he found that she had gone out of the house alone with the city so tense. Elena could imagine the scene he would make, and laughed. Ascony was far too keen on rumour and gossip. What danger could there be here, in her own garden?

Everyone had been living with fear and dismay throughout the long winter months. Try as she might Elena could not keep her nerves taut any longer. She simply trusted that the great city walls of Constantinople would keep them all safe, and got on with her life.

Business at the glassworks was good and this evening little Milo was already fast asleep upstairs, despite a constant hum from the rough and ready multitude camped outside the city walls.

The 'Crusaders' as they called themselves were on their way to free the pilgrim routes of the Holy Land. Unfortunately, once the Emperor of Constantinople had seen the sort of men that had been sent to embark from his city port, he got cold feet. He had ordered that the city gates be slammed shut in their faces.

It was bad enough having Seljuk Turks terrorising the area, but the Pope's Crusaders didn't seem much better themselves. They had funny ways. The Emperor had taken one in after a shipwreck last autumn, and if rumours were true it was no wonder he had been put off entertaining the rest. People said that the rescued Crusader wouldn't take a bath, and ate with his hands. And he was supposed to be the King of France's brother.

Elena stopped to look into the black marble water-courses that ornamented her garden. Once she had found a frog there, but not today. Khar kept everything too neat and tidy for that.

The wall-trained apricots and peaches were wreathed with blushing blossom. Elena wondered if Khar would mind if she snipped a few of the polished twigs for the house. A good tuft of little irises grew behind the arbour. In pebbles and moss with fruit blossom they would make a pretty arrangement come Easter Day.

Her mind full of flowers, Elena did not notice the bushes behind the arbour trembling until it was too late.

The attack was sudden. A hand had clamped over her mouth before she could scream and in an instant Elena was dragged behind the arbour and hidden from the house.

The man who held her muttered a few words in a foreign tongue. He was breathing quickly, his pulse racing against her cheek. Elena could not move—fear had paralysed her muscles and all she could do was wait for the unspeakable horror that was about to befall her.

Nothing happened for a long while. Terrified by the overpowering smell of leatherwork and metal dressing, Elena lay still in her captor's grasp. Finally he managed a little breathless French.

'Keep quiet. I won't hurt you. Do you understand?'

When she nodded but did not struggle or try to cry out his fingers began to relax from her mouth. He seemed as relieved to let go of Elena as she was to free herself, and she saw that grabbing her had sapped much of his failing strength.

She faced her attacker with icy disdain. 'What do you want of me?'

He was a tall young man, painfully thin with features worn by famine and war. Leaning heavily against the garden wall, he pressed one hand to his left thigh. Hopelessness hunted his expression and the dark eyes were nervous.

'I need assistance, and I have no Greek.'

The young man continued in French. He looked at Elena, knowing that punishment for his trespass would be severe. She did not need to be told where he had come from. The other side of the city wall. The Crusader camp.

'You came to thieve,' Elena said shortly. 'Thieving and trespassing, when we were given assurances that your people had come to Constantinople to help our empire.'

'We need food. Your people are starving us to death. For months they have kept us waiting outside the city. Now your Emperor has cut down our meagre supplies even further.'

Elena drew herself up to her full height. No unshaven ragamuffin was going to come into her garden and start ordering the facts to suit himself. 'Only because your leaders will not promise to obey every word of the Emperor Alexius.'

'I'm starving and injured,' the young man burst out at last, 'I need help, not politics!'

He was in a bad way. His left leg was twisted and could not bear his weight. As Elena watched he flagged against the garden wall, trying to ride out the pain.

'Nothing to eat for three days...managed the city wall, but your garden wall was too much. Mossy and wet... I slipped...'

'Nothing to eat for three days? Not even water?' Elena was horrified.

'Rain. That's all.' He swayed unsteadily. 'Food? A crust—anything. Then I'll go. I won't make any trouble...'

Elena looked him up and down carefully. His clothes were sodden wet and clinging to his gaunt frame. Mud buttered his cracked and shabby boots and his teeth chattered convulsively in a chilling breeze off the sea.

'Does anyone else know that you have come here?'

He shook his head sharply. 'Bad enough that one should be caught, without dragging in friends.'

Gone was the desperate terrorist reduced to snatching at innocent women. More like a child caught stealing apples, Elena thought, with his downcast face and sudden loss of bravado. Although she was cross at the fright he had given her, Elena couldn't help but feel a little sorry for him.

'You will be quite safe here for a moment or two. I shall fetch Ascony, and he can sort out what must be done.'

The young Crusader put one hand to his brow. Any resistance was out of the question in his condition. With a hopeless gesture he withdrew a knife from his belt and thrust it at Elena, handle first.

'Thank you—I think.' Elena accepted the offering warily, holding it at arm's length.

There would be little danger that the young man's arrival had been seen. On one side of Elena's house was the city wall. Beyond this was a clear view over nothing very much to the waters of the Golden Horn. On the other side, Elena's only immediate neighbour was spending Lent and Easter away from home with friends.

Ascony was enjoying a joke in the kitchens while the Khars prepared Elena's dinner. One look at her and the knife she carried brought them all to their feet.

'Upstairs, lady. If there is to be trouble, then Khar and I will manage.'

The thin, mercurial Ascony and his lardy friend Khar would be too much of a good thing with the scent of battle in their nostrils. Elena waved away their directions and drew Ascony aside. Explaining the situation, she ignored his increasing fury and laid out the problem as she saw it.

'We won't be able to take him out of the front door. The city is too nervous. He'll have to go back the way he came, by darkness, after we've patched him up.'

'It cannot be safe, lady.' Ascony flared his nostrils in a fine fit of pique. 'All these men—they are exactly the same. He means no good, and will be trouble from the first instant. I don't know how you can expect me to deal with such a dreadful state of affairs.'

'You'll manage.' Elena smiled sweetly. 'You always do.'

She took Ascony's arm and escorted him out through the dining-room. He seethed silently, but it cut no ice with Elena. When they reached the arbour, Ascony began to drop back a little.

'I should have brought my sword, lady.'

'If it's practice that you want, try your luck on the other side of the wall with the real Crusaders. I don't think our friend here will put up much resistance.'

Ascony straightened his robe, cleared his throat and marched behind the arbour. For a moment there was silence, then came a savage whisper.

'What shall I say to the dog, lady?'

Elena followed him behind the arbour at this, and a sorry sight met her eyes. The Crusader had flattened himself against the garden wall. His eyes were shut and he was breathing rapidly like a frail gaze-hound that had overreached itself.

'Be quick,' he said softly, and Elena realised that he was fingering the blackened rosary about his neck. In a score of years her own Milo might be in such a position. Who was this Crusader but some other mother's son? Elena went forward and laid her hand upon his shoulder.

'It's all right. He's not going to kill you, although goodness knows you might deserve it. We only wish to help. What is your name?'

The young man opened his eyes, which showed up large and hunted in his thin face.

'Emil... Selest... From the Moselle...'

'And I am Elena Rethel, Emil.'

In reply Selest winced as he tried to move.

'Rethel...? That—is not a Greek name, lady...'

'My husband came from France on a pilgrimage here, and settled. That is the essence of a very long story.' She smiled and pushed the damp dark hair back from his face. 'Ascony can fill you in on the gossip while he's doing something for your leg.' Elena stood back to give her servant room. 'I'm sure he'll find something that

will have you as right as rain in a moment. Leave it to
Ascony. He'll carry you in and make you comfortable——'

'No!'

So much foreboding spilled from the word that Elena
put her hand back to comfort Selest. He was glowering
at her now, but with a failing defiance.

'We've been told—what they do to the men in
Constantinople. It's not happening to me.'

Elena was puzzled and shook her head. It took Selest
a little while to find sufficient words, and when he did
speak Elena could barely make out his embarrassed
mutter.

'I'm not being gelded.'

Elena laughed at his agitated expression. 'It isn't a
condition of entry to the city, Emil.'

'They've done it to King Phillip's brother, the Lord
Hugh of Vermandois——'

'Oh, don't be so ridiculous. Of course they haven't.'

'That's why they keep him hidden away in the palace.
Nobody outside has seen hide or hair of him since he
was "rescued," and that was months ago.'

'He is an honoured guest of our dear Emperor.'

'Huh.'

Selest was determined that he was right. He knew what
went on in these places. Everybody knew—it was
common knowledge out in the camp—and it wasn't going
to happen to him. He intended to leave with everything
that he had arrived with, and said so. As Ascony inspected and prodded at his injured leg, Selest kept up
an ever-weakening tirade against the decadence and
moral decay of his hosts.

'Noisy pup, isn't he?' Ascony said when interest in
the case had overcome his annoyance.

'Then I hope our manners are better, Ascony,' Elena
replied in French. 'From now on there is to be no Greek
spoken in front of our guest, as he does not understand.'

Emil Selest stopped complaining. He looked at Elena warily, then at Ascony who now hauled him up ready to be helped inside.

'Thank you,' he said with stiff formality. 'It will be a great help to me if you and your husband will converse in my language.'

'Oh, Ascony isn't my husband, he's a——' Elena began with a laugh, then thought that what Emil Selest didn't realise wouldn't upset him. 'He looks after me. My husband died some time ago. Ascony is the most senior member of my household staff.'

Ascony grinned broadly, took Emil's weight and risked a quick question in his native language.

'Shall I tell him what I am, lady?'

'You dare,' Elena threatened. 'We don't want to frighten him to death, on top of everything else.'

She apologised to Emil for the lapse, but he was too curled up with pain to pay much attention. At last Khar had to be called to help. Between them all they man-handled the young knight through the garden doors and into the dining-room.

'He must have landed with his leg beneath him.' Ascony said as they laid Selest down on a soft couch. 'A dislocation of the left knee certainly, and it feels as though the ankle may be damaged, too. I'm afraid you'll have to forget all thoughts of throwing him back over the wall for quite some time, lady.'

Selest moaned in bitter dismay. 'I shall be left behind when they move on——'

'No chance of that happening yet, worse luck. And what about us?' Elena looked around in distraction. 'The Emperor has forbidden entry to you Crusaders, and now here we are harbouring one under our very roof!'

Ascony began to strip away Selest's tattered clothes. Despite the cold and the pain and Elena's predicament the young soldier could think of only one thing.

'Hamelin—my friend—he'll be worried when I'm not back at camp tonight...'

'I'll get a message to him.'

'No!' Emil bit his lip as Ascony started to cut away his left boot. 'It's too dangerous . . . if either side realises that there's yet another hostage held here they'll tear the city apart . . .'

Elena comforted him quietly. The fragments of ancient clothing that Ascony was removing from the patient gave her no such comfort herself.

'Emil must have a bath before he comes any further into this house, Ascony. See to his injuries first, but I'm not having him in any of my guest rooms in that state. Arrange it while I fetch him something clean to wear. Only when he is clean does he get anything to eat.'

Selest's face crumpled as Ascony worked the tattered clothing down past waist-level. With a chance to show off his calm efficiency the Senior Member Of The Household Staff was in his element.

'Indeed, lady. We shall start as we mean to go on, young Emil. In this household, the Lady Elena's word is law. Remember that, and you and I should get on very well together.'

'Then I have a similar request.' Selest gasped as Ascony finished exposing the injured limb. 'I will be addressed with the formality that is my due.'

Ascony looked at Elena and pulled a face, but she shook her head to forestall his sharp tongue.

'Of course, my lord.'

With a gracious nod Elena left them to it, but she was not happy. This Emil Selest might be all right while he was injured, and not at fighting strength. What would happen when he recovered? If he didn't try to fight his way out, his friends might stage a rescue attempt.

Elena's concern was all for her son. Poor little Milo. She would do anything to keep him safe. For the Crusader to find out about this one weakness of hers would give him power over the whole household. Milo must be kept out of his way at all costs.

Her town house was square, everything except the front and garden doors opening on to a cool arcaded corridor that ran around a gravelled courtyard. This was open to the sky, and a small fountain leapt and chattered within it among a filigree of greenery. Hardly the sort of establishment to hide a fugitive from the Emperor, Elena thought.

Even a fugitive with such dark, haunting eyes. She frowned at the idea and went on. At the top of the wide gilt and marble stairway, she entered the first great bedchamber on the left.

It seemed strange to think that Henry had been dead for over two years. They had told Ascony to clear the house for her then, but he hadn't. Not entirely. There was still this room that Elena could come to from time to time.

She opened a linen chest and took out three towels and two robes. Upon a red robe she fancied—only for a minute—that some half-remembered fragrance lingered. Refolding it carefully, she put that one back.

There was a mirror of polished bronze in the room and Elena went towards it. Her reflection was mixed up and scattered in light from the one lamp that she had lit. Memories and fantasies had all become mixed up too, long ago. Once there had been a kind man who had loved her dearly, but now he was gone.

It was a little while before Elena emerged from the bedchamber. An argument down in the marble hall alerted her and she hurried down to restrain Ascony.

'I told you he would be trouble, lady...'

'Quiet.' Elena looked at Selest for an explanation. He was naked now and clinging to the gilded banister for support. Swaying at the foot of the stairs, he looked up sullenly as she spoke. 'What trouble are you causing now, my lord?'

'He's trying to take me over to that room and I'm not going, lady.'

'To the bath?' Elena shook out one of the thick towels she carried and wrapped it about Selest's narrow waist. 'It will be a bit different from what you're used to, I expect. That's all.'

Emil unwound one hand from the banister and pressed it to his thigh again. Black and purple bruises were already staining his left leg. He looked very sick and ill, and most of all uncertain. Elena tried her best to reassure him.

'My husband told me all about France, my lord. They do many things very differently there, but even he was fond of our baths. He had one built here especially. All you have to do is stand in that little room next to the kitchen. The heat will cleanse your skin, then Ascony will soap and rinse you. It won't hurt!'

Selest looked at her doubtfully, his skin rippled by shivers.

'Then can I have food?'

'As much as you can eat.'

This seemed to satisfy him and he allowed Ascony to support him to the bath house. Elena went into the best guest room and started to rearrange the furniture.

Khar could light a fire. Elena never bothered to ask for one normally, but she did love to see flickering firelight dancing over the porcelain and cutlery on grand occasions. Elena determined to make this a grand occasion. Company was a rare treat these days.

It was too dark to fetch flowers for the table now, but instead Elena laid out her best white tablecloth. The Troubles had stopped her family travelling in to spend Lent and Easter with her and even a Crusader would be better company than nothing.

She drew two soft pink couches up to the low table. It felt strange to be dining in the company of a lone man after such a long time. She hoped that Selest would have stories from France the equal of those that Henry used to tell her—princes, demons and changeling children. She heard so little news nowadays. In return Selest might be pleased and amazed at the little luxuries of Byzantine life, as Henry had been so many years before.

Ascony and Khar carried Selest into the room, none the worse for his new experience. He was clean, but very pale. A shave and haircut had done much to reveal faint remnants of striking good looks. Without knowing why, Elena felt a pang of strange uncertainty.

Before Ascony sat Selest down on the couch, Elena made to pass one of Henry's silk robes about the Crusader's shoulders.

'I'm not wearing that.' Selest had recovered sufficiently to make no bones about the matter.

'If you don't, then there will be no dinner.'

His wasted body showed that there was no defence. While Ascony bound up his knee and ankle, Elena arranged the folds of the robe around him.

'Women's clothes,' he muttered darkly, looking about with unease at the opulent guest room.

'Not at all. Silk is quite the best fabric for the climate. There is a second robe here should you want it, and also furs and cushions about if you still feel the cold.'

The room had grown gloomy. Elena called for lamps and they arrived just before the silver dinner trays. While Khar set the lamps about the room and laid a fire, Ascony placed the largest tray before Selest and removed its figured silver dome.

A gale of lemon scent billowed up from soft mountains of steamed rice. With an exclamation of delight Selest dug both hands in and started eating without delay.

Ascony was so horrified that he was quite robbed of speech. The Crusader did not notice. He was too busy shovelling great inroads through the fluffy rice.

Elena had no intention of embarrassing her guest, but was worried that too much food so suddenly might harm him. She leaned towards him and spoke quietly.

'My lord——'

He stopped. As he looked up he seemed to realise that the rough manners of a soldier were for outside the city gates. They had no place in this polite society.

'Oh...sorry...' It was the first genuine allowance he had made to his hosts. 'I was so hungry, I didn't think.'

With sarcastic gallantry he pushed the tray towards Elena, but she told him to continue.

'Don't worry about it. There is no time for manners when a man is dying of hunger.'

'Who is to say that his manners are any better in the ordinary run of things?' Ascony sneered. 'He was surly and unhelpful when I was bathing him, lady. And now he puts on this sort of exhibition——'

'What's the matter? Never seen a man eat before?' Selest looked as though he would be up from the couch at any retort, despite his injuries. Elena waded in.

'Our guest is from a far country, Ascony—you know very well that their customs are different from ours. Khar—fetch a basin of water and some extra napkins. You, Ascony,' Elena said in a voice cold with meaning, 'will take your dinner in the kitchen. Now.'

Ascony swept off, silk gown rustling furiously. Khar finished with the fire and after bringing warm water and napkins left the two diners alone. Elena gestured to the silver dishes in front of them.

'Don't tell me you've lost your appetite, my lord.' She uncovered two of the smaller dishes, one containing peas and beans, the other asparagus and mushrooms. 'Try something else.'

'I regret causing offence, lady.' The first ravenous disregard for manners had left him, and he was distantly formal.

'Don't worry about it. Eat up—I'm only sorry it isn't more substantial fare. The meat is all put by for Easter Day.'

Elena helped herself to a plateful of rice from the half-empty salver in front of Selest. Adding a selection of the other vegetables, she sprinkled chopped nuts over the top, then, slipping off her lacy sandals, curled up on her couch, much to Selest's amazement.

'What sort of a place is it where women lie down to eat?'

'Not only the women, my lord. Everyone likes to take their ease as well as their time over an enjoyable meal.'

He stared at her wriggling bare toes with uncertainty. Elena half remembered something Henry had said—that in Frankish lands only women who were no better than they should be went without stockings. She pulled the folds of her flimsy overtunic down to cover her feet.

'If only I hadn't been so stupid——' Selest sighed, looking at the array of food.

'You'll be all right here. Better off than your fellows, I dare say.'

Hunger overcame the Crusader once more and he tried a few of the vegetable dishes. His manner now was less abrasive than regretful.

'Did you ever send word to Hamelin?'

'No. I expect he thinks you've found yourself a girl-friend, or something.'

Selest was shocked to the core. 'And leave him wounded, on his own in the cold?'

That put a different light on matters. Elena poured them each a glass of orange juice and placed the clear pitcher down carefully. Selest was torn between distaste at her suggestion and wonderment at vessels seemingly made out of rigid bubbles. Elena saw him try the glass with his teeth when he thought she wasn't looking.

'Is your friend badly hurt, my lord?'

'I don't know.' Selest shook his head, dark eyes veiled. 'We went out to help with a bit of a sortie——'

'A wicked raiding party,' Elena interrupted quickly. 'And not the first.'

Selest continued, plucking at his borrowed robe with distraction. 'That is the only way we can find enough food to live. Hamelin got hit in the face by the corner of someone's jacket. It looked all right, but then his eye started to close up. He doesn't complain, but it looks dreadful.'

'A jacket with metal rings, like the one that you were almost wearing?'

He nodded. Firelight hollowed his face, painting deep lines of care about his eyes. At that moment he looked as old as Methuselah, but Elena guessed his real age to be less than thirty.

'We wear the ringed jackets all the time, over as much clothes as we can get on. It's been so cold and wet. The days are unbearable, but the nights are worse. Hamelin must be suffering, but he never complains. I was going to find him a bit of food and get back before anyone saw me.'

He gave a soft laugh and put one hand to the rosary that had been replaced about his neck. 'But fortune wasn't with me, and here I am. I thought that if Hamelin could have just one good hot meal he might rally...'

There were thousands of Crusaders camped outside the city, all with their own tales of woe. The Emperor had been quite explicit—if they could not behave decently, then they could not come in and they certainly would not eat. Elena tried to harden her heart, but it wasn't in her nature.

'Ascony and I will sort something out. A little simple charity surely cannot be refused.'

Elena had felt Selest studying her carefully as she had been eating. Now he took up the spoon and pronged instrument that had been laid for him and copied her movements. She smiled at him encouragingly, and he returned her glance.

'What is your story, then, Lady Elena? I suppose that I must at least be civil while you keep me here.'

He smiled, and once more Elena felt uncertain. Henry had told her that not all of his countrymen were to be trusted. This one made her wary. He spoke well enough when he had a mind to, but there always seemed to be a hint of scorn somewhere.

'Henry said that he was always a worry to his family,' Elena began cautiously, then smiled at the memory of his voice. 'They were relieved when he decided on a pilgrimage here to Constantinople. What they couldn't have foreseen was what would befall him on the way.'

She laughed, tugging at her four heavy plaits. 'He said that he had come across many poor little barefoot goose girls in his time, but I was the poorest and the littlest. Barely eight years old! He offered us money because we were so poor. Unfortunately, my family spoke no French—and, like you, Henry spoke no Greek then. Seeing me perched on the saddle of his horse clutching a purse full of coins, Mamma jumped to the obvious conclusion——'

Selest was shaking his head in disbelief. Elena rocked with laughter at his expression, rings and bangles jangling against the curved gilt arm of her couch.

'Oh, no—you misunderstand! Mamma has a formidable Orthodox faith. She thought her prayers for a rich, handsome husband for me had come true. Here he was with the dowry!'

'And this Henry took you?'

At his tone Elena stopped laughing and looked at him sharply.

'Don't say it like that, my lord. He was kind and we had nine wonderful years together——'

'But you were only a child! What sort of monster would do such a thing?'

Selest threw his cutlery down on to the marble table, making the silver dishes ring with fright. Fingering the network of bracelets about her wrist, Elena tried to keep her temper.

'My husband was a good man. He did not realise that he was expected to marry me until it was too late, but made the best of it and brought me to Constantinople. He treated me then only as a daughter.' She smiled at the thought. 'In fact he and his friends had no idea of how to bring up a child, but they did their best. I lived on pancakes, sweets and watered wine. They took me with them everywhere. When Henry won a little glass-making shop at a dice game he decided to settle here permanently. That was just as well, for when his parents found out about me they disowned him.'

'Forced to choose, your husband stayed with you in this strange land?'

'Of course. That was the sort of man he was.'

The firelight ran streaks of dark gold through Selest's auburn hair, throwing the pale alabaster of his skin into even harsher relief.

'Then we Franks are not all animals by nature, as your man Ascony seems to think,' he said, taking a long drink of orange juice.

Elena laughed lightly, refilling his glass. 'I think poor Ascony is jealous of you!'

It was Selest's turn for amusement. He had good teeth and a merry laugh, Elena noticed. It was a wonder that he had kept either with the hardships the Crusaders had faced over the past few months.

'Ascony would seem to have everything that I lack— a proper job, settled lodgings, security—I can't see that anyone so fortunate could be jealous of a man who has barely two yards of sodden earth to lie upon at night! Hamelin and I would change places with him right now.'

Elena smiled, twisting her wedding-ring absently.

'I don't think you would, my lord. You see, Ascony is a eunuch.'

Selest was completely wrong-footed. For a moment he smiled, waiting for her to laugh and confess it was all a joke. When she did not his nervous irritability returned.

'They warned us what went on here. I was right—this is all a plot—you must lure men in. The food—it's poisoned——'

'Oh, be quiet, do!' Elena lost her patience and flung down her napkin. 'I've got better things to do with my time. Ascony's always been the same. Since he was a baby, I suppose. It is a decision often made by parents here. It gives younger sons the chance of a good career, untroubled by ambitious thoughts for their heirs. That is all—we are not in the habit of carving up our dinner guests, however unwelcome their arrival may have been.'

Selest toyed with his last piece of asparagus. 'Is that true?'

'Every word.' She pushed the fruit basket towards him irritably. It did not appeal to her to discuss such a matter further over supper. 'Here, have some figs. From my own garden. They were particularly fine last year.'

He took one large sun-dried fruit from its nest of plaited straw. It sat on his plate for a moment while he waited for Elena to demonstrate how one ate figs in polite society. When instead she picked out a pear and started to peel it expertly with knife and prongs he summoned the nerve to ask.

'Use your hands, my lord. If you are to be a guest here, then you should eat in exactly the way you wish. My only reservation is that you do it tidily. My husband learned our manners, but then he was faced with Ascony's scorn day after day and week after week. Ascony is inclined to pay too much attention to the Right Way of Doing Things, if given half a chance.'

'Thank you, Lady Elena.' Selest paused, then picked up the fig and nibbled it thoughtfully. He seemed to find it to his liking and finished it in a few bites. Beginning to relax at last he made to move backwards on the couch but stopped with a sharp exclamation.

'The pain isn't as bad as it was before your Ascony attacked it, true enough,' he said, hissing through his teeth. 'But it can still take a hold.'

'Being overtired will make it worse. As soon as you have finished here I'll call for Ascony to take you up to bed.'

Selest was immediately suspicious. 'Where?'

'Upstairs in one of the guest bedrooms, of course. Where else—out in the courtyard?'

He shook his head in disbelief. 'I came here to beg, or at worst steal. Instead of being killed I'm fed like a fighting cock. Rather than putting me to lodge on the floor you say you're going to put me in a guest room. What sort of a place is this?'

Elena smiled, wondering if all the other Franks shared his sad lack of faith in human nature.

'I hope that this is a good God-fearing house,' she said simply, 'and with only a few days left until Easter Day it is the least that we can do.'

If Selest had been amazed by his reception downstairs, what awaited him upstairs took his breath away
completely. Ascony and Khar carried him into a large
room decorated in shades of pale green. Sweet-scented
lamps shed a soft warm glow in the peace of the room.
Painted silk hangings covered the walls and thick rugs
were scattered over a floor of polished marble tiles. The
bed was freshly made with crackling-new linen sheets
and the mouse-like Mrs Khar removed hot blocks from
between them just before the Crusader was helped into
bed.

He lay back in a cloud of pillows, studying the antics
of painted cherubs and doves that fluttered about the
ceiling. A metal fireguard served to support the bedclothes away from his injuries and in his borrowed robe
he looked almost regal. His attitude, though, was far
from gracious. Such extravagance made him question
the morals of the Byzantine empire even more. His
sidelong glances at Ascony didn't help matters, either.

'You must, of course, hand me over to the authorities?' he said when Elena arrived later with Lent-
forbidden hot milk and fruit cake in honour of his frailty.

'Not if we can get you back secretly.'

'I pray it's possible,' he said fervently. 'My lord—the
Duke Godfrey of Lorraine—he's not the sort you can
cheat and get away from.'

Elena pursed her lips. 'Oh, dear. As bad as that?'

'I wouldn't like to put him to the test,' Selest said,
chasing the last few cake crumbs around his plate. 'They
say he's never done a wrong thing in his life. He certainly makes one expression suit all occasions.' At this
Selest pulled such a face of world-weary cynicism as an
impression that Elena had to laugh.

'You ought to laugh more often, lady. It suits you.'
Suddenly he looked towards one of the heavily curtained
walls. 'What was that?'

Elena shrugged. 'I didn't hear anything.'

There was silence for a moment, then a thin, high
sound from outside. From her room across the

courtyard. Of all the things to happen—just when it was so important that he should remain silent, Milo was having another nightmare. Elena stood up. She could not pretend that she had not heard this time. Pushing behind the curtains, she closed the fretwork doors that led out on to a little veranda.

'Nothing. Probably only a cat. Pull the bedclothes over your head.' She stood back from the window and closed the curtains again. 'The doors will let in enough fresh air with no danger of any cats coming to visit. My room is opposite this one—not far away. Ring the bell beside your bed should you need anything.'

'I shan't sleep a wink,' he said sharply, finishing the cup of milk. 'There's something not right about this place—it makes me feel uncomfortable. Inside the City of Sin. I won't sleep. I know I won't.'

'Then that will make two of us, my lord.' Elena walked quickly to the door but paused with one hand on the latch. 'If you play halma and should like a partner, I am always at a loss for something to fill the dark hours.'

She watched him try to decide whether or not she was serious. In the end he made no reply, and she left him alone with his thoughts.

# CHAPTER TWO

ELENA went to midnight mass that night out of desperation, rather than habit. Muffled up from head to foot in black silk she tried to look invisible. Every passing minute was a torture. As if on pins she waited for someone to challenge her as the woman hiding a Crusader in her house, although thankfully nothing came but kind words and murmured conversations. This was a respectable area. What would people think if they knew, or even suspected?

No one said anything remotely sinister. The rites and ceremonies progressed around the church and received the worship of the devout. Elena made trips to a couple of the icons then slipped from the church quickly. It was a shame they didn't have a picture for the good of those who were overtaken by events, she thought. Elena felt that control of her life was slipping away with every minute that the unwelcome guest stayed.

When Selest was still asleep late next morning Elena let Ascony and the Khars go to their own prayers. They dropped Milo off at school on their way, which saved Elena the worry of leaving the house guest unattended.

Selest slept for so long that eventually Elena woke him, taking in a bowl of vegetable broth. He took a moment or two to remember where he was, then pulled himself up into a sitting position with a mutter of discomfort.

'I hope you don't intend keeping me here for the duration, Lady Elena? What would the lads say if they knew that I had been confined to my bed for so long by such an exotic beauty?' He laughed, persuading his copper chestnut curls into some sort of order with a weary hand.

'Such loose talk is uncalled for, sir. For the life of me I don't know why I risk my good reputation sheltering such a scoundrel...'

'Because you are the heart and soul of Christian generosity. Come—sit and talk with me, my little jewel of the Orient.'

He accepted the bowl of broth and also, to Elena's relief, the spoon that she offered.

'I am not of the Orient, my lord.' Elena tried to cover her confusion with a harsh tone. 'I am from the slopes of the Rhodope, as are all my family——'

'Ah, yes, I remember passing through those mountains. Littered with uncommonly airy stone temples. Now they *will* look nice when they're finished!'

'No, my lord, no—they are all very ancient. Finished with... falling down...'

With steady amusement he watched her bewildered expression and small fluttering hands. 'I know, Lady Elena. It was a joke.'

When she did not appear to understand he gave a sudden short laugh. Elena took a step back towards the door. Now that Selest was rested he was too noisy and his humour—if that was what it could be called—too boisterous. Yet something made her stay. A mysterious light in his hazel eyes, or the pure jollity of his laughter. It was a long time since the house had been racketed by a man's good humour.

Elena stood in uncomfortable silence as Selest finished the vegetable broth. He made no move to return the empty bowl and in the end Elena was forced to advance. She paused, half fearful, but he spread his hands wide in a gesture of innocence. Elena reached for the bowl but in a flash he had caught her tentative hand and held it fast.

Elena panicked like a trapped bird, squeaking and fluttering amid her gauzes and silks. Laughing, he pulled her down beside him on the bed.

'Oh, now, hush, little one! What do you think is going to happen? I only want to look——'

As Elena cowered away from him, silenced by fright, he took both of her hands and turned them palm downward.

'Paint? You paint your hands as well as your faces?' He was delighted at this new wonder, and grinned. 'When I saw you first I thought you must surely have been decked out for a masquerading party. Today you are as gilded as ever. Right down to the fingertips!'

Elena endured in silence as he trailed one finger around the delicate tracery decorating the backs of her hands. Relieved when he did not seem in a hurry to progress further, Elena found her voice.

'It is the fashion, my lord. Plant juices stain the skin. My friend Gulzun does it for me, and I for her...'

'And does she paint the rest of your skin with glowing honey? Your hair the sloe-deep hue of a winter night? Fleck your dark eyes with stars?'

'No, my lord—she is too busy with her work...'

He leaned forward. Elena could retreat no further and could not help but feel the warmth of his skin near her neck as he whispered in her ear.

'It was another joke, Lady Elena.'

Elena did not like his jokes. When he released her she bounded from the bed like a startled kitten. Without stopping to retrieve his empty bowl, she ran out of the room, Selest's laughter in her ears. She did not stop running until she reached the sanctuary of her own room and could slam the door on his wickedness.

When Ascony and the Khars returned much later, Elena was sitting in the kitchen slicing cabbage. Putting down the knife she had been using, she wiped her hands.

'You and I have an errand to do before we can enjoy our lunch, Ascony. While you were away Gulzun came, and I persuaded her to take a message up to the palace for me. The reply has been received that it will be perfectly in order to take greetings to a kinsman of my dear late husband. Even if he is camped outside of the city walls.'

Ascony was puzzled. 'I did not know that the Lord Henry's family had ever contacted you, lady.'

'They haven't. But they have a new member. His name is Hamelin, and he is in need of our help.'

'The rascal's friend? Oh, no, lady. You cannot go out there on some whim—they are dangerous men! Armed and with murderous intent!' He shook himself with distaste.

Elena was having none of his nonsense. 'There are two blankets and a cape here on the table. You carry them, and I've hidden a few little things within the bundle of Selest's old clothes—I thought we'd return them to prove our story.'

Ascony was not happy. He moaned all the time that they were getting ready to leave, and then he moaned all the way from the house.

'It won't work. We'll be cut down, I know it. We ought to take some Pechenegs with us——'

Elena waved a greeting to some of the native Muslims who acted as policemen for the city.

'They'd be slaughtered. You've said yourself that those men outside the gates are not like us, Ascony. They've been whipped up into this "Crusading Frenzy". If that wasn't enough they've then had to endure hundreds of miles of travelling during the worst of the weather—all they want to do is kill Muslims now, not pass the time of day with them.'

Ascony shivered and fell silent with foreboding. Elena patted his arm, regretting her hasty, unconsidered words.

'You'll be all right with me.'

The eunuch smiled at her, but was visibly uneasy. Dishonesty was not in his nature and he knew that no good would come of their mission.

Constantinople's great metropolis formed a bridgehead between Europe and Asia. It guarded the great trade routes bringing silks, perfumes and porcelain from the Orient, furs from northern lands, jewels and ivory from India and exotic fruits and spices from shadowy lands overseas. The city formed a lifeline for merchants desperate for new and costly luxuries to tempt the jaded purses of rich clients. Such a position had given it absolute power.

For hundreds of years Constantinople had been able to pick and choose from the best from all cultures. Now it was threatened. The ancient Christian stronghold with its cosmopolitan attitude to other faiths was under attack from the young and vital force of the Seljuk Turks, who were eager to win the whole world for Islam alone. An aloof, ageing queen of a city, Constantinople and her Byzantine empire realised that subtlety and sly diplomacy were no longer enough. She had to call in the young champions of the newest Christian empires— England, France and Germany.

Even though the city had taken fright at the raw eagerness of these Frankish Crusaders, her people were not unduly worried by the hordes of foreigners camped outside. A stout wall protected Constantinople on the landward side while on the other three sides the Sea of Marmara, the waters of the Golden Horn and the Bosphorous lapped at its coastlines like loyal guard dogs. The city was safe, and well provisioned from its port. The Crusaders had no such line of supply. They starved while the inhabitants of Constantinople thrived.

Inside the city walls life was going on as usual. The Mese, a broad marbled way, swept from Constantinople's golden gates all the way to the Emperor's palace, some miles away. This main highway was always busy with people. With the help of their note Elena and Ascony slipped out of the city barely noticed amid the usual traffic that the Crusaders were unwilling to prevent yet could not profit by.

The Crusading army was camped much further from the city walls than Elena had imagined. The closer she and Ascony got to the camp, the more apparent it became that these were no ordinary soldiers, but something altogether different.

It was as though a great hurricane had swept down through Frankish lands. Many thousands of knights, pilgrims, ruffians, women and children had been snatched up, carried, then dumped all higgledy-piggledy outside Constantinople. Horses, carts, camp fires and forges too were all strewn about the gathering carelessly, as though the ramshackle 'army' lacked organisation and hope as well as food.

A great blue marquee fluttering with pennons dominated the shabby scene. All about it were small tents, bowed and soggy with recent rain. Those who could not afford that standard of luxury crouched behind evil-smelling old fish crates scavenged from the coast. Other lucky ones managed to find shelter beneath the many hundreds of ox carts, now quite empty of provisions.

Many more had nothing at all. Some stood about, staring up dull-eyed at the city that kept them out. Others simply lay where they had fallen, too weak to move. The most appalling thing, more shocking than the poverty and hopelessness, was the smell. Sweat and ordure and sickness carried along in the smoulder of wet, fish-fragranced wood. The old crates were the only things left to burn in the soggy camp. All the dry wood had been used up long ago.

'Let us go back, lady.' Ascony's words were muffled by the sleeve he held over his mouth and nose. Elena paused but then pulled her gauze veil about her face and carried on. There was no point in taking on a task if she didn't see it to the bitter end.

'He won't be grateful, lady. None of these dogs are. If they were they would be biddable to the rule of Emperor Alexius.'

'It is not their choice, Ascony. They can only do as their master orders.'

People of all descriptions were huddled alone or in groups. The meanest beggars had little enough comfort, but the knights were forced to stand around in full rusting armour for fear that once put down it might be stolen.

The crowd was dispirited, but not too tired to offer a few catcalls and jeers to Elena and Ascony as the only trace of civilisation in their hell on earth.

Elena decided that there was nothing for it but to go straight to the top. Ignoring the leering crowd, she picked her way towards the blue marquee. Ascony could do nothing but follow in her wake. Gestures and guttural remarks thrown at them by the ruffians were easy enough to interpret, even if most were in German rather than French.

Duck-boards had been laid about the marquee and the lines of expensive horses parked beside it. Grateful for a solid footing at last, Elena lifted one foot to step on to the planking. Before she could set it down a ringing of swords and rough voices stopped her.

'Was' want?'

Elena caught the recognisable words through a chorus of different languages and dialects. Men were spilling through the horse lines from all directions to bar her way.

'I wish to speak to the leader of this——' here she stopped and scanned the ill-assorted throng '—assembly.'

The men peered at Elena. It was clear that they had understood little of her speech even though her French was fluent. They looked the Byzantine couple up and down then chuckled with scorn to conceal their ignorance.

Their sniggering stopped as a flap in the marquee was lifted and a vision of heroism emerged. Tall and fair with eyes of ice, this was undoubtedly a leader of men. His tunic of laced metal rings showed no sign of rust— only the glow of frequent polishing. When he spoke to the ruffians they melted away in silence. Godfrey, Duke of Lorraine was not a man to stand for the slightest disobedience.

He regarded Elena without a great deal of enthusiasm.

'I take it that you come as yet another envoy of sorts from Emperor Alexius.'

'No, my lord. I come upon a personal matter.'

'Is that not the same thing, then?'

The French he spoke was heavily accented and expressionless with effort. Elena looked up, afraid of what he might be thinking. Godfrey's cold eyes showed neither lust nor scorn. If anything there might have been the faintest trace of amusement.

'I believe one of my kinsmen may be suffering in your employ, my lord.'

She spoke fearlessly now, for although dressed for war the duke carried no sword. That had given her confidence.

'I suppose you had better come in, then,' he said at length, but turned away as Elena held out her hand to be escorted. She was left to make her own way into the marquee. Ascony stayed close behind, complaining loudly at such barbarous treatment.

It was a relief to be out of the biting wind, but icy draughts still whipped about at ankle-level. Canvas sucked and cracked as the marquee battled against spring gusts.

The duke had gone to sit on the edge of a large trestle-table. Around him sprawled the remains of a meagre meal and two loutish young men. They stopped carving chunks from the table as Elena entered and sniggered as the guards had done.

One of them leered, picking his teeth with the tip of his knife, but was silenced with a vigorous command.

The duke folded his arms. 'Madam—as you see, this is no place for a woman. Be brief, then be on your way.'

Elena refused to be intimidated despite the harshness of his voice.

'I have come on an errand of mercy.'

'Then you have not heard that only melt-water runs in my veins, not human blood?'

'Yes, but your heart can be of only the purest ice, my lord. You are widely accepted as the perfect model of a true Christian knight.'

He snapped his fingers imperiously, never taking his eyes from Elena's face. Two guards appeared in the doorway. 'Perfection is reserved for our Lord, madam, not mere mortal man. That sort of flattery offends my beliefs.'

Godfrey turned from Elena to pour himself a cup of watered wine. When at last he addressed the guards it was again in halting French.

'Escort these people back to the gates of their city. And keep the other men quiet as you do so.'

'But lord—what about my kinsman?'

'What about him?'

'He is the reason that I came out to this hellish——'

'Ah! No such language in Holy Week, if you please!' He spat out violently. His companions laughed, but Elena was determined not to be put off.

'I came out here to see my kinsman. Not you, my lord.'

Godfrey fastidiously removed a hair from his wine then took a delicate sip. 'And I cannot be seen to allow favours to individuals.'

'Yet you can sit in comfort here while your men are soaked to the skin and blown senseless by the wind? They are dying of cold and hunger, lord, yet you would deny one of them a kind deed.' Elena was more indignant than awed now. 'No, lord, the people are wrong. You haven't a speck of Christian decency in you!'

Ascony drew in a sharp breath, as did Godfrey's kinsmen. Only Elena in her rage could bear to look at the duke. She glared at him, fuming, until he began to smile. It could not thaw the deep winter of his soul, yet touched his eyes kindly.

'Guards, do as I say and escort the lady from our presence.'

Elena leapt forward, but Godfrey had turned aside to put down his goblet of wine.

'And should you stumble across her kinsman on the way, then I do not wish to know about it.'

Elena and Ascony had no time to be astonished. The tent flap was pulled back and they were ushered out, the audience at an end.

It took them a long time to find Hamelin among the multitude. Going only on Selest's vague description of where he had been camped, they had much ground to search.

Moving among the dispirited hordes, Elena realised just how cosmopolitan the Crusaders were. Sweeping down through Europe, Godfrey's Lorrainers had gathered Germans, Poles, Slavs and any number of other nationalities that neither Ascony nor Elena could understand.

The guards had been searching, too, and soon one held up his hand. Going to join him Elena and Ascony saw only a bundle of rags. It was cowering beneath a shelter made from two battered shields and some chunks of driftwood. Elena was horrified.

'All on his own now, poor lad,' a tattered French neighbour said with feeling. 'He did have a friend—Emil—nice chap, but he's gone off now.'

From his tone the Frenchman obviously considered that Emil Selest was gone for good. Elena went to the sorry little heap squeezed into the furthest corner of its shelter. Lifting one corner of a tattered blanket, she gasped.

'Oh, Ascony, he's only a little boy——'

Hamelin put up a filthy paw to shield his injured eye. One side of his face was swollen and crusted with infection, giving a lop-sided look to his pale, pinched features. He seemed barely out of babyhood.

'Hamelin—here, I've brought you some things...'

Henry's cape would go two or three times around the little waif, Elena thought with pity. There was no doubt that the things she had brought were welcome. Smelling food, Hamelin started to move towards her like a little blind kitten, hand outstretched. At the last moment he stopped, and face crumpling he gave out a thin, desperate wail.

'Mi!'

'Ssh!' While Ascony waited at a respectful distance, Elena wriggled into the shelter to quieten Hamelin. Kneeling on damp, beaten earth, she put down her pile of things and sorted out a small pot of vegetable broth.

It was barely warm now after the time wasted with Godfrey.

'Mi?' Hamelin repeated, then added more jagged jabberings of his own language. He continued through mouthfuls of broth, the word 'Mi' surfacing time and again.

'Emil?'

'Mi.' Hamelin nodded briefly, cheeks bulging with food. There was no hope of finding a translator. Any hint that another one of the Crusaders was inside the city might provoke a riot.

'Emil's all right,' Elena whispered, hoping that Hamelin would understand her tone if not the words. 'He went over the wall, fell and hurt himself but now he's safe in my house.'

She accompanied the story with suitable gestures, pointing towards the wall and rubbing her ankle. Hamelin looked puzzled, but when Elena repeated the mime a look of delight appeared on his face. That matter settled he pounced on a herb loaf that Elena gave him.

When he had finished Elena brought out items for treating his eye. Seeing the array of cloths, bottles and scissors, Hamelin shrank back nervously. Elena sat down under the low shelter and patted her lap.

'I only want a look, Hamelin. I'll be very gentle.' Her tone was calm and quiet, willing him to understand.

The boy shook his head and again put his hand protectively to his face. In two strides and an easy movement Ascony grasped the reluctant child, who barely had chance to scream.

'It's all right, Hamelin.' Elena stroked the tousled blond head in her lap as Hamelin fought against Ascony's restraint. Eventually her cool hands calmed him and she was able to clean part of his face with salt water. All the time she worked he whimpered with fear, but gave no sharp cries of pain, which was encouraging. Only when Elena began to ease his eyelid open did Hamelin start to wail in earnest. The eye had been made red and sore with rubbing, but Elena could see no permanent damage. Persevering despite his cries, she worked a good quantity of cooling salve into the eye then bound on a protective pad.

The moment he was released Hamelin's hand flew up to claw at the padding. Elena caught both his hands in hers, raised them to his face and squeezed them hard, shaking her head as she did so.

'Don't scratch. Use this.' She handed him the salve pot with an elaborate pantomime of gestures, and to her relief Hamelin nodded gravely. Leaving him the bundle that they had brought, she gave a little wave of farewell. Hamelin reached across and slipped his hand into hers in a gesture that needed no interpretation. Beneath the ingrained grime his face shone with simple trust.

'No, sweetheart,' Elena said sadly. She couldn't help thinking of her own little Milo, well fed, healthy and safe at his lessons. The line between comfort and disaster was very fine. She was lucky for the moment—Hamelin was not. It had been her duty to come and try to help him, but her feelings went deeper than that now. Peeling his fingers from her hand, she mimed her next words.

'You—stay here with your friends. When you're all let into the city I'll come and fetch you to stay in my house. Then you'll be with Emil,' she finished in a whisper. Patting Hamelin's shoulder, Elena hardened her heart and backed out of the shelter. She walked away quickly, Ascony in tow.

'He's still watching after us, verminous wretch,' Ascony said with a shudder. 'I hope we haven't brought any unwelcome visitors home with us, lady.'

Elena sighed, but could not bear to look back. 'I wish I could have brought home a welcome visitor, Ascony. Poor little mite.'

Ascony snorted dismissively. 'They're all as filthy as one another. The smell of him clings still—I hope the sea breezes can diffuse it, lady.'

'He can't help it, Ascony,' Elena countered as they went back into the city. 'After three months of living out here it's a wonder he's still alive.'

Much later, scrubbed from head to foot and in a clean silk robe, Elena sat on the very end of Selest's bed, well out of reach, and told him what had happened. She did not feel able to visit Selest alone now, so Khar sat beside the fire working on a new rag rug. Elena and Selest were idling through a game of halma to no particular conclusion.

Selest roared with laughter to hear of the exchange with Duke Godfrey. When Elena asked him about Hamelin he became more thoughtful.

'I don't think he's had much of a life. From what I understand, when his parents realised he was a bit lacking they didn't want anything to do with him. Peasants can't afford to support those who can't pull their weight. He lived as a swineherd for a time, then picked up with the Crusaders. It's taken me the best part of three weeks to make him understand what we're here for.'

He sighed and leaned back against the pillows. Good food had brought some colour back to his skin but dark shadows of deprivation still remained beneath his eyes. Elena looked at his hands resting on the coverlet and thought how wasted and thin they were.

'Sufficient to dispatch the enemy,' he began, reading her thoughts with a quiet laugh. 'Or to gentle a lady, as you already know. I regret that I have not been in a position to repay your kindness more positively, lady, but if you would draw nearer once more I may be able to suggest a suitable arrangement...'

'Khar does not speak any French, my lord. What is it that needs to be said in such confidence that it must be whispered?'

He smiled at her knowingly, strong aristocratic features giving him an air of authority.

'A healthy young woman left alone for two years? Come, lady, despite your pretty struggles this morning no doubt you are as eager in your pursuit of pleasure now as you were in the days of your marriage——'

'No, sir!' Elena stood up in surprise and Khar started at her movement.

'Then why do you come visiting a man in his chamber clad only in your chemise? And a very flimsy one at that,' he added appreciatively, causing Elena to draw the garment around her in shame.

'Khar is here as my chaperon. And in any case, a true gentleman would not think such ill of a lady,' she began nervously. At that moment she became very conscious of her loneliness. The animal attraction of Selest's warm, taut body had taunted her before, but this was the first time that Elena had admitted such a longing to herself. He had put her guilty fantasies into words and it brought deep shame, not relief.

'My life was devoted to my husband, my lord. No man could presume to take his place, then or now.'

Emil Selest continued to smile at her with undisguised appreciation. Though watchful, Khar had made no move to caution him and this gave Selest confidence.

'Come now, lady. Who would know if you were to share my lonely bed for a while? Send your man away on some pretext. No one pays any heed to the gossip of servants, as long as they cannot give the evidence of their own eyes. And I dare say that it wouldn't be the first time that you had spoiled yourself with a little idle pleasure...'

'I have told you, my lord. My husband comes—came first and last with me.'

Selest stopped smiling. His expression was growing hard and unyielding, heavy with threat.

'That seems an odd notion, lady. Perhaps there are other reasons why I do not appeal. Is it because I am a foreigner? Or in view of the poverty of my circumstances? Ah, that must be it. A poor man, especially if he is a foreigner, is not good enough for you.'

'No—no, it isn't that...'

'What's stopping you, then?' He gave a low chuckle and held out his hand to her. 'You needn't worry that my leg will prove a hindrance. There are more ways of——'

'After all our hospitality you treat me like one of your low Frankish women? I wish I had told Duke Godfrey about you now. He is a good man, and would have known how to treat a scoundrel like you.'

Elena moved well away from the bed and with a few words sent Khar scurrying off to fetch Ascony.

'You seem set to leave too, lady. Wait—not so fast. Should it come to involving the good duke, who do you think he would believe? One of his loyal countrymen or a foreign temptress decked out to lure poor innocents into the forbidden city?'

'Oh, but you came here to steal! You know that I didn't entice you!'

Selest was not in the slightest bit concerned by her agitation. He even had confidence enough to throw back the bedclothes. 'My word against yours, lady.'

'And that of my household.'

'You don't put your faith in servants?' He patted the bed with delight. 'It's bred into them to be base and sly.'

'My staff have always proved trustworthy in the past.'

'Ah, but the duke will have only his own experience to go by.' Selest showed his confidence by leaning back against the pillows nonchalantly. 'His servants are as shiftless and lazy a bunch of brigands as you are likely to meet.'

'Of course. They are Franks,' Elena said with a new confidence as she edged towards the door. 'This is Constantinople, and we do things differently here. Staff are held to their masters by loyalty, not mortal fear. We all work together, not in opposition.'

'Then this is indeed a most wondrous place, lady.'

This time Elena refused to let his taunts and sarcasm frighten her. Selest was injured, after all. He was unable to get out of the bed without assistance and could prove no threat unless she got within his reach. Besides, he was for the moment a stranger in a strange place. He was bound to be unsettled, and foolish as she felt it was surely her place as hostess to make allowances for him.

The sun had moved around and shadows were drawing their veils. Going to the window, Elena started to release the heavy drapes and shut out the evening, but Selest stopped her.

'I fancy I can hear the camp. Faintly—the wind must be in the right direction...'

'Then you must be mistaken, my lord. If the wind was bringing their sound then it would bring their fragrance too, and I fear that we should both be suffering.'

She did not close the curtains, but stood looking down at the cool greenery of the courtyard. At last he spoke through the dusk closing about them.

'The camp is not a place for decent women. You should not have risked going there.'

'I'm glad I did,' Elena said without hesitation. 'Poor little Hamelin. What possessed such a child to travel all this way?'

'He had no life at home. The Crusade offered him travel, and a certain amount of food. The chance of a new life in new lands——'

'But you've only come to help out. You're not expected to stay here.'

Elena's statement surprised him. Suddenly he was alert, sitting up and fixing her with eyes that almost glowed in the gloom. 'That's what you all think, is it? That we would leave our stinking hovels at home, come and make you lot secure in your idle decadence then go back to our poverty without reward, like good little boys?'

'You would have the knowledge that you had saved the cradle of Christianity from those evil enough to want to destroy it.'

'Knowledge of that sort doesn't put food into empty bellies.'

'And so Hamelin is more fortunate to be starving outside the gates of Constantinople than in some French hovel?'

'He's German,' Selest snapped. 'And a few sticks short of a bundle, too, although I'll not have foreigners laugh at him for that.'

'I wouldn't, my lord,' Elena murmured, sorry that she might have given that impression.

'He's too slow in the wits to be out there on his own.' Selest picked at a loose thread in the bedclothes, his face turned towards the pale shape of the window. 'It's so difficult for him to understand people, or make himself understood.'

'Yet he and I got on well enough together, my lord, even though I have no German.' Lighting a taper, Elena went about the room, bringing the scented candles to life. When the bed was flooded in a pool of welcome light Elena saw that Selest had arranged the bedclothes neatly once more. Thoughts of Hamelin had managed to take his mind off romance for a while.

'How did he seem?' Selest asked at last, voice soft as a whisper.

'Frail, small and lonely. He still has a good appetite, though, and ate well.' Elena remembered something with a smile. 'What *does* "Mi" mean in the German tongue?'

Selest's face was suffused with happy memory. 'Nothing. That's the nearest he can get to "Emil", no matter how often I repeat it.'

All further talk was cut short by a blood-curdling scream from downstairs. Elena sighed.

'Mrs Khar. She's either heard of your perfidy or another lizard has found its way into the pantry.'

But the scream was followed by distant muffled cries and a slamming door. Elena was out of the bedroom and down the stairs before she at least remembered her manners and called back to assure Selest that she would return.

The kitchen was full to bursting with the two Khars. They were running in hysterical circles, snatching up pokers and kitchen knives and pots and pans in frenzy. The worst was happening—the Crusaders were coming over the wall! They were in the garden! Ascony had rushed out to stop them, and now he was going to be killed!

Elena could hear nothing but the screams of Mrs Khar and the oaths of her husband. It would be up to Elena to take control, and her first thoughts were for little Milo playing happily in the living-room. She would have to stop the Crusaders reaching him whatever else happened.

Taking a deep breath, she went out into the hall and quickly through to the dining-room. Only Ascony's voice was to be heard, accompanied by the gentle tapping of the unlatched garden doors. The eunuch seemed angry, rather than frightened. Elena took courage from this and dashed out to confront the hordes that he must be holding at bay.

At first sight the garden was deserted. There were certainly no signs of a bloodthirsty rebel army. Only Ascony's breathless tirade of rage interrupted the dim twilight, coming from beside the little stone arbour.

'And I suppose you've come snivelling around here for sympathy. Well, it won't work, do you hear?'

'Ascony?'

'Aha! Now we'll see you brought to account, wretch!' Ascony gloated over the huddled form crouching inside the arbour as Elena strode forward. Ascony had Hamelin cornered and was towering over him in a spectacular rage.

'Shh!' Elena gave her servant a gentle shove. 'Why don't you get the Imam to have our business cried from the rooftops? You'll get us all hung, drawn and quartered!'

Her urgent warning came too late. Prancing hoof-beats rattled up the lane between Elena's garden and the city walls. Both Elena and Ascony froze with fear, but

Hamelin filled their silence with a ragged burble of appeals.

'Ssh!' Elena put her finger to his lips and pointed at the garden wall. At once Hamelin fell quiet, but the damage was done. Deep Turkish tones rang out from the other side of the wall.

It was the voice of a Pecheneg.

# CHAPTER THREE

'EVERYTHING all right in there?'

Elena felt her mouth go dry. She tried to clear her throat, but could only croak unsteadily. 'Yes, Officer. Only a spot of trouble with the staff. You know how it is...'

The Pecheneg laughed. 'No problem. I'll come around the front and sort it out for you, my lady.'

With appalling dread they heard him back his horse and turn to go.

'Er—no, no—it's quite all right, Officer. I can manage, and the evening's turning chill. Save yourself the trouble and get back into the warm!'

Elena thought her legs would fail her as the Pecheneg laughed once more then rode away cheerfully. She let her breath out in one long gasp.

'Making all that noise! Ascony, have you got no sense?'

'Me? Me? Lady, you should have heard the racket this wretch made throwing his rubbish over our wall!'

Two sinister-looking bundles lurked where they had been dropped and Ascony pointed at them as though he were presenting exhibits in a court case.

'I barely had time to get out of the bath house and pull on a robe before chaos ran amok. Mrs Khar was in a fine flurry, thinking the worst after seeing him climb over the wall.'

Hamelin pitched in with some ugly jabbering of his own at this point. He had lost the pad covering his eye and the bandage hung forlornly about his neck. Only when Elena held out her hand to him did the boy forget all his petulant complaints. He smiled at her trustingly.

43

'Come on, sweetheart. Now you're here we might as well try and make you welcome.'

'I've said it before and I'll say it again—no good will come of this.' Ascony sniffed haughtily. 'If I had my way the little guttersnipe would be thrown back over the wall right this instant!'

To finish he cuffed Hamelin sharply.

'Ascony! Leave him alone! Get inside and arrange for him to be cleaned up and fed.'

'Nasty little sneak, creeping in here like a burglar. He'll make off with everything that isn't nailed down. You mark my words—we'll be ruined!'

'Ascony!' Elena said sharply, putting one arm around Hamelin. 'Go and do as I say.'

Ascony moved off grudgingly, but left Elena in no doubt of his feelings towards Hamelin. He neither liked him nor trusted him one inch.

It was some time before Elena got back to Selest with the news. He was eager to see Hamelin, but Elena explained that it might be some time before they could meet. Hamelin was going to be cleaned up, but when Elena had shown him a bowl of water, soap and a towel he had been totally bewildered. In the end she had bullied Ascony into taking the boy into the bath house with him.

'My troubles weren't over then.' The smile died from Elena's lips as she rearranged counters on the halma board again. 'At the thought of going off with Ascony he started to cry and cling to me as though his life depended on it. It was awful.'

'I hope you didn't put up with it.' Selest looked at her sternly. 'He's got to learn discipline. If someone is kind to him he's pathetically grateful. It's unmanly. Don't pander to him.'

'Unmanly? He's only a poor little thing!' Elena laughed, then saw that he was serious for once. She placed the halma board on Selest's lap and sat down out of his reach. 'How did you two meet up?'

'He was wandering through the camp, begging for food.'

'And you shared yours with him?' Elena smiled warmly, but Selest gave her a hard stare.

'Did I say that?' He tapped a halma counter against the board with irritated embarrassment. 'If he's going to survive in this world he's got to be able to fend for himself. And a word of warning, lady. He's not as much of a child as he looks, and even if he was children should not be indulged. Do not lavish kind words and caresses upon Hamelin. It will be misinterpreted.'

'I can look after myself, you know,' Elena said sharply. 'And even if he is a little slow in the wits I'm sure he can tell the difference between mere friendship and approaches of a—a different kind.'

'Don't be too sure about that, lady. Remember, he's been living with animals and is now no more than an animal himself. Uncivilised, uncontrolled——'

'He's only a little boy, my lord,' Elena interrupted firmly. 'If he has failings then they must be corrected, but with kindness. If you don't intend to offer him that then you must teach me sufficient German to take on the task.'

She stood up, a little warm and uncomfortable from the exchange. Emil Selest was the most unforgiving brute imaginable, and it was as well that she was managing to keep Milo's existence a secret.

'If you would excuse me, my lord, I feel that I may be of more use downstairs. I will have Hamelin sent up to you directly——'

There was no need. With a rush and a clatter the boy burst into the room, Ascony close behind. Engulfed in a huge towel, Hamelin was pink and glowing from his bath. Nearly reclaimed after years of neglect, his freshly washed hair stood out from his head like a dandelion clock. Beaming at Elena, he flung himself on top of Selest.

'Mi!'

Selest hugged his young friend, then, seeing Elena's grin, pushed the boy away with a few rough words.

'You will have to speak up if you expect the child to hear you, my lord,' Ascony said smugly. 'After all, he is very nearly deaf.'

That explained a great deal.

'How do you know that?' Piqued, Selest glowered at Ascony suspiciously. 'You're only a Greek.'

'He took too little notice when Mrs Khar dropped her cooking pots. Presumably with delight at the sight of another welcome visitor,' Ascony murmured to Elena as an ironic aside. 'And we talked, or rather he gabbled on when I turned away or my words were too quiet for him to hear. I have a little knowledge of the German tongue, you see, my lord. One never knows when exotic languages might be of use, living in Constantinople,' Ascony finished, folding his hands beneath the long, ornate sleeves of his gown.

Selest didn't think much of the eunuch's attitude and was openly hostile.

'Well, I'm the only friend Hamelin's got, and he's never told me.'

Elena had been thinking. 'I don't believe he knows that anything is amiss, my lord. As he has learnt some speech in the past perhaps the loss was sudden, after his banishment. Without human company he may not realise that the sounds that he is missing are words.'

Elena watched Selest consider her words. With one hand he was patting Hamelin while with the other he tried to stop his young friend eating the halma counters. This reminded Elena of an important thing.

'Ascony, go and fetch Hamelin food and drink. Something nice, and plenty of it. My lord Selest, could you tell poor Hamelin that he will be sleeping here with you, but must remain in this room and not wander?'

'I would have thought you and your sign-language would have been better qualified to tell him,' Selest said coldly. His expression was no longer merry but harshly disapproving as Elena bent to make a fuss of Hamelin and help him beneath the bedclothes.

'You're going to let him spoil your expensive bedding?' Selest queried darkly.

'He has had a bath and is now as clean as you, my lord.'

The Frank snorted. 'Not in his habits.'

Cheered by being the centre of attention, Hamelin burbled something to Selest, who translated it with a slow grin.

'He says that this is a very funny place to have no straw on the floor.'

Speaking to the boy again, he laughed out loud at the reply he received.

'I asked him if he'd ever been in such a beautiful house before. He asked me what a house was.'

'You shouldn't laugh at him!' Elena snapped, but Hamelin didn't seem very bothered. He was looking about the room distractedly. All of a sudden he clambered out of bed and wandered away into a quiet corner. With the instincts bred of motherhood Elena watched him go, then swooped like a chicken hawk as he started to squat.

Selest was in fits of laughter. 'I told you! Living with pigs means he's no better than one himself!'

'Be quiet.' Elena hustled the grizzling Hamelin behind a screen set up beside the bed for Selest's own privacy. 'Don't be horrible, my lord. The child can't help it if he doesn't know any better. We'll have to teach him.'

'You're mad! How much mess is he going to make in the process? He'll spoil all your lovely things and then you'll be sorry. Let him sleep on the floor—he's used to it and it's more easily cleaned.'

'No, my lord. Hamelin is a guest, like you. We must all help him to learn. It's only a matter of using a different place.'

Ascony arrived with food for Hamelin who, back in bed once his hands had been forcibly washed, threw himself at vegetable casserole and rye bread.

'Like a duck on dough-boys,' Elena observed, spreading the bath towel over Hamelin's lap to catch any waste. There was none. Hamelin didn't intend losing the smallest morsel as he choked back stew and great hunks of bread as fast as he could cram the food into his mouth.

'I suppose you're going to blame me for his table manners?' Selest leaned back in the bed and eyed Elena with amusement.

'Not at all, my lord. Swine cannot be the easiest of dining companions.'

He read sarcasm in her words where there was none.

'What? A painted heathen calls me a swine?'

Elena held up her hands to calm his anger, taken aback that he should be so touchy.

'No, no, my lord. I referred only to Hamelin's past life. It is not the habit here to insult our guests. We believe in gentler jests, and then only between friends.'

His anger subsided, but he did not apologise. Instead he looked back to Hamelin, who was licking his empty broth bowl with quick, eager little movements.

'Fetch him some more, Ascony. Being Lenten food it is plain, and should not upset him.'

Too late Elena realised that her order meant being left alone with Selest. In fact he was too interested in talking to Hamelin in loud, slow German.

'How did he get into the city, my lord? We are supposed to be perfectly safe and well defended in here.'

'He got in the same way that I did. You know the beggarmen that fish from the seashore? Each evening I and others would try and persuade——'

'Threaten, more like——'

'No, my lady. The one knight who tried rough tactics was soon dealt with by a horde of beggars protecting their own. As I was saying, each night I would ask if they could spare any of their pitiful catch. Of course it was hopeless, but the other evening while—engaged in necessary business against the wall,' he smiled at her but Elena looked away in embarrassment, 'I noticed that a small fissure ran up through joints in the stones. Earth movements have affected rubble packing the double skinned city wall. Under the guise of begging I was able to remove a stone now and then, while a poor, scabby briar growing in the mortar shielded my efforts. Then by last evening there was a hole big enough for my poor, wasted body to slip into the interior of the wall.'

He paused, smiling at Hamelin's grimace of indigestion as the boy started on the second bowl of casserole that Ascony now brought him.

'After that it was easy. A quick scramble up the tumble of masonry packed inside the wall——'

'Like a rat up roughcast,' Elena interrupted, but he carried on.

'—and then a few sharp blows where the plaster felt hollow on the inner face and I was through. It was quite a drop down into the lane behind your garden, but that was easy. It was climbing the garden wall that exhausted me, and you know the rest.'

'How were you intending to get away with your ill-gotten gains?' Elena asked, curiosity and amazement at his cunning overcoming her natural reticence.

'That was why I had my ringed jacket on inside out. It would have passed for normal beggar's wear, and I could have mingled with the crowds trailing out of the city gates next morning.'

Elena sat back and stared at the two Franks, one fully intending to return to his young charge with food, even though he might have been able to linger in well-fed safety within the city walls, the other so young and trusting that he had followed his friend into the city that despised him.

When Hamelin had finally finished his meal, Elena treated his eye once more and bound it up for the night. She spoke little to the child and even less to his older companion. Emil Selest had succeeded in surprising her. He was proving to be a very curious manifestation of these murderous Franks.

After settling the two young soldiers Elena sent Ascony out to tell the authorities that she was worried about the condition of the city wall beyond her garden. That would ensure they had no more unwelcome visitors.

She had an early night, going to bed as soon as she had tucked Milo up in his alcove.

Mind uneasy, she barely slept and rose very early. Eager to find some occupation to take her mind off the danger of her situation, she turned to the kitchen and cooking.

Weeks of dull Lenten rations had sharpened her appetite for Easter celebrations. With so many fancy dishes to be prepared for the feasts ahead there was always plenty to do.

First she wrung out a large clean towel in water warmed over the slumbering fire. Laying the cloth in a tray, she covered it with a thick layer of wheat grains. Covering the whole with another damp towel she set it beside the hearth. In a few days' time the sprouted grains, when mixed and baked with honey and grated carrot, would make a rich, sticky cake.

A large muslin bag hung over a basin in the coolest part of the airy kitchen. Elena untied it and removed a soft ball of curds, wrapped in more muslin. Tightening these bandages to compress the developing cheese further, she replaced it to drip out more whey and mature.

Elena hardly dared think as far ahead as Easter Day. All these preparations might be in vain. If the pair they were hiding upstairs were to be discovered——

The arrival of Mrs Khar from the staff quarters made her jump. The sign of a guilty conscience, Elena thought as she relinquished the kitchen work into the cook's more capable hands. After returning upstairs to wake and bathe Milo, she sent him down to have breakfast while she went about her own toilet.

It wasn't difficult to understand why Selest stared at her so much. Henry had told her often enough how Frankish women dressed in drab, shapeless clothes, tied around the middle with cord. He said they looked like bags of turnips compared to the women of the East.

Selest's scrutiny always made her blush, so giving him more cause for merriment. Elena decided to try and find something dull, boring and more Frankish in design to wear.

It was very difficult. Henry had lavished her with expensive clothes in his lifetime, but they had all been chosen with his newly acquired tastes in mind. All of Elena's pairs of soft, voluminous trousers were made of gossamer-fine materials, as were all her blouses. Some of the pinafores and overtunics might have been modest enough in design, but Elena thought of Duke Godfrey's wintry expression as he had scrutinised her the day before. Neither the pastel shades nor bright colours she had worn then had raised anything other than a look of scorn. Perhaps the Franks were too used to sludge colours.

Finally she chose grey silk trousers, a matching high-necked blouse and a cherry-red overtunic with three-quarter-length sleeves. The sheer floor-length veil she chose only had a little gold thread, Elena reasoned. And the edging of little gold discs were only necessary weights to keep it in place.

It took Elena some time to get the kohl about her eyes exactly right. For some reason her hands were a little unsteady that morning. The black would smudge into the pink ochre of her eyeshadow, and in wiping it off she always seemed to dislodge too many of the tiny specks of glitter dusted about her brows and cheeks.

Without her normal amount of make-up Elena felt almost naked and unwilling to face the world. She would have to paint up afresh before she could venture on to the streets, or people might begin to suspect that she was ill.

She remembered that Selest had stared at her feet. Instead of her normal open-work sandals she pulled on a pair of red tsourapia. 'Foot mittens' Ascony would sneer, but then he was a snob. They might only be worn in the country and not in polite society, but Elena valued them in the winter against the chill of marble floors. Besides, Elena's relatives knitted her pair after pair. They could afford nothing more for Christmas presents, and so Elena wore them out of loyalty as well as choice.

Preparations complete, she skipped down the stairs to find Milo waiting for her at the bottom. She scooped him up in her arms with a giggle.

'You're getting too heavy for this, sprout. Why, what's the matter?'

Milo had inherited his mother's large dark eyes, and they were troubled now. Lower lip trembling, he threw his chubby arms around Elena's neck, pressing his face against hers.

'Ascony's cross with me.'

Elena sat down on the bottom step, Milo on her lap.

'Oh, no. What mischief have you been up to now?'

'Nothing, Mummy!'

'Milo——?'

The plump little child squirmed around to sit on her lap more comfortably, and Elena brushed through his tousled hair with her fingers.

'Mrs Khar gave me some bread to dip in my whey. Then Ascony came and shouted at me to go out. I didn't do anything this time, Mummy...promise! 'Cept...'

'Ye-es?'

'I was frightened. I dropped my bread on the floor. Now Khar will be cross, too.'

The kitchen door burst open and Milo flinched. Hands twisting painfully in his mother's plaits, he lay waiting quietly for his punishment.

'Lady Elena. Something—terrible...has happened.'

Ascony stood in the doorway. All trace of efficiency had been swept away by the tears running down his cheeks. Elena knew that it must be something truly devastating, for only once before had she seen Ascony in such a state—the night men had come with the news of Henry's death. This was no tantrum over a child's mischief.

Patting Milo, Elena set him down and stood up.

'Go and find your Noah's ark, sweetheart. You can play with it quietly in the dining-room until it's time to leave for school. Don't put anything on the table. It might get scratched, and you know what happened last time...'

Milo's usual excitement was dulled by his new wariness of Ascony. One small finger in his mouth, he sidled past the eunuch, eyes never once leaving Ascony's face. Once safely out of reach he bolted for the safety of the dining-room and slammed the door behind him.

Elena took Ascony by the arm and helped him into the kitchen. Mrs Khar was slumped over the table, weeping. Khar himself was standing in front of the fire, back towards them all. Milo's bread lay forgotten where he had dropped it.

'Lady...we are at war...'

'What?' Elena's mind flew to the store cupboard. Mercifully all the shopping was either done or on order awaiting collection.

Ascony knuckled his eyes and continued.

'Last evening, under cover of darkness, two Pechenegs arrived at the city gates. They were from a group sent out to aid villages being terrorised by the Franks. On the way they ran into an ambush laid by these so-called "Crusaders".' Ascony's eyes burned now with a savage fire. 'It was one of the louts we met yesterday, lady— Baldwin, they say his name is—it was his doing. He wanted the Pechenegs captured alive, although the two that managed to get back here are barely living. Baldwin intends to mutilate his hostages and send one back for every day the Crusaders have been kept waiting outside the city.'

Elena subsided on to the bench beside Mrs Khar. All she could think of was the rich laugh of the kind officer who had offered his assistance the night before. Was he one of the hostages?

'Why? Why the Pechenegs? What have they ever done except be honest and dutiful to the Emperor?'

'They are Muslims, lady. That is enough for these Franks. In their eyes the only good Muslim is a dead one.' Ascony spat.

Elena knew she would have to rally her household despite the secret dread she was feeling.

'Listen, all of you. This was just a cowardly move by the Franks and not necessarily the start of war. Our Emperor is too cultured and courteous to stoop to their base level. And you saw the state these ruffians are in, Ascony—they wouldn't dare attack. We shall be safe enough here.'

Ascony shook his head. It was some time before words would come to him again.

'The news gets worse, lady. The Lord Baldwin was so delighted with his good fortune in capturing our friends that he has persuaded his brother Godfrey to move the forces right up to the walls of the city. The ragged rabble are even now fitting up their siege machines outside the city gates.'

A growing horror twined its way about Elena's heart. Ascony and the Khars were Muslims. And there were two Franks in the guest room upstairs.

'The Emperor will never let them attack us!' she said with more conviction than she felt. 'The Pope sent us these Crusaders to help out against the Seljuk, that's all. We have no quarrel with anyone else. There's no earthly reason why the Crusaders should turn against us!'

'You will be safe, of course, lady. But the Crusaders are demanding that all Muslims in the city be sent out to them. They see the extermination of our people as their holy duty——'

'Well, you three aren't going. You are all staying right here.'

The three Muslims looked at each other, but Ascony was left as spokesman.

'Many of our people have gone to shelter under the Imam's protection, lady. I know that Mrs Khar would feel safer on holy ground.'

A look passed between Elena and Ascony. Both had heard what the Crusaders had done to Jews in their own countries. Those who had escaped the riots had been burnt alive as they sheltered in their synagogues.

'Nonsense. Things won't come to that. We'll all be perfectly safe, you'll see. Nobody will get past the walls.'

The thought struck all four of them at the same time. Two Franks had already breached the wall. How long before thousands more zealots did the same?

'Emperor Alexius will put paid to their fancy ideas. There's absolutely nothing to be afraid of.'

Her words were in vain. Ascony and the Khars were already afraid. The small figure they all saw standing on the kitchen threshold had brought fear to their eyes as surely as if it had been the entire Crusading hordes. Elena took control.

'It's all right. It's only Hamelin. He's the same poor little lad he has always been, and couldn't have understood our speech even if he had been able to hear. Come here, Hamelin.'

She smiled and beckoned to the boy. He came forward, miming hunger by rubbing his stomach.

'What are you all waiting for? Fetch our guest something. Sit down here, Hamelin.'

Milo would be safe enough next door with his toys, and would be unlikely to risk coming back into the kitchen. Elena put her arm about Hamelin as plain bread and water were brought for him. A meagre portion at that, Elena noticed, but did not reproach her staff.

Hamelin lunged at the food. Still expecting it to be stolen from him at any minute, he continued cramming food into his mouth until he could barely chew.

'Will you explain to the Franks what has happened, Lady Elena?' Ascony hissed as Hamelin choked back the last morsels of his food like a hungry hawk.

'I must.'

She stood up, motioning that Ascony and Hamelin follow her out into the hallway. With the kitchen door closed and Milo safely shut away in the dining-room, she confided in Ascony.

'Even Selest can't fail to sympathise when he hears what has been going on. If there is to be trouble, Ascony,

I would rather we were in this house with two Franks
on our side than have them in ignorance and against us.'

Ascony was not convinced. As they walked across the
hallway he muttered mutinously, casting the occasional
sidelong glance at Hamelin.

'Don't worry about him.' Elena squeezed Hamelin's
arm companionably. 'He's just an old woman.'

Although he could not understand, Hamelin burbled
something in reply and, putting his arm about Elena,
hugged her. At that moment a door slammed somewhere in a light breeze, causing Ascony to jump violently.

'It's only the wind, Ascony! I think rampaging
Crusaders would make a bit more noise than that.' She
smiled kindly at him. 'Now, take Milo off to school while
I settle this little lad in the guest room. Then I'll ask you
and Khar to carry Selest down here as well.'

Ascony looked at her doubtfully, wondering if the
Frank was to be taken up and downstairs on a regular
basis. Elena opened the guest room and, removing a key
from beneath the door-handle, invited Hamelin to enter.

'There should be no more little surprises and sudden
appearances if they are lodged in here, Ascony. This
room has a lock and key.'

An hour or so later Selest was again lounging on one
of the silk-covered couches in the guest room. Before
him was a roaring log fire, driving the chill of early spring
from the large, high-ceilinged room. Behind him a semi-
circle of pink and apricot painted screens protected him
from draughts and would shield the Franks from sight
should the best guest room door be left carelessly ajar.

Selest and Hamelin had couches of the finest quality,
and an elegant marble table of the like never seen back
at home. Unfortunately, they had barely anything else.
There was little for them to do except sleep or sit and
look at each other.

After a long consultation with her staff, Elena went
with Ascony to tell the Franks of the recent ambush.
When they arrived Hamelin was crouched in the hearth
watching the leaping fire while Selest spun a halma

counter on the table with tedious regularity. He slapped
it down with a snap as they appeared in his little
sanctuary.

'I'm starving. Any chance of breakfast? And there's
no need to lock the door, Lady Elena. We aren't animals
in a menagerie.'

Elena stood before him, hands clasped, and tried to
gain some comfort from the icon looking down on them
all from the cornice. Henry had made it for her from
hundreds of waste glass fragments and now it leapt with
the reflected light of the spring morning and the busy
fire.

'The door will be secured until I have received your
word that you will not allow Hamelin to roam as he did
earlier this morning. It is my house, and you are welcome
to hospitality only as long as you respect my wishes.'

At this Selest shrugged and sighed. 'Very well. I
suppose you can be forgiven for expecting that much.
Now, how about my breakfast?'

Elena summoned up her courage and looked him directly in the eyes.

'There will be breakfast, my lord, but from now on
meals will not be quite as lavish as they were. Circumstances have changed. Although we always have plenty
of food in store, when seven must live as five——'

She hesitated, but he made no comment that Elena
plus her three staff made only four. Either he knew
nothing of arithmetic, or he had missed the reference.
Moving on quickly, Elena told him of the disaster that
had befallen the Pechenegs. To her dismay and Ascony's
horror he was delighted.

'How many did they get? Oh, tremendous! Never fear,
Lady Elena, the lords of Lorraine will cut through these
infidel like a knife through warm butter. We'll soon have
these Muslims on the run!'

Elena looked at Ascony as Selest showed his delight.
Her servant was pale, but his eyes no longer registered
terror. There was only a dull, helpless acceptance of the
fate he knew awaited him. Feeling Elena's glance upon

him, Ascony turned to her and spoke in the Greek that Selest could not understand.

'I—the Khars—all our people . . . we are dead . . .'

Elena went to his side. Taking his arm, she led her servant to the unoccupied couch beside the fire and sat him down.

'Listen. The Crusaders outside are as close to us as they are going to get while they are in this murderous mood. And these two are unarmed, Ascony. They cannot hurt you. I will not let them,' she whispered quietly.

Turning to face Selest, Elena continued aloud in French. It was difficult to keep the hatred of Selest's principles from her voice but she had been taught that civility cost nothing except strained nerves.

'My lord. I know little enough of your culture, but it would seem that you know even less of life here for all your three-month stay. Our problems are not caused by all Muslims, only one particular sect. We share the city here with people of many races and creeds, and have done for hundreds of years. Why do your people waste time persecuting us and our friends?'

'Because your Emperor is an unreasonable, blinkered man and so it seems that we must take matters into our own hands.'

'You would do better to bury your foolish, bigoted ideas and accept our people, all of them, for what they are. Honourable, hard-working and—and willing to risk their lives by harbouring you two!'

Elena glared at Selest but was in turn held by some inner magnetism that crackled from his eyes. Only with difficulty did she marshal her wits and tear free from his gaze.

'Ascony. If you would be so kind as to clear the dining-room. I think I will take my meals in there today, and not with our guests.'

With a slight bow Ascony took his leave. He studiously refused to acknowledge Selest. When the door had closed, Selest's expression changed to one of amused indulgence and he stroked the silken couch beside him.

'Come, my lady. It seems strange that I alone should be seated while such a selfless lady is left to stand.'

Elena hesitated, then in a rustle of silk and gauze went to sit on the couch at the furthest point from Selest. The Frank laughed—a soft, intimate sound in the quiet room. Hamelin looked up from his job of feeding the fire with sticks. At a few words from Selest he laughed, too, but it was an unmodulated, broken sound. Elena shivered.

'You do not ask what we say, Lady Elena.'

'It was clearly not suitable for my ears. Private jokes are better kept as such.'

With one finger Elena traced the outline of an embroidered lily on her veil. Looking down so intently she did not notice Selest slide across the couch to draw a little closer to her. Before she could resist he had lifted her hand away from the gauze.

'Lady,' Selest murmured softly, 'I merely told him that you were in need of a little education.'

Elena looked up nervously. She knew that she had been foolish in sitting beside him, but... his eyes were the deep dark of forest pools. There was no anger in them now, only mystery. Something stirred deep within Elena, thoughts that she had not acknowledged since Henry had been lost to her. She looked away.

In the brief glimpse she had taken, Elena had noticed that Selest was quite a different shape from Henry. He filled out the borrowed robe in a way that the slight Henry could never have done. In particular the silk clasped Selest firmly over his still muscular shoulders. Every movement of his hand upon her wrist had been mirrored by ripples in the taut fabric. Elena began to wish that she had not dismissed Ascony so readily.

'Pretty bangles,' Selest said with a smile in his voice. He jangled the array of silver and enamel bracelets at her wrist. One for each year of her marriage to Henry— the ninth one broken to signify widowhood and held to the others by a fine gold chain.

The chain that still binds me to Henry, Elena thought, but did not stop Selest's finger idling over her wrist. He had her trapped, but by something far more effective than brute force.

'Put aside all these foolish infidel fashions, lady. Has no man ever praised you for being yourself, beneath all the paint and gilding?'

'Everyone dresses well here, my lord,' she said in a small voice. 'I dressed carefully today in the hope that you would not be offended again by our fashions. If I were to venture out so plainly attired everyone would talk——'

'"Everyone"? Who is this "everyone"? You are the widow of a Frankish lord, my lady, and so by association you have become almost one of us. Pay no heed to the foreign fancies of this land. They are for the infidel. Dress and act like a woman. There is no need to paint up and display yourself like some ignorant savage...'

While talking, he had cunningly released the ribbons securing two of her plaits. Elena felt faint alarm with the easing of tension at the nape of her neck, but could do nothing. The sweet hypnotism of his voice and caressing touch had robbed her of all power.

'I tell you what we'll do. Send the servants off to take refuge wherever it is they go. It won't be too long before our lads break any resistance. There might be a bit of trouble to begin with, but this place seems solidly built. We'll be quite safe here until the kill—until everything's over.'

He paused to fluff out the mane of her dark hair that he had released.

'There! Only the braids on either side to take out now and you'll be looking almost human, not like some little painted doll. Your gentlemen callers won't recognise you!'

'I have no "gentlemen callers", my lord.'

'What?' Selest gave another intimate little chuckle. 'You don't tell the whole truth, my lady. I bet they're queueing up to visit you during the long winter afternoons.'

Leaping away from him like a startled fawn, Elena tried to escape. It was impossible. Selest was sitting between her and the door. He caught her wrist again and held it deftly.

'Now, now, what's all this? Living among the infidel seems to have made my lady very nervous.'

'I cannot stay and hear the loose talk that you seem to delight in, my lord!'

'Loose talk? What harm is there in a little polite enquiry? I'm not the sort of man who would even think of kissing another chap's girl.'

Selest's tone belied the firm grip that he had on her arm. A mocking smile dared Elena to continue her attempts to escape.

'It is hardly polite to talk of——' Elena tried squirming against his grasp but it was useless. His grip was as resolute as ever. Petrified of being held so tightly, Elena really began to panic as Hamelin's ragged laughter joined in from the hearth. If she cried out for help Ascony wouldn't hear—the heavy guest room doors were closed and would have trapped all sound.

In desperation Elena made one last lunge with all her might. The surprise almost pulled Selest upright but his size and strength worked for him. Instead it was Elena who overbalanced and fell heavily on top of him. Real terror gripped her now and as Selest clutched at her she lost her head and started to scream.

'Shh! Hush!' He was still laughing but now held her pressed tightly against his chest. Elena could feel the amusement bubbling within him even as he fended off her blows. 'And I thought that you were just another pretty little butterfly. There, now. No need to make all this dreadful fuss. Hush. There—isn't it nicer when you don't struggle?'

Elena managed to free her face from the folds of his clothing.

'Let me go this instant. I shall report you to the authorities.'

'And risk a charge of harbouring the enemy? I think not, little butterfly. The sooner you accept the fact that you are all going to have to learn proper Frankish ways, the better. Now, simmer down and tell me what you are in such a terrible bate about.'

'You accuse me of having gentlemen callers then call me a liar when I try to defend my honour. Now you intend to have your way with me. Have you no shame?'

'Probably not.' Selest shrugged impishly, adjusting her weight well away from his injured left leg. 'Although it seems that you suffer from an overheated imagination, my lady. I merely tried to restrain you from a hasty action—you fell. That is all there is to it.'

'Then why do you insist on continuing to clutch at me?'

'Because, my lady,' Selest hugged her even closer to him, 'I'm beginning to enjoy it.'

He whispered these words deep in her ear with evident glee. Elena did not react with the laughter that he had expected. Instead she lay completely limp in his arms, feeling the rapid pulse of his life. After a few moments of stillness he relaxed his grip and looked down at her.

'Still alive?' He was smiling with apparent innocence. 'I was beginning to wonder. This isn't so very painful an ordeal, is it?'

At that point Elena knew she was lost. She would have to comply with all his demands. Although he held her lightly now, hidden power was hinted at in the spread of his broad shoulders and the determined set of his chin. All her struggles would be useless against him.

Elena was indeed nothing more than a frail butterfly in his hands.

## CHAPTER FOUR

ELENA swallowed hard and found a voice from somewhere.

'May I—may I be permitted one favour, my lord?'

'Certainly, my lady.'

'Not in front of the child. Send Hamelin out of sight.'

'It's a bit late now,' Selest said sharply, and Elena noticed a trace of uncertainty in his voice. 'It looks as though he's seen the best bit.'

He sent Hamelin out from their sanctuary and into the main body of the guest room. Once the boy had disappeared there was an uncomfortable pause. Elena had her eyes tightly shut. It was a long time before she risked opening them.

'Well, my lord?'

He was staring over her head towards the cheerful fireplace and did not answer. Time had revived Elena's wits and spirit. She was no longer feeling such a helpless victim, and, trying to rise, found that he did not hinder her. She was able to scramble to her feet.

As she straightened her dress and picked up the two discarded hair ribbons he roused from his reverie.

'That was an undignified way to begin, Lady Elena. All our beginnings seem doomed. Shall we try again?'

Elena still had to get past him to reach the door. There was no option but to do as he wished. She sat down meekly beside Selest while he set up the halma counters for a game. His movements were at first deft and swift, but they soon became slow and more thoughtful.

'You go first, Lady Elena.'

Perched upon the very edge of the couch, Elena could not move. Only after repeated urging from Selest did she finally reach out and slide one carved counter across the board.

Selest spent a long time in contemplation of her move. At last he bent forward, muttering something as he did so.

'Pardon, my lord? I didn't quite catch——'

'Can I put my arm around you?' he snapped crossly.

The horror would take forever at this rate. Elena felt herself tighten with dread.

'Of course, my lord.'

Selest turned to her as though startled, but the moment soon passed. He cleared his throat, in any other circumstances Elena would have said nervously. After a little while he did indeed lay his arm about her waist.

'It—it won't be long before Duke Godfrey frees the city, my lady.'

'We had freedom enough and to spare before the good duke arrived,' Elena said coldly, pushing another counter out of her line in response to his attack. Selest's hand began to fret up and down her rib-cage.

'You can't possibly live here properly with all these infidel...'

'We can and do, my lord. We have done for some time, and will continue to do so. If that causes your people distress then I am afraid that's their problem.'

'I want to make love to you, not discuss your stupid city!' he burst out.

Elena was unimpressed. 'If it hadn't been for your hopeless attempts at burglary none of us would be in this appalling mess and my honour would still be unblemished.'

His caresses became more insistent and suddenly he manoeuvred nearer her. As he was unable to use his left foot as leverage, Selest's movements were clumsy. For a moment his thigh was pressed tightly against Elena's, startling her, but his arm tightened around her waist. It drew her into an enveloping embrace almost before she realised. Then he was kissing her.

His kiss was slow and sweet, lingering on her lips but without insistence. Elena felt her will-power draining away as gentle caresses to her hair and back brushed away all remaining resistance. Suddenly she was kissing him with an unknown, unbidden hunger.

'No!' She broke away, gasping. 'I can't! Anything but that——'

'You were enjoying it!' Selest said with amusement and gave her a sly squeeze.

'I wasn't!'

He leant forward until his nose touched hers. 'Go on— you were!'

Amber glints in his eyes showed that he saw through her indignant pretence.

'No...no, never! If it weren't for the sake of my household I would never have agreed to your—your blackmail in a million years!'

'Oh, now, that's a rash thing to say! When have I ever threatened you with blackmail?'

Elena had to look away. He confused her, unsettling her with his deep dark eyes and sensuous mouth. Taut with the effort of trying to keep up appearances, she began to tremble.

Almost at once Selest's expression changed. Amusement melted away to be replaced by distaste. His arm slipped from her waist, the tide of his ardour leaving its high watermark.

'Perhaps I need to remind you that we are not all barbarians, Lady Elena,' he said flatly. 'Although I don't apologise for what I did. We both enjoyed the moment, even if your spirit will deny your body. What do you intend to do now?'

Elena stood up. Rearranging her clothes and dignity, she half turned from him and began to divide her dishevelled hair for replaiting.

'It is Easter. There are many things to be done about the house——'

'I meant, what to you intend to do about us? Do what you like with me, but in the spirit of Christian charity——' He looked up at her, guilt tinged with embarrassment. 'Don't punish the boy for my failings. Don't give him away. Please...'

Elena's fingers slipped from her plaiting and she looked at him directly. He really was worried, but not for himself. Why did he have to be so nearly irresistible? Elena had to steel herself against getting involved. Selest would have to be kept at rather more than arm's length in future. She shrugged, trying to keep her voice free from emotion.

'I am as much to blame on this occasion, my lord. But I will not be forced into being chaperoned inside my own house. You must learn to keep your—failings——' she blushed at the word '—under better control. I don't expect to be seduced every time I offer aid.'

'Very well.' He bobbed his head in a mock bow. 'I shall take care never to inflame your seething passions again.'

He was laughing at her. Elena scowled and wrenched her hair ribbon tight.

'I am the respectable widow of a noted businessman, my lord. I am not allowed passions.'

Instead of taking notice of her words, Selest laughed out loud. Elena was mortified. How dared he? From now on, Elena vowed, I'll show him. No more the frightened butterfly. I'll become as wily and artful as he is. He won't catch me with fear again.

Selest had turned his attention to fingering the mother-of-pearl inlay on the halma board.

'You need not worry about the Crusaders outside for the moment, my lady. Whatever happens there will be no attack in Holy Week.'

Elena stopped adjusting her hair and looked at him keenly. The matter had worried them all.

'Are you sure?'

'Positive. As you know, the duke is a very religious man. He would never countenance it.'

Instead of reassuring Elena, Selest's words only made her worry more. What, then, would happen after Holy Week?

Elena busied herself in the kitchen for a while. She had sent Ascony and Khar out to escort Milo to school and then collect the meats that had been ordered for the Easter celebrations. When the two men staggered back under the weight of their purchases, it was with more disturbing news.

The city was in turmoil. Panic was tearing through the streets and running riot through the shops. Fearing for the future, the Byzantines had already emptied the shops of food. Those without the hoarding instinct would go hungry until the next shipments arrived.

Rather than stay at home and worry, Elena went out to visit her own shop.

The glass business had been the making of her husband Henry. With the help of loyal staff he had become quite a financial genius. When he died, jealous rivals had been quick to pounce on Elena, trying to frighten her with stories of unpaid bills and missing orders. Expecting the young widow to yield to their extortion, they had been in for a shock. Elena had not intended to let the business Henry had built up slip away.

To the amazement of everyone she had arrived at the shop the same day that the threats were received. Eban the supervisor had been wary. His doubts were only dispelled when Elena had taken up a sweeping brush, so freeing one of the apprentices for more important work.

Milo had been made to do his part, too. When poor young Elena arrived at palace or apartment with the latest delivery on a tiny donkey and her poor fatherless mite in her arms there was always a little something added to payments 'for the baby'.

Ascony had been horrified. Elena was more realistic. The extra cash meant she never had to dip into the business account to feed and clothe Milo. Every little helped when so much had to go to cheating 'creditors'.

Elena had kept nothing for herself. Poverty had been no stranger to her before, and she bore it again.

As she turned into the Mese, Elena gasped. The highway was one solid mass of people. Men shouted, women cried, dogs barked and children thieved. Suddenly, above all the racket rose one sound more horrifying than all the rest put together. It reared up from the other side of the city wall. The sound of sword on shield. A rapping, tapping, chorus of insistence. Men at the ready.

Elena jostled with the crowd, elbowing her way through the thronging struggle. Finally she was forced through the door of her shop by the sheer press of people milling along outside.

'Eban! You're still here! Why aren't you out there with the rest of them?'

'No need, lady,' the Turk said quietly. 'My wife always has enough food laid in for a siege at the best of times. I've sent the apprentices out for whatever they want, but they're welcome to come and share ours if things get too tight.'

'I should shut up shop if I were you, Eban. People aren't interested in glassware today—only what goes into it.'

A small, elderly man with knowing eyes, Eban looked at Elena kindly as she watched the heaving crowd outside.

'If you'd like to wait while I put up the shutters, Lady Elena, I'll see you safe home again. The lads took a key with them.'

The crowds seemed to increase with every passing moment. Eban closed the shutters one by one until only thin shafts of sunlight could enter the shop. Dust motes spiralled slowly up to the ceiling, the shop feeling warm and secure against the pressing masses outside.

'I sent Milo off to Father Johann's this morning. Even though I was in two minds after the ambush——'

'Awful business,' Eban said, tutting. 'Nothing but lying barbarians, only pretending to come and help us. All those Franks see in Constantinople is rich pickings.'

He made a noise of disgust, then went to pat Elena's arm. 'The little lad will be as safe at Father Johann's as anywhere, Lady Elena. He'll be all right, as long as I take care of his mamma.'

Taking Elena by the arm, he led her into the street and locked the door. At that moment they were both forced back into the doorway by a tidal wave of people and noise. A small number of the imperial guard were struggling against the tide, trying to reach the city gates. They were armed to the teeth, and the atmosphere became as tense as a bowstring.

'The Crusaders won't fight! Not today—it's Holy Thursday!'

'Begging your pardon, lady, but that racket they're making says differently.'

The sound of sword on shield was a noisy crescendo of evil intent. Only the city walls stood between the innocent citizens of Constantinople and thousands of Frankish soldiers inflamed with blood lust. People began to sense disaster, like animals panicking before an earthquake. They began to run.

The tattoo of swords stopped as suddenly as it had started, and the people froze with terror.

Constantinople's golden gates burst open like a ripe peach as the first roar of battering rams tore down the Mese. Only the sheer weight of people packing the highway prevented an immediate Frankish invasion. There wasn't room for the gates to open wide enough to admit an army. One knight kicked his horse through the gap but was seized and dashed to the ground. He disappeared beneath a screaming rabble while his horse plunged and kicked through the terrified citizens in its way.

A couple of Crusaders burst in while the Byzantines were distracted by the fleeing horse. Flailing wildly with broadswords, they accounted for several innocents before being overwhelmed by a flood of citizens. The Frankish infantry threw its weight against the doors, trying to prise them further apart. For minutes as long as hours the struggle went back and forth, push against shove. Constantinople was fuelled by a desperation of fear and after terrible agonies the gates were slammed shut and barred once and for all.

The rattling challenge began again from outside. Sick with fear Elena pressed on, almost outpacing Eban. Rumours were already flying past with the fleeing crowds— Byzantines killed by Franks or trampled underfoot in the terrible panic. And on a holy day.

'He said Duke Godfrey wouldn't let them attack before Easter...'

'Who, Lady Elena?'

'Oh...A—a kinsman of Henry's. He is with the Frankish Crusaders. I took him a few home comforts the other day...'

'Have nothing to do with any of them, Lady Elena,' Eban said sternly. 'It's a bad business when you can't even trust the poor master's kin, I know, but they're none of them to be trusted. Franks? Animals, more like. No—that's disrespectful to animals——'

He stopped. Even from the end of Father Johann's lane they could both see that his ever open door was now firmly shut.

The sound of sword on shield from outside increased.

'Why, they're all safe and secure inside, lady. You come along home. Young Milo will be safe enough with his little friends——'

Elena would not be put off. Breaking away from Eban, she ran down the lane and hammered on the great black door. There was no reply—the door was locked and the windows shuttered. Elena called out, hoping her voice would brook the fear and suspicion within. Nothing.

There came no reassuring sound from inside, even though Elena pressed her ear hard against each shutter in turn.

'I expect Father Johann's sent all the little lads home, Lady Elena. Come on—the quicker we get there the sooner we find out.'

Taking her more firmly by the arm, he marched Elena towards her home in the next street. He could not have guessed at her horror when they saw a Pecheneg horse tied up outside the house.

It took some time for Ascony to reach the door, to Elena's growing frenzy. Then the key grated ominously in its lock before the door was eased open a tiny crack.

'Ascony? Where's Milo? What's happening?'

Ascony's breath came out in a rush of relief. 'Oh, lady—it's . . .'

He caught sight of Eban just in time.

'. . . quite all right.'

Ascony laughed, but it was a tightly unnatural sound.

'If you would care to take some refreshment with us, Eban . . .' Elena said, hoping that he wouldn't. Sensing that this was not the right time, Eban made his escape with Elena's thanks for his help. Once he had been waved out of sight Ascony whisked Elena into the house.

'The Franks are——'

'I don't care about them! Where's Milo?'

'School was cancelled today, lady. Father Johann brought him back, and they are in the second guest room.'

Elena began to run towards it, able to breathe easily again at last.

'There is someone else with them, too, lady.'

'A Pecheneg? What does he want?'

'"Who" might be nearer the mark.'

Elena's eyes opened wide with horror but Ascony put a finger to his lips as he pushed open the double doors of the second guest room.

Ascony's restrained announcement was quite at odds with Elena's entrance. She dashed to Milo, veils fluttering, and flung her arms about him. Her relief was only matched by his joy at the thought of a day off school.

'Pecheneg let me ride on his horse, Mummy. Can I have one? Can I?'

'We'll see. When you're older, sweetheart.'

Elena kissed her son then turned a dazzling smile on her guests.

'Thank you both so much for bringing him home. I hope my staff have kept you entertained in my absence?'

She tried to inject a tone of 'Isn't it time you were going?' into her voice, but neither of her visitors took the bait. Instead Father Johann settled himself more comfortably in his seat and stroked his long white beard thoughtfully.

'Milo's been telling us all about his new friend.'

Elena studied the top of Milo's head, brushing the dark hair into order.

'Oh, yes? And who's that, sweetheart?'

Looking up at her, Milo struck quite innocently but with devastating effect.

'I don't know his name, Mummy. He came and played with my Noah's ark this morning. He likes piggies best. But he doesn't call them piggies.'

Milo sighed heavily, which was nothing compared to what Elena felt like doing. She pinned on a wobbly smile and tried it out on the Pecheneg officer. He did not immediately produce manacles, so it must have been more convincing than it felt.

'Sorry to trouble you with this, Lady Elena, but we've had a few reports of Franks trying to get in on the quiet. Best to clear this up first as last, in case. Have you noticed anything missing—food, wine—that's what they'll be after? At first,' he finished darkly. An unmistakable look passed between him and Ascony.

'The stores seem all right, don't they, Ascony? There, Officer. Nothing to worry about. I expect it's just a bit of romancing——'

Milo pulled at her tunic insistently and stamped his foot. 'It isn't, Mummy, it isn't! You know him. Last night Ascony was telling him off in the garden...'

Elena laughed carelessly. 'That's right, sweetheart, of course he was. It was a nasty person to come creeping round here, wasn't it?' Pointedly she put her hand to Milo's forehead as though testing for a high temperature. 'I think you'd better run along to the kitchen for a cup of kefir. All this excitement with the Crusaders is proving a bit too much for him, Officer.'

Ascony stepped forward and led Milo away firmly. The eunuch's expression said clearly that, as Elena had got them all into the mess, she had better get them out of it.

The Pecheneg officer cleared his throat.

'All the same, Lady Elena. Young Milo seemed to have too vivid a description for it to be a complete fantasy. We can't be too careful with these murderous Franks about. Mind if I take a quick look around? These old houses are full of nooks and crannies where a chap might hide. If he only came out at night to feed, like a 'roach, you might not know he was here. I'll start with the garden, if it's all the same to you.'

He stood up, straightening his jacket. With a polite bow he invited Elena to show the way while he followed. Merry with curiosity, Father Johann accompanied them, although the last thing Elena needed was company.

To reach the garden doors in the dining-room they had to pass the room where Selest and the cause of all the trouble were trapped. Hamelin. He must have come across Milo while searching for the kitchen. Elena wondered how she would manage to keep her hands off the boy when they next met. Then she remembered that, if they were found out, the imperial guard would wreak vengeance enough on all of them.

The Pecheneg cast a professional eye over the dining-room. It was neat and tastefully furnished, the only possible hiding-place behind its long, flowing curtains. He nudged these about carefully with his sabre, then went out into the garden.

There was little cover here, either. The Pecheneg strolled around the little stone summerhouse then returned, smiling.

'Nothing here, although there's plenty of fresh water and a fish or two that would keep him going.'

'A childish fantasy, then. Nothing more.' Father Johann chuckled. 'I was too hasty in bringing it to your attention, Officer.'

'Ah, you never can tell, Father. "Hair like straw and skin like pastry." That's what the lad said. Sounds like a Frank to me.'

Elena trailed along behind the two men as they headed for the kitchen. As well as the Khars, Ascony and Milo were in there. Mrs Khar burst into another spasm of wailing at the sight of the Pecheneg, but he was used to that and withdrew hurriedly.

'We seem to have that effect on people.' He smiled ruefully, then went upstairs. Each bedroom was given a quick, methodical search. All the balconies overlooking the quadrangle were checked. There was nothing to be found.

The Pecheneg walked slowly, each step feeling like a lifetime to Elena. He seemed to have forgotten about the first guest room. Elena prayed that he would go before remembering, but it was not to be.

'Now, there's just that other room downstairs and the quadrangle to check, Lady Elena.'

Her stomach plummeted.

'I'm sorry, Officer.' Elena twisted her veil appealingly as they trooped downstairs again. 'You see, what with all the panic the first guest room is in a bit of a state. Housework not done, you know. But I was in there myself not an hour ago——'

Father Johann laughed indulgently as the Pecheneg poked about the greenery of the quadrangle. 'My house-keeper is just the same, Officer. Place as neat as a new pin, yet still she worries.'

This was a nightmare, without hope of being able to wake. Elena stood transfixed as the Pecheneg went into the first guest room. She could not run, or hide, or even appeal to his better nature. Pechenegs only had one nature, and that was to be professional to the fingertips.

He was inside the room for a very long time. Father Johann tried to make polite conversation, but Elena could not concentrate. How could she, when cold beads of perspiration were trickling down the small of her back?

Finally the Pecheneg strolled out.

'Shouldn't waste the nice fire you've got in there, Lady Elena.'

'It's—er—to dry out the wall. Damp, you know...' Elena gabbled half in fear and half in relief.

'I do indeed. You want to get that seen to, Lady Elena. Only last year we had to pay the landlord a fat sum to have our roof put right...' His voice faltered, died away then returned with a burst of enthusiasm. 'That's it! That's where he's hiding! Up on the roof. May I, Lady Elena?'

Elena showed him to the trapdoor giving access to the flat roof above. As he began fiddling with its catch, Ascony materialised at the foot of the stairs.

'You were unsuccessful in your search, then, Officer?'

'Until now. There's one last place I didn't check. The roof.'

'Ah, now that would be unwise. We have had a little trouble with it over the winter, and I fear that it may be unsafe. We are going to get it checked.'

The Pecheneg turned to Elena almost suspiciously.

'You never said, lady.'

'I didn't know,' Elena floundered as Ascony threw her a furious glare. 'Ascony takes care of things like that.'

The eunuch's black eyes flashed. 'Not for very much longer,' he spat at Elena, coming up the stairs to stand behind her.

Once he had managed to open the hatch the Pecheneg had another observation to make.

'Better look to your chimney pots too, lady. This one has rolled off against the hatch. A wonder it didn't smash.'

The Crusaders were still battering sword against shield and a wave of sound rose up as though from a mighty sea.

'Look at that lot,' the Pecheneg sneered openly. 'More Franks than the French exchequer. Sent here on a mission of mercy yet all they can think of is attacking the very ones they've come to help.'

'We were sorry to hear about your people,' Elena said, relieved to see that the roof seemed empty.

'No matter.' He turned on his heel, kindly manner replaced for an instant by cold, hard arrogance. 'They will ascend directly to heaven, having died in a righteous struggle.'

'Doesn't it make you bitter towards the rest of us Christians?'

The Pecheneg laughed, teeth flashing white against his Turkish tan. 'No. Only the Crusading dogs. To account for just one of them, even though I were to die in the attempt—ah, can you think of a more glorious way to die, lady?'

'No,' Elena said untruthfully, hoping that she would be saved from the Pecheneg idea of justice.

The Turk strolled around the flat roof, enjoying his view of the Crusaders. They were getting hotter and more irritable by the minute as they tried to keep up their rattling tattoo of fear. Elena was hot and bothered too, but for quite a different reason. She suggested lemonade in the quadrangle for them all, which her guests accepted graciously.

With a last look over each edge of the roof to assure himself of the forty-foot drop, the Pecheneg went to the door and back down into the house.

Ascony looked at Elena with dread. He evidently didn't know where the Franks were now, either.

At any other time Elena would have been delighted to entertain Father Johann and the Pecheneg officer. They were amiable company and the quadrangle was a pleasant place to sit and drink. Today time crawled past as they talked of this and that, business, pleasure and Milo's progress at baby school.

Elena wisely managed to steer the conversation away from everyone's favourite topic, which was religion.

Father Johann seemed of the same mind, speaking only of the extra time he would have that day to spend in his garden. In such a civilised setting it hardly seemed possible that barbarian hordes were set to burst into the city at any moment.

When at last the two men rose to go Elena barely had strength enough left to see them to the door. She shut the front door behind them with more relief than she would have thought possible.

She was still gathering her scattered wits when Ascony rippled down the staircase to meet her. When he saw Elena's shattered expression he marched straight up to her, tight-lipped and petulant.

'Let this be an awful warning to you.'

Spinning on his heel, he strode off towards the kitchen, but Elena called him back. He obeyed, but with an insolent tilt to his chin. Elena was ready for him.

'I'll not have you speaking to me like that.'

'How would you prefer that I addressed you, lady? With sly seductions like the Crusading dog?'

Elena slapped his face. Ascony reeled, but more through shock than pain.

'Remember who pays your wages, eunuch.'

Bewilderment replaced the arrogance in Ascony's eyes and he backed off towards the kitchen. Only when he put his hand to the door-handle did Elena force herself to look at him again.

'Come here, Ascony.'

He did as ordered, but not willingly. When he stopped in front of her Elena had to look down at her toes in shame.

'I'm sorry, Ascony. That was uncalled for.'

She looked up in time to see relief cross his face before he could conceal it. Almost at once his air of calm efficiency returned.

'The fault was entirely mine, lady. I spoke churlishly.'

'Where the Franks are concerned perhaps it ought to be a case of "least said, soonest mended". They mustn't come between us, not after all this time. Are we friends again?'

She looked into Ascony's face. Her hope was rewarded with a wide grin.

'Of course, lady.'

There were thumps and rustling shuffles from the head of the stairs and Ascony bowed low to her.

'If you will excuse me, lady. I must ask Khar to stoke up the kitchen fire. Another bath is in order for our guest.'

Elena followed him towards the kitchen but stopped short at the foot of the stairs. She could go no further. It was all she could do to stop herself from laughing out loud.

'My lord! Look at you—you're duskier than a Turk!'

Selest sat on the top step while Hamelin closed the hatch. He was plastered with soot and embroidered with a rich mixture of twigs, straw and feathers. Scowling furiously, he was not amused.

'Your chimneys need sweeping.'

'It looks as though you have done an admirable job already, my lord.' Elena looked curiously to Hamelin, who was still reasonably neat and tidy.

'He jumped across to your neighbour's roof. The gap was too wide for me with this damned leg.' He winced, and at once Elena put aside all thoughts of his earlier behaviour. Running up the stairs, she took one arm while Hamelin supported the invalid on his other side. Together they made slow progress down the wide staircase.

'You have only yourself to blame, my lord. None of this would have happened if you had kept an eye on Hamelin. Letting him wander about—it's a wonder he didn't get out into the street.'

'It's not my fault. He said he'd found a baby—how was I to know that your precious child was old enough to talk?'

Selest was snatching breaths in ragged gasps. He was clearly in great pain, so Elena forgave his abrupt tone. Reaching the foot of the stairs, she stopped Hamelin so that Selest could gather his strength. At rest he leaned more heavily on Hamelin, giving Elena a break too.

'I need a doctor.'

'Ascony is all we have for the moment. He's very good.'

'I am in pain. I need a leech!'

Elena could feel his hand clenching and unclenching as it rested against her shoulder. Perspiration from his arm about her neck was already dampening her tunic. This was serious.

Ascony took charge as soon as he came out of the kitchen.

'Sit down, my lord.'

'I can't. I can't move——'

Calmly Ascony took Elena's place and lowered Selest down to sit on the stairs. The Frank tried to contain his agony but it burst out in one sharp cry. Head down he clutched at his left leg, fingers digging into the pale skin savagely.

'All that clambering about hasn't helped. The pain will probably pass away of its own accord, but I'll take a look in case.'

Ascony began to tug at the knots securing Selest's bandages, but the patient writhed at his rough handling.

'Let me try.' Distressed by his distress, Elena moved forward, searching in the purse at her waist for a small pair of scissors. Selest lay back against the stairs, eyes closed and breathing quickly. His pain seemed little affected as Elena cut through the knots of linen rather than pulling at them. She unwrapped his ankle.

It seemed worse than before. The swelling had increased and bruising had painted a wide black stripe along the outer edge of his foot.

'As I thought.' Ascony allowed himself the smallest of smirks. 'My lord has been the architect of his own downfall once again.'

'It was that or death by Pecheneg sabre, Ascony. Perhaps we shouldn't judge him too harshly.'

'I—need—something for the—pain.'

'There is nothing. I am not a doctor.'

Ascony stood up and with Hamelin's help took Selest towards the bath house door.

'When you are clean, my lord, I shall set the ankle in sand. That will ease some of the pain, but I regret that you will not be able to move from the guest room again for some time. If we are searched a second time, nothing will save you. Or us,' Ascony finished in a whisper.

'I don't—care. Anything, but—stop this awful pain! Can't you—send out for something?'

'To do so would arouse suspicion, my lord.'

Elena watched Ascony's face. He was trying to conceal a hint of satisfaction at the suffering of one of the hated Franks, but Selest wasn't in a position to notice. His pain was clearly increased tenfold by the shame he felt at losing control in front of strangers.

'Ascony, what about the medicine you gave me when they told us that Henry...' She still did not like to use the word.

'That is too strong, lady.' He shrugged without looking at her. Elena wondered if he thought that a little pain might not be good for Frankish souls.

'Very well, Ascony.' She went to offer some little comfort to Selest. 'But if I find that there is any other reason why you withhold it——'

'Of course, lady.' Ascony gave her an innocent smile as he manhandled Selest into the bath house, and Elena silently scolded her suspicious mind.

She went to find Milo. Under Mrs Khar's watchful eye he was busy making shapes out of flour and water dough.

'Mummy?' His voice was querulous and he scrambled off the kitchen bench to run to her. 'I have got a new friend, Mummy. Really. I wasn't pretending.'

'I know, sweetheart.'

To lie to a child was unforgivable. Milo might as well know some of the truth. Elena had already decided that she would keep him home from school for the foreseeable future.

'He's staying here for a little while, Milo. We're looking after his friend. Only we don't want anybody to know about it. It's our special secret.'

'Why, Mummy?'

Elena wished she had a drachma for every time she'd heard that question. Biting back 'Because I say so,' which never got her anywhere, she thought of another ploy.

'Because—well, because some people aren't lucky enough to have a nice house like this to stay in. They will be cross to think that two Fra—two gentlemen could come and stay here. They'd come and knock on the doors and peep through the windows, and say "Why can't we come in, too?"'

Milo looked very uneasy. He was a nervous child with a horror of people coming to the house. Elena knew he would keep the secret now, and, taking his hand, led him out into the hall.

Hamelin was sitting on the floor outside the bath house door. At the sight of Milo he sprang up and the two boys greeted each other in their own way. Hamelin was much the taller of the two and a good six years separated their ages. If Selest was anything to go by the Franks dragged their children up rather than bringing them up. Elena had misgivings about the friendship, but she let Milo take Hamelin off to play. She had other things to worry about.

Pink and perspiring, Ascony emerged from the bath house.

'It is no good, lady. I must do as you suggest and arrange medication for the Frank. Even I cannot stand by and watch such suffering, but must help the in-fidel——'

'Hush!' Elena cut in quickly. 'There's to be none of that talk here. I'll look to the Frank while you arrange matters. Be quick!'

Looking from Elena to Selest's discarded clothing outside the bath house, Ascony was horrified.

'But—lady—you alone in there with him? He's all...undressed! It can't be decent...'

'You had him prancing through the hall without a stitch on the first day he was here, Ascony. I don't remember him having anything that I haven't seen before.' She waved aside Ascony's complaints and slipped off her tunic and tsourapia. Taking towels from a chest beside the bath house door, Elena plunged into the stifling washroom.

There was barely room for one and an assistant in the tiny room, which was little bigger than a cupboard. Selest was slumped against the back wall, one hand over his eyes. Elena knew that she had to be brisk or Selest would dissolve before her. That was a fate that no man—especially a brave Crusader—could be expected to endure.

'Come along, my lord. There's no time to waste. Ascony won't be long, but he'll expect to find you ready to go.'

'You shouldn't be in here,' Selest managed mutinously, hand still at his face and head down.

'Why not? It's my house, and you know what I said about being free in my own house.' She wrapped one of the towels around his waist. 'Did he finish washing you?'

Selest grimaced. 'All except my foot.'

'Right, I'll do that quickly now——'

'No!' Her would-be seducer now had the expression of a frightened child.

'Don't be silly. You're worse than my little Milo. It has to be clean before we start.'

The effect of her words on Selest was dramatic. Closing his eyes, he drew himself up as much as possible and began to clutch at the rosary about his neck. Elena was unimpressed and knelt down before him.

'Rest your foot in my lap as much as you can, so that I've got something to work against.'

Wordlessly he touched the sole of his foot against her knees. He could put barely any pressure on it before gasping in pain. Soaping her hands, Elena ran them so lightly over his foot that he barely winced. To rinse it she trickled clean water over the skin then stroked it dry with a silk kerchief from her waist.

Only when Selest had finished with his prayers did he look to see what she was doing.

'Why do you bother?'

'Because you are so grateful.'

Elena looked up at him quickly and smiled. Instead of responding he laid his head back against the wall, dark curls thrown into sharp relief against the blank white wall.

'Takes so long,' he muttered to himself at last. 'I know—I've held others down before while it's done to them...and to be brought down to such shame in front of foreigners——'

'They're not so bad. I'm giving house room to a couple at the moment, don't forget.'

Selest wasn't listening to her. In a nightmare world of his own he continued.

'I've seen the state others get into when they realise...but it's not happening to me. I won't give them the satisfaction...' His fist thumped the wall in defiance.

'Oh, for heaven's sake,' Elena said crossly. 'Anybody would think Ascony was going to chop your leg off.'

There was a very long pause.

'Isn't he?'

'Isn't he what?'

'Going to take my leg off?'

'And your head, too, if he's got any sense.'

Elena bit her tongue as soon as the words were out. The prayers, the defiance—it had been because he thought that the worst was coming. And Elena had made fun of him.

# CHAPTER FIVE

ELENA took her time dabbing Selest's injured foot dry as though extra care would make up for his earlier torment. No speech passed between them until Ascony knocked on the door. There was no room for him to enter, only just enough for him to pass a goblet through to Elena.

She handed the warm cup to Selest. 'It's not very nice, so drink it down quickly. Don't let it touch the sides.'

Selest gripped the goblet, looking into the liquid.

'It isn't a trick?'

'As if we would!'

Once more Elena regretted her hasty words.

'I promise.'

He winced as another wave of pain made the decision for him. The cup went to his lips and he drained it quickly.

When Elena had passed the goblet out to Ascony she stood up.

'What happens now?' Selest asked roughly, wiping the back of his hand across his lips. Elena handed him a towel and he repeated the movement, a little sheepish at his ill manners.

'You will begin to feel tired, in a little while. It dulls the senses. That's all. Would you be easier leaning against me, my lord? It seems uncomfortable for you to be balanced there like that.'

Selest shrugged. For a moment he resisted, then let her take a little of his weight. They stood together without speaking, listening to Ascony tidying up outside. At last Selest broke the silence.

'I'm sorry—about what happened this morning, I mean...'

84

Elena's heart warmed towards him. Even barbarians had finer feelings, then.

'Don't mention it, my lord. Think of it as a simple misunderstanding.'

'Then...you won't tell anyone? Hamelin?'

'Of course not, my lord. As if I would. Why would I want to tell Hamelin anyway?'

Selest sighed. It was such a childlike sound that Elena looked up at him. Ascony's medicine was having an effect. Selest's pupils were growing large, dimming his brown eyes into new softness.

'Hamelin thinks I'm...' He sighed again, and the weight of his arm increased around Elena's neck. 'Hamelin thinks I'm wonderful. He's never seen me fail with a woman. Come to that, I've never seen me fail with a woman before.'

Elena knew now what he meant. All he worried about was his image. He hadn't spared a thought for her feelings and very real distress at his advances.

The Pecheneg was right, she thought with feeling. You are infidel dogs, the lot of you.

With a violent rap on the door Elena summoned Ascony to open it. When they had eased the rapidly wearying Selest out into the hall Elena left Ascony to it. For the present Elena had little sympathy with the Frankish cuckoos in her nest. Her only thoughts were for Milo and the effects that such barbarians might have on him.

The dining-room sounded suspiciously quiet. Elena went to the door and eased it open, but the boys were too absorbed in their game to pay any attention. They were laid down on the floor while pairs of wooden animals grazed over rolling plains of green rug. Elena withdrew quietly, before any deluge.

Mrs Khar was getting on quite happily with the cooking. Most of it was finished now, and Elena would only be in her way.

There seemed little else for her to do. She went into the guest room.

Selest was already propped up on the couch, his left leg supported on two chairs. Ascony and Khar had taken the front off a packing case and were fashioning a way of encasing Selest's ankle in sand with the least mess.

'I think your Crusader could do with a little moral support,' Ascony said in reply to her offer of help. His smirk of distaste showed him as eager for Selest's conversation as Elena was.

She sat down on the couch with an air of obligation. Selest turned his head slowly on its cushion, watching her with the air of quiet resignation that she had seen in Milo when he was suffering. He raised his hand weakly as though reaching for something.

'How much longer?'

'Quite a long time yet.' She spoke sharply, the bitterness of his perfidy still rankling.

'What are they doing now?'

'Look for yourself.'

His eyes closed whenever he stopped fighting against the drug. Sleep tried to ease him but he would not accept its embrace.

'I can't.'

'Then go to sleep.'

He shook his head, forcing his eyes open to look at her directly. 'Bad dreams... Wake up and my foot—it'll be gone...'

Elena took hold of his hand. It must be a habit of the Franks to always look on the black side.

'I've told you what they're going to do. Now go to sleep.'

He continued to look at her, but found it difficult to focus. Even so, he would not sleep.

'Would you want a man with only one foot?'

Elena thought of an answer to that, but it wasn't one fitting to a sick-room.

'I wouldn't want you at all.'

His eyes opened a little wider. 'How can you say that?'

'Very easily. Khar has told me all about Crusaders. I know what you're like.'

'You—you hardly know me...'

A ghost of a smile flickered across his face but he had no strength to sustain it.

'Khar says that Franks spit on their babies to baptise them.'

'I—I have to disappoint you there, Lady Elena. I've never known of that.'

Selest gave a weak cry of pain as Ascony settled the Crusader's lower leg in the hastily made trough.

'Khar should know better than to relay gossip, lady.' Ascony gave his companion an angry stare. 'I hope that that was the extent of his scaremongering.'

'Oh, no,' Elena said, made bold by Ascony's dismay. 'He told me that the Franks wash their clothes in their cooking pots, eat vermin and they drink blood—and...well, worse things, too...'

Elena stuttered to a halt, realising from Ascony's expression that she had gone too far. Selest made a small noise, and she looked down to find that he was trying to laugh.

'Lady Elena,' he slapped his spare hand to his heart with a loose-limbed movement, 'I cannot tell a lie. I've done all that—and probably the worse things, too...'

He seemed quite unrepentant. Now it was Elena's turn to be shocked. While Ascony and Khar busied around and scowled at each other she tried to think of something to say. Nothing, but nothing seemed adequate.

'You can't begin to understand.' A sudden spasm of pain seized him as Ascony began packing sand around his injured foot. Only when the bulk of sand was sufficient to take the pressure from his torn muscles did the pain ease enough for him to continue.

'We don't do that sort of thing—at home. Only on the road. Been on the road for months...when you're hungry and thirsty to the very death you'll try anything...anything...' His voice faded away, then returned slowly. 'When you're starving—not that you'll remember anything about that—even a mouse's child is tasty. Cats...sparrows...urchins——'

Elena screamed in horror, 'Cannibal!'

'No, no...silly child. Like...' he drew an expansive picture in the air with his hands '...big mice—with prickles. Two mouthfuls,' he added with relish before drifting off for a moment.

Elena fought her revulsion but was left with a morbid curiosity. As Ascony levelled the sand off around Selest's toes Elena nudged the Crusader awake.

'They've finished, my lord. Now, tell me about the blood—— ' she whispered. When the veils of confusion had cleared from his mind, Selest smiled.

'And the "worse things"?'

Elena blushed and looked away, but he started to tell her all the same.

'Hunger is bad enough, but thirst is unendurable. The worst torment of all. You'll do anything to slake it...so, every day that there was no rain to drink...we killed some of the pack ponies, or oxen. And drank the blood.'

'You didn't enjoy it?'

He managed a look of disgust. 'Of course not. And as for the other stuff...' Laughing, he squeezed her hand. 'I didn't bother. It gets saltier every time, they say, making the thirst much worse. And as I say, we don't carry on like that—at home...'

Drifting away again, he merely nodded as Ascony and Khar took their leave. His eyes only opened properly when Elena arranged a blanket over him.

'They won't—come back and...' He struggled, but was overcome by weariness.

'No. You sleep and save your strength, my lord. The sooner you're able to walk out of here and all our lives, the better.'

Selest slipped away into a deep sleep. Ragged, nervous gasps were gradually replaced by deep, even breathing and for the first time peace lay over his features. Elena watched as he slept, marvelling at the length of his dark lashes or the softness of his skin as she tended him. It didn't seem right to leave him alone when he was so vulnerable.

Mealtimes came and went, but Elena remained at his side. Someone had to stoke up the fire, she told herself. The real reason had more to do with his strong, handsome features. His was the attraction of the unknown, although Elena would not admit it to herself.

When Selest showed signs of stirring Elena sent for Milo and Hamelin. They could play in front of the fire where she could keep an eye on them.

Milo's first sight of Selest was when he ran to see his mother, and he was not pleased. He stopped and eyed the sleeping Crusader, but would not approach. Elena held out her hand.

'Come and kiss me, then, sweetheart. He won't bite.'

Milo shook his head, even though Selest had by now opened his eyes and was smiling at him. To have a stranger in the house was unsettling enough for Milo. To see his mother fussing with the newcomer as she only ever did with him was even more distressing. Milo stuck one finger in his mouth and scowled furiously. Hamelin's arrival with their toys did nothing to distract him.

The German boy knelt down before the fire with Milo's large wooden ark. He began unloading all the animals, singing a disjointed melody to himself.

'Go and play with Hamelin, then, my love.'

Milo continued to stare balefully at the smiling Selest. Instead of going to play he went forward and scrambled on to his mother's lap. Pulling her hand away from Selest, he clutched it firmly.

'Mummy, play with me.'

Elena explained that she was busy, but would be there to watch him. Grizzling, Milo squirmed against her, his petulant little whimpers loud enough to rouse Selest fully. As Elena stroked her son's hair and laughed at his jealousy Selest's rough male voice interrupted.

'You'll spoil that child, if you haven't already.'

'Oh, but he's only a baby, my lord. Not even three years old, yet.'

'Time enough to be spoiled by rich food and an indulgent mother. Well-born Franks are sent from home

at four to become pages. By then they're hardened
enough to wait at tables and live with the hounds. That
soon puts some character into them. Sink or swim.'

'I don't doubt it, my lord. Yet what sort of people
raise their children among animals? Pages with dogs,
and poor Hamelin with swine——'

'People whose men are more than milk and water. Men
who will fight for what they know is right, and will not
dress in effeminate fashions and pretty themselves with
a woman's care.'

'You may sneer at the good people of Constantinople,
my lord, but our noble heritage goes back a great deal
further than a few boatloads of looting pirates.'

'That hasn't stopped your Emperor begging us for
help, though, has it? He knows which side his bread is
buttered. There isn't a decent man worthy of the name
in his entire empire. A lot of mother's boys and holy
Joes, eh, my lad?'

He reached over and poked Milo in the ribs. Startled,
the child jumped and started to cry. At once Elena
cradled him to her with low crooning noises. Selest was
astonished.

'I barely touched the child, lady! Oh, put him down,
for heaven's sake.'

Hamelin gave a ragged laugh at Milo's dismay and
bounded forward. Two frights in quick succession were
quite enough for Milo and he hid his face in the folds
of his mother's robe.

'I knew it was a mistake to mix Milo up in this.'

Elena stood, but Selest put out his hand to stop her
leaving.

'Put the child down.'

'I won't let you harm him.'

Selest pulled a face. 'I'm not going to harm him. Just
toughen him up a bit. Make him into a real boy. Here,
Podge!'

He reached up and shook one of Milo's sandalled feet.
Waves rippled through the little boy's chubby calf, and

Milo hugged in closer to his mother's neck. Selest spoke first to Hamelin then, laughing, turned to Elena.

'Put the child down, Lady Elena. Hamelin will see that his little friend comes to no harm.'

Elena was undecided. Hamelin seemed a good boy at heart, and now he smiled at her openly. This gave her a false sense of security and she almost weakened.

'Milo speaks only Greek, my lord, and has no French...'

'That won't matter.'

Unseen by Elena, Selest winked at Hamelin mischievously.

Despite Milo's complaints, Elena untangled his fists from her plaits and set him down at Selest's side. Then she stepped back from her son.

'Now then, Podge. Hamelin and I are going to have a game. Do you know what a game is?'

Milo stuck one finger into his rosebud mouth and stared at Selest suspiciously.

'No, thought not.' Selest shrugged, then with a few words to Hamelin put up his hands. Used to the game, Hamelin advanced and began to punch into the palms of his friend's hands to much amused encouragement from Selest. He seemed unimpressed with Hamelin's skill and suddenly snapped his hands shut over the boy's fists. In the good-natured tussle that followed Hamelin was pulled over on to the couch. With much laughter and useless flailing of Hamelin's limbs the two wrestled for some minutes. Despite Selest's handicap of a secured leg he won easily, pinning his young friend upside-down on his lap. After a moment he tipped Hamelin off to land in a giggling heap on the rug.

'Come on, then, young Milo. Your turn.'

Despite the laughter of his friend Hamelin, Milo gave his mother a look of deep misgiving as Selest held up his hands once more. Only Hamelin prevented the little boy escaping back to his mother's arms. He crawled to Milo's side, showing the Byzantine boy how to make a fist from his podgy little fingers.

Milo's dark eyes grew larger and larger, filling up with bewilderment.

'He doesn't like it . . .' Elena began weakly.

'Rubbish. All boys like rough games,' Selest snapped, poking Milo gently first here, then there in an attempt to get him to join in. When the pats and prods became too insistent Milo sat down in fright. The usual wailing for his mother was cut short as Selest pulled the little boy upright again by his tunic, none too gently.

'Come on, my lad! None of that——' Selest's brave words ended in a savage yell.

Milo had sunk his teeth gum-deep into the hand that taunted him. Instinctively Selest cuffed the child off, and Milo ran screaming to his mother. The Crusader was now more interested in the bright blood bounding from his hand. His fury was not helped by Hamelin's laughter, and the German boy got first a warning then a cuffed ear. That didn't stop Hamelin laughing at his friend's discomfort. He merely moved out of range.

'Animal! Did you see what your precious son did? He bit me!'

'Serves you right,' Elena said shortly over Milo's sobbing shoulder. 'We don't agree with that sort of rough play here.'

'No, but you're quick enough to call on others to do your dirty work when necessary.'

He sucked his wound and spat viciously across the floor, to Elena's horror.

'What's wrong? It's only to get the poison out. Human bites are the worst kind. They mortify quicker than anything.'

'He's only a child.' Elena swung the sobbing Milo around to her hip. 'I'll fetch some thyme oil for you to clean the wound, if you're so bothered. And you'll have to get Hamelin to wipe up the disgusting mess you've made. We aren't doing it for you.'

She stepped past him pointedly, but Ascony rushed into the room to meet her before she could reach the door.

'News, lady! Good news!' His beady eyes were bright, speaking of a major piece of gossip. It was too important to be spilled in front of the Franks, that was for sure, so Elena allowed herself to be hustled out into the hall.

Sending Milo off to the kitchen, Elena closed the guest room door so that Ascony could speak freely.

'Emperor Alexius is sending nearly all the imperial guard up to the gates,' he said with glee. 'The very sight of our glorious army should put paid to the ragamuffins outside.'

'What if it doesn't?' Elena wondered aloud. 'If they are forced to fight during Lent, that will make us as shameless as the Franks.'

Ascony tapped the side of his nose with one forefinger. 'Rumour has it that they've thought of that. There are more ways of solving a problem than murdering men,' he finished mysteriously.

Elena immediately thought of Selest and Hamelin. They, and more particularly the Lord Hugh of Vermandois up at the palace, were hostages in all but name. Perhaps such hostages would be used as bargaining counters between the two sides.

Human beings used as currency. The thought revolted Elena. She made up her mind that their lodgers, however unwelcome they might be, would not suffer that indignity.

The next day was Good Friday. Trying to explain to Milo what was good about it with two fugitives in the guest room and a murderous rabble laying siege to the city was not easy.

After the events of the day before Milo was reluctant to go near Selest. Although Elena had told him that the Frank was unable to move from his seat Milo still hesitated. When she went into the guest room that morning, Milo stayed hovering in the threshold. Hamelin's laughter couldn't coax him in, but Selest stopped Elena going to fetch her son.

A plaintive little cry when his mother did not reappear from behind the screen was repeated, growing louder.

'Pay no attention to him,' Selest said sternly. 'My guess is that he won't want to be parted from you for a moment longer than necessary.'

Sure enough the sad little voice came nearer. In fits and starts it grew closer until Hamelin got up, went behind the screen and began jabbering to his little friend.

'Mummy? What's he saying?'

'He says come and be friends with us.'

The sound of small sandals kicking at the screen reverberated through the guest room.

'Mummy? Is monster still there?'

'Yes.' The kicking stopped. 'But he says he's going to be a nice monster today.'

After a short silence there was a scuffing along the screen and Milo peered around it anxiously. When Selest beckoned him he went forward, but only as far as his mother.

Elena sat beside Selest, embroidering a new jacket for Milo. When her small son put his hand on her knee for reassurance Elena petted him, to Selest's amusement, then held up the new jacket with a sigh.

'Milo's such a bonny child——'

'Fat,' Selest cut in abruptly. 'You're a real little butterball, aren't you, Podge? What on earth do you feed him on, lady?'

'He gets the best of everything, my lord. A well-built child has more strength to resist plague.'

'Milo looks strong enough to ward off the other three horsemen single-handed, too. Do him a favour, lady. Cut the size of his meals in half. He's got a real prison pallor to my mind, too. Doesn't he ever go out in the sun? I'll bet he doesn't get a lot of exercise either, does he?

'He walks to and from Father Johann's every day.'

'And where's that?'

'In the next street.'

Selest sighed in despair. 'Doesn't he ride, or swim? He certainly doesn't know how to fight, that's for sure.'

'I keep telling you, my lord, he's only a little boy.'

'I'm surprised he doesn't still sleep in your room!'

Elena looked away to her sewing.

'Oho! He does, doesn't he? That's it. Now there's a thing!'

'He keeps me company,' Elena said, indignant in the face of Selest's growing amusement.

'You're not going to tell me he still shares your bed as well?'

'Certainly not!'

'Thank goodness for that. I do so hate crowds.'

Elena frowned in puzzlement but before she had worked out that Selest was being shameless again he continued.

'I tell you what. Let him sleep down here tonight, with us. Tell him it's a big adventure, and he'll love it.'

'But he won't,' Elena said firmly, stroking Milo's hair. 'And I'm not having him so far away. He has night-mares, and always needs a feed before he'll settle again——'

'You can't baby the lad all his life, Lady Elena. We'll look after him.'

'But he'll never settle if he's kept hungry——'

'I doubt young Podge here knows what it's like to be hungry. Waking up is only a habit he's got into—one you encourage by giving him midnight feasts.' Selest did seem to notice Elena's distress at this point and patted her hand comfortingly. 'If he really is hungry, lady, I promise to send Hamelin to the kitchen for something. Satisfied?'

At this Elena gave him a look of withering scorn. 'Although Milo's not yet three, my lord, night-time is the only meal of milk he takes.'

'All right—so Hamelin can fetch him some...' Selest ground to a halt as he realised what she meant. His brown eyes lost their merriment and widened in complete amazement. 'Good grief, woman! You can't be serious?'

Elena was mystified. 'What about, my lord?'

'You don't still feed him yourself?'

'Of course! What would be the point of employing a wet-nurse for the tiny amount that he takes now?'

'But the child's big enough to fend for himself!' Selest burst out. 'That has to be the most disgusting thing I've ever heard! Why hasn't he been properly weaned?'

Elena smiled, intrigued at his attitude.

'It's easy to see that you aren't a father, my lord. Children need milk to grow. If a little brother or sister doesn't come along, many take it until they're four years old or more. Milo's very forward,' she said proudly. 'If it weren't for his nightmares he would have finished with me a year or more ago. It's only his little comfort now.'

'No wonder the Byzantines are a peculiar lot.' Selest shook his head in bewilderment. 'All the more reason why Milo should come and sleep with us, Lady Elena.'

'You will teach him rough ways.'

'We'll teach him to be a proper little man, not a mother's pet.'

'Oh, but he's only a baby, my lord——'

'Not yet three. Yes, I know.'

A knock at the door interrupted any reply Elena might have had. Ascony entered bearing a silver tray laid with glasses of orange juice.

'I regret that the tray is late, lady, but Khar and I have been up on the roof. It really has been most entertaining.' Looking up at Selest from beneath hooded lids, Ascony placed the tray down in front of them.

'Thank you, Ascony. I suppose we might as well hear your news, too, as you are plainly so keen to tell.'

Elena had been roused by Selest's scorn of her mothering and wanted to hurt him with a Byzantine triumph.

'The rascals have been well and truly routed from beneath the walls, lady! Everything went according to plan. When the attack came our archers rained down arrows from the city walls, aiming only to confuse, not kill. When the Franks persisted in their wickedness our men shot the horses from under them! The Emperor decreed that there would be no killing of men on this day, and so it was. The imperial guard made a lightning strike out of the city at their flank, which threw the Franks into disarray. They have scattered and fled,' Ascony finished with a triumphant smile at Selest.

The Crusader slumped back with a moan. 'Duke Godfrey wanted to be in Jerusalem by Easter. We won't even be in Constantinople by Christmas at this rate. We'll be stuck here until hell itself freezes over.'

'I do hope not,' Elena said shortly, putting down her embroidery and following Ascony from the room. Milo trotted after her but was gently turned back at the door while his mother spoke to Ascony outside. After a few whines and a little foot-stamping from Milo, Elena returned. Lifting him up, she carried him back to her seat beside Selest.

'Your boy loses the use of his legs every now and again, does he?'

Elena chose to ignore the Crusader's remark. 'Ascony agrees that Milo can stay here with you tonight. Although I want it understood that I'm not happy with the arrangement, my lord.'

'Do you consult your eunuch about everything, Lady Elena?'

'Most things, yes, I do.'

'And what, I wonder,' Selest picked up her forgotten embroidery, 'does he think of me?'

Elena was candid. 'Not much. He thinks that you are a dangerous indulgence of mine.'

'Ah, like cream on fresh fruit, or some other sinful luxury? I'll take that as a compliment! Thank you, Lady Elena!'

His smile was playful, but Elena was in no mood for his games.

'I'm surprised that you aren't more concerned for your comrades in the field, my lord.'

'They'll be back,' he said with steady-eyed assurance. 'Refreshed, reformed and ready to attack as soon as Easter is past.'

\* \* \*

Like all the other Christians in the city, Elena went out to mass that afternoon. With so much uncertainty the Good Friday rituals were even gloomier than usual.

Eban, the workshop manager, was almost as keen as Ascony on gossip and had the advantage of living closer to the palace. Elena had sent Ascony off to Eban's for more news so it was not unusual that Khar opened the door for her when she reached home. What was strange was the fact that Milo was not hanging on the doorknob waiting for her return. Before she could panic he came tumbling out of the guest room and flung himself into her arms.

'Look!' He uncurled a grubby hand and showed his prize. 'A new animal for my ark. A heliflump.'

'Elephant. El-e-phant.'

'Elefump!' Milo put his hands over his face to contain spluttering giggles. 'Emil's still making Mrs Effiplump——'

'Now you're being silly.'

He pulled at her hand, eager to get back to the guest room.

'Come and see, Mummy.'

Dragging his mother behind him, Milo dashed as far as the protective screen behind Selest, then stopped. The Crusader looked up from his carving as Elena appeared and smiled.

'Going to get him to come a bit closer? We had a bit of excitement here earlier, so he's a bit wary now.'

Elena was horrified. 'What have you been up to?'

'Nothing that wasn't long overdue. We'll soon see if it's had any effect.'

Blowing flakes of wood from the animal that he had been whittling, Selest held it at arm's length to admire the workmanship.

'Milo?'

In answer to Selest's stern voice the little boy looked up at his mother.

'Milo, come here.'

Selest spoke in French but slowly so that Milo could try and understand. The child took his tone as threatening and tried to pretend he wasn't there.

'Bring him forward, then, Lady Elena.'

'He's afraid...'

'Rubbish. He doesn't know what I'm going to do, yet.'

'You won't hurt him?'

'You'll make the child as nervous as yourself, lady!' Selest snapped. 'He'll never learn if you insist on holding him back.'

Reluctantly Elena eased Milo in front of her and took him to stand beside Selest. The child's trembling made Elena nervous, too, and she stroked him for comfort. To her surprise Selest began by giving Milo his most gentle smile and ruffling his hair. The tiny boy flinched as though expecting a blow.

'Your toy is finished, Milo. Here is the elephant.' He held out the small wooden figure.

Selest had never seen an elephant, only heard tell of them. The carving bore as much resemblance to the real thing as a pig did a partridge, but Milo's eyes shone. He reached out and took it.

'What do you say, Milo?'

The child immediately looked up at his mother.

'Don't help him, Lady Elena. He knows.' Selest leaned forward to Milo and whispered, 'Thank——'

'Thank you, Emil!' the child blurted out in relief. He hugged both animals to him as though guessing what would come next.

'Well done, Milo! Good boy!' Selest sat back on the couch. 'Now give the elephants to Hamelin.'

Milo clutched the toys even tighter and glared across to Hamelin, who was sitting on the floor beside Selest. There was no doubt that the Greek boy understood what was asked of him, and there was also no doubt that he wasn't going to obey.

'Give the elephants to Hamelin, Milo.'

Repeating the phrase patiently and pointing at the German boy, Selest glanced at Elena, who laughed.

'Don't tease him, my lord!'

'He'll have them straight back. As soon as he learns to share.'

Once more Selest told Milo to hand over the toys. The little boy stayed still and sullen.

'You've already had one smack from me this morning for throwing a tantrum, Master Milo. You're going the right way about getting another one——'

'No!'

'He has to learn, Lady Elena. Children are like pups in that respect. Teach them the right way from the start and they won't grow up as unmanageable brutes.'

As he spoke Selest reached out and took a firm hold on the toys and repeated his request to Milo. Challenged by Selest's strength and about to lose his treasures, Milo screamed in pure rage. He tried to bite, but Selest was ready. In the twinkling of an eye he had dragged the child on to his lap, pulled up Milo's gown, delivered a sharp smack where it would do least damage and cast the child aside. The Frank had moved so quickly that Elena hadn't had time to save her son. She could only kneel where he had fallen, weeping piteously.

'Oh, my angel! My poor little pet! What's he done to you?'

'Don't pander to him, woman! It's only surprise. I doubt he felt a thing, padded with all that blubber.'

'You—you evil animal! You—dog!'

'Steady on.' Selest sat back, grinning at the unhappy pair on the floor. 'He might have to suffer worse than that before I've finished with him.'

'You've finished with him now!' Elena's dark eyes flashed fury at Selest as she stood up to take Milo away.

'Come on, little one. Let Mummy put you to bed——'

Still snivelling, Milo dragged himself upright. He raised his arms to be picked up, but Selest caught one of his hands.

'He's not going anywhere yet.' The Crusader picked up the forgotten toys and handed them to Milo.

'Thank...you...Emil...' Milo sobbed automatically, hiccupping with grief.

'Good boy.' Selest patted him kindly. 'Now give the toys to Hamelin.'

Teardrops were spilling from Milo's huge eyes, beading the lashes before dripping down his cheeks. Chest heaving with distress, he looked down at the toys then across at Hamelin. The German boy solemnly held out his hand.

One eye on Selest, Milo edged forward and gave the elephants to Hamelin.

'Good boy! Well done!'

Smiling, Selest ruffled Milo's hair vigorously. To Elena's amazement the little boy responded with a broad grin, licking away his tears. Hamelin returned the toys and the lesson of give and take was repeated. This time Milo showed no hesitation and received a tiny morsel of dried fig as well as unstinting praise.

'Oh, don't be mean, my lord! Give him the whole fruit!'

'Ah, no, lady. No more of this gorging when he thinks he will. From now on young Milo eats only at proper mealtimes. The rest of the time he has to wait, like everybody else. Perhaps a titbit now and again, if he's good, but otherwise nothing. We'll soon have you as fit as a flea, won't we, Milo?'

The child smiled shyly, still wary of Selest. When his mother tried to take him off to bed, however, he grizzled and hung back.

'Now, Milo, none of that.' Selest compressed his features into an angry scowl. 'I thought he was to sleep with us tonight, lady?'

'Not if you're going to beat him.'

Elena pulled her veil around Milo protectively while Selest folded his arms and treated her to a look of mock anger.

'I don't beat anything. Much less the innocent child of a pretty girl. When Milo behaves he is treated kindly enough, as you've seen. It's only when he rebels that I am firm with him. It's no kindness either to yourself or others to let the child rule you, Lady Elena.' He was looking up at her with those dark, twinkling eyes that had proved her downfall before. 'Ask the child if he'd like to sleep down here with us tonight. Go on—make it sound like a great adventure. He'll love it.'

Highly dubious, Elena knelt down beside Milo and explained Selest's plan to him in Greek. She wasn't happy, and Milo sensed it.

'You're doing it again, Lady Elena. Making the child nervous. I'm sure I heard Ascony come back—fetch him and he can try.'

To Elena's dismay Ascony was still as keen on the idea as Selest and translated willingly. Egged on by his companions Milo was at first undecided, then shyly keen.

'Can I, Mummy? Please?'

'But what about all your bad dreams?'

'It might be better not to put ideas into the child's head, lady,' Ascony said carefully, then added to Milo, 'You'll have company, little one. The Lord Selest and Hamelin will keep you safe.'

He added a grim warning in French for Selest's encouragement.

Milo had been downcast at his mother's words but now he beamed happily.

'Can I, then, Mummy?'

Elena stroked his cheek. 'Very well, sweetheart. Just remember that I'm not far away. I'll leave the doors open so that I can hear if you're in distress. Call me if you need me.'

'He won't,' Ascony sighed almost with regret. 'You'll see.'

# CHAPTER SIX

ELENA stumbled out of bed, still asleep. When she found that Milo's little alcove was empty there was a flash of pure panic until she remembered.

He was crying for her, downstairs. Pulling on a robe, Elena dashed out on to the landing. The stairs were all darkness, lit only by Milo's muffled grizzling. Elena had reached the guest room door before she realised how cold the marble tiles were to bare feet.

As the door swung wide Selest's voice cut through the warm darkness in an urgent whisper.

'Go back to bed, Lady Elena.'

'But Milo...he's woken up...'

'Not really. Come to him now and he will, though. Go back upstairs and he'll settle down again.'

A ragged sob had Elena dashing forward before Selest's words could stop her. 'It's all right, sweetheart. Mummy's here——'

At the sound of her voice Milo started to wail in earnest. The firelight was too poor to make much out, so Elena lit a candle, much to Selest's annoyance.

The boys were laid on the couch beside Selest, jumbled together like puppies. Milo blinked through sleepy tears as she approached while Hamelin tried to burrow away from the light.

'You should have left the child. He didn't really wake, only cried out in his sleep.'

'How do you know?'

'I was here, Lady Elena.'

'And I'm his mother.'

Selest smirked at her appreciatively in the candlelight, and Elena coloured. Setting the candlestick down on the table she held out her hands to Milo.

'Come here, sweetheart. Let me make it better.'

He stumbled over Hamelin, who grunted at the clumsy placing of small feet. Falling into his mother's arms, Milo was carried to the couch beside the fire, where Elena settled herself down comfortably.

'My God! You're not going to do it here and now?'

'Of course, my lord. Hamelin is asleep, and if it bothers you, simply look away.'

'It's never natural...'

'On the contrary, my lord.' Elena began arranging her robe, causing Selest to look away quickly. 'It's the most natural thing in the world. If you ever get to walk in the streets of Constantinople you'll come across women doing this all the time. Look—there's nothing to see. Don't the Frankish women do this?'

'Ye-es.' Selest turned his head back towards her slowly. 'But only to babies. Not grown-up children——'

He stopped. Elena was not listening to his complaints. Caressed by gentle firelight she seemed asleep, still cradling Milo protectively in her arms. As she had said there was nothing for Selest to see except a picture of complete contentment.

'Are you asleep?' he whispered across after a time. Elena stretched her bare legs luxuriously and opened her eyes.

'Nearly. Milo's well away, though,' she murmured. 'I'll carry him back up to bed——'

'No, bring him here. I'll have him back.'

Elena worked her robe back behind Milo's nodding head and stood up.

'I—I don't know...'

'He was enjoying himself with us.' Selest smiled through the shadows. 'Let him wake up here.'

She went towards Selest, who held his arms out for the child. As she reached the edge of the rug beside him she stopped, something holding her back.

'No. I can't come any closer.'

'What's the matter?'

'I—we must smell of baby...'

'And I thought it was perfume,' he said softly. 'Don't worry. Bring the child here to me, Lady Elena.'

Bare feet whispering on the thick rug, she crept forward. To pass Milo into his arms she had to lean very close to Selest, but he made no comment. He laid the child back beside Hamelin.

'He'll sleep until morning now, you say?'

Elena nodded. She could see her little baby growing up and slipping away from her forever, and her heart was too full for her to speak.

'Off you go, then, my lady. You and I need our sleep, too.'

Looking back to Elena after settling Milo, Selest smiled, reaching forward to pat her hand.

There was nothing sinister in the gesture at all. For once Elena found herself wishing that there had been.

The next day dawned bright and clear. Elena lay on her bed, wondering what was wrong. Then she realised. It was suspiciously quiet.

With the doors thrown open as they were now, a low agitation could always be heard from the Crusader camp. Until this morning. Nothing now disturbed the clean, still morning air.

Pulling on her robe once more, Elena slipped out of her room and up on to the flat roof. Ascony had beaten her to it.

'Have they gone?'

'No, lady. Look.'

Dawn was barely brushing the eastern sky as he peered into the distance. The Crusaders' camp had contracted into a brooding huddle, and had moved a long way back from the city walls. Here and there a grey thread of smoke hung suspended in the air above a camp fire, but all was horribly silent.

'It's a trick,' Ascony said firmly. 'They'll play on our nerves until we send a party to investigate and then— phut!'

'What can the Emperor do?'

'Nothing. Your friend the Frank has touching faith in his theory that his cronies will wait until Easter is over. If so, that only gives us until the day after tomorrow.' Ascony's resolve broke. He hung his head in desperation. 'Oh, lady, what is to become of us?'

Elena put her arm around his hard, unyielding shoulders. She was at a loss herself. Thousands of Franks were outside the city threatening Constantinople's very existence while inside her own home one was trying to spirit away her little son.

'What is it you've always said to me through these long months, Ascony? "Trust in the Emperor. He won't let us down." '

Leading him towards the trapdoor, Elena tried to push thoughts of disaster back by telling Ascony the events of the night. That did manage to lighten the atmosphere a little.

'Perhaps it is a good thing that Milo is to be taken in hand, lady,' he said as they went downstairs together.

'Ascony! What do you mean?'

The eunuch squirmed a little under the cross-examination. 'He can be a little—er—wilful at times, lady. And while he could of course have no finer mother, perhaps the little fellow needs a firmer spirit now and again. At last I am beginning to think that there might be some use in the Frank, however unwelcome he may have been.'

He stepped before her to open the guest room door, but paused.

'Perhaps I may be allowed to add one word of caution, lady. The Franks will not be with us for much longer. Either we will be overrun, or he will be discovered, or his people will submit and travel onward...'

'What are you trying to say?'

'That you should take care, dear lady. Do not become involved in something that can have no future. Think of the little one.'

Without a word Elena stepped past him and into the guest room. Going to the apricot velvet drapes, she pulled them back, flooding the room with air and faint light.

'It seems a pity to disturb so pretty a picture.' Ascony smiled as he unstuck the grease-crusted candlestick from the table.

Selest was watchful, but could not move. Both children were still fast asleep. Hamelin had his head in Selest's lap while Milo was held in the Crusader's arms.

'Here, take your "baby", madam,' Selest growled crossly at Elena. 'I thought you said he would settle? The wretched child would only sleep in this position. My arm's been asleep most of the night, which is more than can be said for the rest of me.'

'Come on, then, sprout.' Elena retrieved her burden gratefully as Milo began to stir. 'Off upstairs to wash and dress. You can come straight back to play, if you like.'

'What does he want a wash for? He hasn't been any-where to get dirty!'

'He is bathed night and morning, my lord, as is only right and proper.'

'Unhealthy, if you ask me. What's wrong with once a week or so?'

'Everything. Ascony washes you every day. Even a brave Crusader should be used to it by now.'

'Er——' The eunuch began to make a hasty exit, but Elena called him back.

'You're looking guilty, Ascony. What is it?'

'I've told you,' Selest interrupted. 'I don't hold with all this washing business. It's one thing to be clean, but I don't go anywhere to get dirty. All I do is sit here.'

'Has he been making things difficult for you, Ascony?'

A look flitted between the two men but neither spoke.

'Very well.' Elena put Milo down and patted him in the direction of the door. 'I shall expect you to be busy here with soap and water by the time I get back. And if you won't do it, Ascony, I shall stand over our guest and shame him into doing it himself.'

Selest put his head on one side and clicked his tongue. 'And I thought that you were going to offer to do it for me, Lady Elena.'

'Correction then reward—that is what you say, isn't it, my lord?' Elena said cheekily before bundling Milo out.

Let Selest think on that and act as he would, Elena thought. Time was running short, as Ascony had pointed out. The eunuch already thought the worst of her over Selest, Elena was sure. That simple remark wasn't going to change his mind one way or the other.

When Elena crept into mass that night she felt lower than a lizard in a cart rut. What had come over her? It was fortunate indeed that Selest hadn't made anything of her rash words. The cold light of day had given her time to lose her nerve, and be ashamed.

Both Selest and Hamelin had been scrubbed clean by the time she had returned to the guest room. No reference had been made to her remark. The day had started off uncomfortably strained, but as it wore on Selest seemed to become less distant. They had eventually spent a happy day trying to teach the boys French.

Her mind full of Hamelin's problems and Milo's disobedience, Elena jumped with a start when the church was suddenly flooded with light and bells shouted the arrival of Easter Day.

She had dropped her candle in surprise and had to have it relit hastily by a neighbour.

There was no doubt that her mind wasn't on the service. Everyone greeted each other joyously enough, but Elena's heart wasn't in it. All her thoughts were back at home. Easter was here, and tomorrow the fighting would begin in earnest if what Selest had said was true.

How could she hope to keep Milo safe from the hideous hordes when they broke into the city? What would happen to Ascony...the Khars...her friend Gulzun? There would be no saving any of them.

Elena looked up at the richly decorated screens about the high altar. Dripping with gold and encrusted with gems—it would take a miracle to save anything from the northern pirates. The city would be pulled to pieces. People would be their last concern.

She took a final look at the glory that was Constantinople, certain that it could not last for much longer. Then she went home to make ready.

The streets were wild with merrymakers. After the deprivations of Lent enjoyment was the order of the night. Inns were already open, providing celebration cakes and wine.

Despite all the noise of singing and shouting, Elena felt quite safe as she walked home alone. There would be little if any trouble. The Byzantines were a naturally happy people, in contrast to the Franks—the foreigners only seemed happy when they had a chip on their shoulders, Elena thought.

Torches flared throughout the crowds clustered at the golden gates, and fear grabbed at Elena. Then darkness descended once more amid laughter and cheers. Elena could breathe again. She ran the rest of the way home, the crowd's excitement and the clatter of church bells both ringing in her ears.

A shifty-looking Khar opened her front door in the absence of Ascony.

'I suppose he's out enjoying *our* celebrations!' Elena laughed ruefully. If there was a chance of free cake and lemonade Ascony would join in, whatever the religion of the party-givers.

Khar slipped away without a proper explanation of where Ascony had gone, and Elena went to the guest room.

'They're asleep?' She looked at the children incredulously.

'Yes, and so was I.' Selest eased himself up on the couch, trying not to disturb his partners in crime.

'It's Easter—they can't sleep! What about their toys?'

'Toys? In the middle of the night?'

'They've all been laid away since the beginning of Lent. Milo's only been allowed his Noah's ark. Now he can have them all.'

She went to a large cupboard built into an alcove. At the jingle of keys as she unlocked it Milo sat up then opened his eyes.

'Easter?'

When Elena nodded he scrambled over the long-suffering Hamelin and across to his mother. The cupboard doors swung open and he plunged into his element, rifling through a rattling, clattering cascade of toys. Selest winced and groaned at the noise, at which point Hamelin woke up too and started to jabber.

'You really don't get much sleep in this house, do you?'

'Don't be so miserable, my lord. This part of Easter is for children. Like Christmas morning.'

A wooden framework crashed down out of the cupboard, making the boys squeal with laughter.

'Mummy! Mummy, put the swing up. Now!'

Milo danced around Elena and Selest moaned again.

'Of all the houses I could have chosen, why did it have to be this one?'

'Ascony can put the swing up at first light, sweetheart. It's too dark out in the garden yet——'

Milo's arguments were soon drowned out. Hamelin had found a drum. Sitting on the floor, he hammered out a tattoo, shrieking with noisy laughter.

Selest put his hands over his ears, but Elena laughed.

'You'll get no more sleep today, my lord. You might as well resign yourself to that. How about a nice cup of tcha?'

'Will it make me as deaf as Hamelin?' Selest yelled over the cacophony. Milo had found a set of Chinese bells and, forgetting the swing, sang now as he shook them.

'Sorry, no. Oh, here's Ascony. Kettle on for a lifesaver, Ascony?'

The eunuch nodded, but his beaming smile was directed at the boys. They were sitting amid a jumble of toys and making as much noise as possible.

When Ascony had gone Elena sat down beside Selest and started to deal out cards for them both. He was at once surprised and amused.

'Playing cards? On a holy day?'

'Only a simple matching game, my lord. Such as children might play. I was brought up at gaming tables, so I never play cards for money. My memory could never be good enough.'

They began laying down cards in turn. Selest moved slowly at first until he realised that many games in the past had sharpened her reflexes. The cards flicked down faster and faster, Elena winning most of the points. It was left to Selest to try and distract her by talking.

'What's Ascony decorating?'

She laughed, and gained another point. 'Nothing! You talk in riddles.'

Selest took the next point, which annoyed Elena intensely.

'Blow! What makes you think he's decorating, anyway?'

'The paint on his gown and hands.'

'Rubbish. You're only trying to put me off!'

The game progressed vigorously until Ascony returned. He brought milk and biscuits for the boys, together with a porcelain pot of tcha and a china bowl each for Elena and Selest.

'Oh, Ascony! You've forgotten the milk jug. We mix it, remember?'

She set one of the small china bowls before Selest while Ascony went back to the kitchen.

'It's like gold dust, this stuff. Tcha bushes grow in the Orient, and locals dry and powder the shoots. It makes an infusion guaranteed to cure all ills and lift the spirits. Henry brought me back a slip of tcha bush from his travels so that I could grow my own. It hasn't worked—

the plant is so slow in growing I still have to save up and buy from the importers after all this time!'

She poured tcha into each of the china bowls. Selest immediately turned up his nose.

'It's black!'

'Wait until you see this.'

Ascony had reappeared with a jug. Adding splashes of milk to each bowl Elena turned the liquid a pale golden tan, stirring each with a carved ivory stick. Selest wasn't keen.

'Any brew that does you good is bound to taste foul.'

'This is a luxury! Make the most of it, my lord. It's easier to get hold of pigeon's ears than a chest of tcha.' Elena sat back and enjoyed her drink. 'Ah, that's better. My first cup since Shrove Tuesday.'

She turned her attention to the eunuch, who was arranging combinations of milk, biscuits, plates and small boys.

'Now, then, Ascony, what are all these spots you're covered in? You might have got them off your hands, but your gown looks as though it's got measles down the back.'

'Ah...' said Ascony, looking at the tcha things for inspiration. 'Some...revelry abroad in the streets, I fear, lady.'

Elena sat up sharply. 'It is paint, and not blood?'

'Oh, yes, lady, it's paint all right,' Ascony said hurriedly, with a strange look at Selest.

The Crusader was sniffing his bowl of tcha and pulling faces.

'My lord, if you're going to be ungrateful give the bowl to Ascony. He likes living dangerously now and again. As long as the Khars don't find out.'

Selest braved a sip, thought about it, then risked a second and a third.

'It's quite nice,' he said in amazement.

'At the price it ought to be,' Elena muttered, pouring herself a second bowl. She looked up when Ascony seemed in no hurry to leave and was surprised.

'Ascony, what's the matter? You're on pins. What is it?'

'Lady—oh, lady, I have done a dreadful thing...'

A dawn chorus of noisy children was not the right accompaniment for a confession. Elena called for silence, but could barely make herself heard above the racket. Selest had more luck. In reward for immediate silence both boys were allowed a sip of his tcha.

'Oh, no, Ascony. What is it now?'

'If you please, lady, I would rather not say in front of——' He nodded towards Selest, who immediately grinned with delight.

'More news?'

'Not of the sort that you would wish to hear, my lord,' Ascony said quietly before rustling out of the room. Elena left the boys under Selest's watchful eye and followed her servant out into the hall.

'I cannot conceal my wickedness, lady. When it becomes common knowledge you will know that I was involved. It was a mad, reckless impulse—but how I regret it now...'

'What on earth have you done?'

'Perhaps you had better come and see, lady.'

He swept off to the front door and Elena followed as instructed.

Despite the hordes camped on the city's doorstep, Constantinople was still fired with joy and excitement. Although it was the early hours of the morning the streets were noisy with goodwill and the incessant clatter of hundreds of Easter bells.

The broad city walls were topped by crowds and crowds of people, illuminated by hundreds of flaming torches. Laughter taunted the Franks outside in their wretched camp. Elena wondered if this was one last act of defiance, or whether there really was any cause for confidence.

Only when Ascony led her into the stream of merrymakers squeezing out through the well-guarded gates did Elena realise why everyone was in such high spirits. The areas of city wall facing the Crusaders had been daubed with crude messages in red paint. Each letter was enormous, and Elena had to turn her head to take it all in.

She read the least offensive offerings aloud, with interest. '"Huns go home!" "We don't need baby-eaters here!" Oh, Ascony...'

Her servant hung his head. 'It is true that I have no defence, lady. Although I wasn't the only one involved. There were many of us.'

'Was it your idea?'

Ascony looked up. Honest remorse was the only expression on his dark, narrow face.

'No, lady.'

Sighing, Elena turned back to the city. 'Very well. Suffering with a guilty conscience looks to be punishment enough for you. We'll say no more about it, Ascony, but I don't want this sort of narrow-mindedness shown off at home. Our guests,' her voice dropped to a whisper as they passed back into the city, 'are to be treated only with kindness.'

'Then it is true. You don't want them to "go home", lady?'

'Never mind what I want.' Elena shoved and chivvied her servant back towards home. 'And don't ever let me catch you doing anything like this again.'

Neither Elena nor Ascony was convinced by her anger. His statement had unsettled her, and he knew it. As they went back into the house Ascony was thoughtful and regarded Elena with something close to scorn.

She sensed then that more difficulties might lie ahead.

Breakfast was early and enormous. Cold sliced lamb and kid, hot minced liver with spiced yoghurt, wheat porridge, jugs of heavy cream, crusty honeycomb, fancy breads burnished dark and shiny as old oak and piles of featherlight cake were ferried into the guest room on silver trays.

Selest and Hamelin were in their element. There was more food offered in one meal here than in a month of

Sundays at home. Milo sat on the floor beside Selest and to Elena's surprise ate what his new friends did.

'Here's some cream for Milo's porridge, my lord. He won't eat it without.'

She went to hand over the jug but Selest shook his head.

'He's doing all right.'

'On plain porridge with no cream or honey? How can he be?'

The faintest hint of jealousy tinged Elena's voice. She couldn't forget the hours spent coaxing Milo to eat, feeding him the choicest morsels with her fingers. What relief when she found something he would accept! Expensive titbits were carried up to him at every opportunity until he refused them in favour of some new fad.

Now he was guzzling wheat and water porridge such as the meanest beggar might eat.

'Children need dairy foods to grow,' she snapped crossly.

'If he grows any more, my lady, he'll burst!'

'Don't try and teach me how to bring up children, my lord. Look to your own charge. What's wrong with him this morning?'

Selest looked at his young friend, but could see nothing out of the ordinary. He was about to say so when Hamelin bent to Milo beside him. As he moved his head so he shook it irritably.

'Don't know.' Selest shrugged. 'Perhaps it's got something to do with being wrong in the head.'

The matter was forgotten almost immediately. The boys finished their breakfast and Hamelin ran to get Elena's box of salves. He looked forward to his few minutes of attention while Elena tended his eye, and climbed readily on to the couch to lay his head in her lap. As he did so on this occasion he flicked his head rapidly several times.

'Ask him what the matter is, my lord.'

Selest did so and laughed at the answer. 'Noises in his head. He wants you to do something about those, too, lady.'

Removing Hamelin's pad and bandage, she stroked the child's hair kindly.

'I don't know anything about that, but you've nearly got two good eyes again.' She caught his hands and squeezed them. 'If you promise not to scratch I'll leave the bandage off today. Fresh air will do it good.'

'I'm impressed,' Selest said, finishing a fourth piece of toast. 'And what treatment would you prescribe for me, my lady?'

'We can do nothing else for your foot, my lord. I don't think anything else ails you, does it? Unless, of course, it is indigestion.'

'Well.' He took care now to dab his lips with the napkin provided before taking a sip of orange juice. 'It's all very fine being fed and tended like this, but there's more to life than sitting around. I need fresh air, exercise, and most of all a little agreeable company.'

The dark amber gold of his hair shone in the early morning light. Elena needed company, too. Selest with his fair skin and happy laughter was the first thing she thought of each morning. More disturbingly, he was often the last thing she thought of in her lonely bed at night.

Trying to think reasonably had no effect. Elena told herself time and again that it was because she felt sorry for him, injured and alone among strangers. She was a respectable widow, and should have only respectable thoughts. What would Henry have said...?

'My friend Gulzun, my lord...her daily work is in providing companionship for gentlemen. Although I must admit, the fewer people that know of your presence here the better——'

'Elena.' He arranged the blanket covering him even more neatly. 'That wasn't the sort of "company" I meant. There's little enough for me to do all day and night but think. I realise now that I may have chosen a bad time before. Perhaps today might be more favourable?'

Elena had three choices. She could be hypocritical and snap, admit to feeling secretly as shameless as Selest or make a quick escape. In the event she dithered.

'You—you would speak so on such a holy day, my lord?'

'Even on a Sunday.'

'My—my husband——'

'Is dead, poor fellow.'

Elena tried to swallow but her dry throat ached with the effort.

'I—love—my husband——'

'You sound as though you are trying to convince yourself, lady. Or am I permitted to call you Elena?'

Head tilted to one side, his dark eyes gleamed seductively beneath their sooty lashes.

'Mummy, I'm still hungry!'

Milo had marched up and tugged at her sleeve. It was the escape that Elena thought she wanted.

'I'll take you to the kitchen and find something right now.' She breathed with relief, but it was short-lived. He grasped her hand and prevented her from leaving his side.

'No, you won't. Elena, now that Easter is here time is running out. For Constantinople, your staff and, most of all, for us. Any minute now Duke Godfrey and his troops will storm the city. The mood they're in they'll take no prisoners...'

'No—don't say that in front of the children——'

'But it's the truth! We can't do anything to save ourselves, let alone them, when the worst happens. We might as well spend the last few hours as pleasantly as we can. Have the swing put up outside for the children. Give the staff the day off...and then come back to me...'

'I can't...' Elena pulled at her plaits in anguish. She knew she had to walk out of the room there and then, take the children and make sure that Hamelin and Milo at least spent their last hours happily. If only Selest wouldn't keep tormenting her——

'You can, Elena. You want to. It's the perfect offer for you—no strings, just a last bit of fun. No one will ever know...'

That decided Elena. '*I* shall know,' she said firmly. 'Come on, boys. Quickly. I'll find you something to eat and then we'll go out to find Gulzun.'

Gathering her robes about her, Elena shook off Selest's hand and caught hold of Milo and Hamelin. She scurried off to the kitchens.

Selest let her go without comment. Within an instant she was back, as he had known she would be.

'How dare you issue orders to my staff?'

'It's your house, Elena. Countermand them.'

'I can't!' Elena bounced with indignation, her sandals shuffling on the rug. 'Ascony agrees with you. He says Milo shouldn't have any more, either.'

'It's a wise woman who controls her own servants,' Selest said with a smirk, then after a suitable pause he added slyly, 'I see you've left the darling babes behind, this time. This must mean you're a little more amenable to my suggestion.'

'I most certainly am not! How can you think of your own pleasure and starve innocent children when you insist we're all under sentence of death?'

'Quite easily. Stubbornness. The same way that you've been able to deny yourself all offers of love and affection.'

'You're unnatural!'

'It takes one to know one, they say.'

Sands were shifting beneath Elena's feet. Selest's merry laugh—those eyes—the cool strength of his attraction—it could all be hers in an instant. With disaster imminent only one thing was now holding her back.

'Henry... what would Henry say?'

Selest snorted with disgust. 'Look, Elena. Your Henry was evidently a perfect husband, father, businessman and all-round shining paragon. I can't challenge him on any of those grounds, and I certainly don't want to. But I can beat him hands down on another. Henry's dead, Elena. He's no longer of any use to you in the way that I could be——'

It was true. One step across the room and she could be in his arms. Every fibre of her body drew the moment of her release nearer but Elena railed against it valiantly. Unable to resist, unwilling to sin, she stood before him in a ferment of turbulent emotions.

Then without warning she froze, rigid.

'Made up your mind? What's it to be?'

'No...no! The Easter bells!' Terror freed her. Only fear was the enemy now.

'They've stopped. What of it?' He shrugged.

'They never stop on Easter Day!'

She fled out of the room despite Selest's order for calm. Out in the hall Ascony, the Khars, Milo and Hamelin were all jabbering at once.

Elena's mind was blank with terror. All she could think of was to herd everyone up on to the roof. Selest couldn't be moved, but at least he was a Frank. Not even they would harm their own, surely?

Once on the roof a staggering sight met their eyes. Nearly the entire population of Constantinople was ranged about the city walls. Thousands and thousands of people stood in total silence. Waiting. Only the mew of kites scavenging over the Crusader camp plucked at the tension.

A tight formation of Frankish horsemen was riding towards the gates of Constantinople. They did not hurry. Even when a group of the imperial guard rode out from the city to meet them, their pace never altered.

For an age the two parties drew together. Nerves were tensed almost beyond endurance. Here and there among the crowds rose the mutter of priests, and many citizens fell to their knees in prayer.

The city of Constantinople watched and waited.

When the opposing forces were still a tournament pitch apart they stopped, facing each other.

No one moved for a very long time, either inside the city or out. A door left open in the breeze banged, and was ignored. Far out in the distance one of the Frankish horses reared and danced sideways, raising a cloud of dust around fluttering pennons.

Still nothing happened. The Byzantine people stared until they ached, each trying to get a hint of what was to come.

Suddenly the imperial guard wheeled their horses. Splitting into three groups, they took up positions behind and to either side of the Frankish party, who had ridden forward.

A great roar burst from the distant camp. It was as though an ants' nest had been disturbed—a number of tiny black figures streaming towards the group of riders. At once all was confusion. Horses plunged and barged as Frank and Byzantine were thrown together in disarray.

One Frankish horseman broke rank and tore back towards his comrades. Even before his standard bearer caught up with him Elena knew that it was Duke Godfrey. Sunlight exploding from his sword, he brandished it over his rabble of followers.

They all stopped dead. Ruffians without number had been held by one man on a horse.

Galloping back to the other horsemen, Godfrey and his standard bearer were soon at the head of a united party of Franks. Without urgency they allowed the imperial guard to escort them towards the city.

As they drew closer a grinding of massive toothed cogs and winding wheels winched open the great golden gates of Constantinople. Good citizens shrank back as the imperial guard opened a route for Godfrey and his kinsmen to take through the multitude.

'Are they going to fight?' Elena pulled at Ascony's sleeve frantically.

'I don't think so. Not yet, anyway. Wonder of wonders, the cursed Franks may even have seen enough sense to consider diplomacy at last.'

'Let's go down!' Elena said in a moment of madness. 'Let's run down to the palace and see them presented!'

'Lady, are you mad? It would be terribly dangerous! The barbarians are armed to the teeth. And look how shiftily they view our city!'

Elena could see. With the exception of Godfrey, who was above such things, the party of Franks were gaping with wonder. Pointing from marble collonades to sculptures and decorations adorned in real silver and gold, the Franks shook their heads and muttered in their strange languages.

'Quick! They're going out of sight!'

Leaving Khar comforting the children and his weeping wife, Elena gathered up her veils and skipped across the gap to her neighbour's flat roof. Ascony could do nothing but follow.

As soon as the last Frankish soldier had entered, the city gates thundered shut behind them. Any retreat cut off, the Franks drew their swords in terror as their horses backed and kicked against the gates. Constantinople cringed in fear, and all was near panic. Then Godfrey raised his hand.

The Franks stopped. It was as simple as that.

The citizens of Constantinople watched the display in sullen silence. Stony-faced, they glowered at Godfrey and his men, but unlike his nervous kinsmen the duke did not seem to have noticed. He began to proclaim in loud, clear Latin.

'"He is the righteous Saviour, and he shall speak peace unto the heathen."'

It was not a very tactful quotation to choose after the accusations he had recently been levelling against the Byzantines. The crowd surged forward, jostling the Franks into another plunging frenzy. Glowing zeal made Godfrey oblivious to danger and he sat his rearing horse with a royal air. Fearing for the foreigners' lives, the imperial guard closed ranks about them, shouldering the crowds away.

Unfortunately for everyone, Godfrey hadn't finished. He drew his fabled sword.

'"Worthy is the Lamb that was slain"!' he roared and suddenly spurred his horse forward. The crowd was surprised, the imperial guard astonished and the Frankish party left behind. They had to put on an undignified spurt to catch up with their duke, who was at last off to see the Emperor.

# CHAPTER SEVEN

AFTER so many weeks and months of worry the citizens of Constantinople heaved a sigh of relief. Their troubles weren't over by any means, but at least talks were in progress. If the worst came to the worst the Emperor could simply hold on to his Frankish guests until they saw sense. With Godfrey and his kinsmen within the city walls the Crusading rabble wouldn't dare attack.

Tensions in the city may have eased a little but within Elena's house they were as taut as ever. Milo was irritable with hunger, Hamelin would keep twitching, and as for Selest...

He had her cornered, and knew it. Every smile, every kind word or joke he shared with Elena was calculated to play her like a little fish on a line.

Selest knew that her craving for real affection was almost the equal of her loyalty for the dead Henry.

Elena tried to think of ways to avoid him, but it was hopeless. She went out to the shop to check that no damage had been done during the excitement of the night before. That was a waste of time. Eban always fixed the shutters up most carefully. She couldn't even hang about inside with the excuse of cleaning up. The apprentices kept everything wonderfully neat and tidy. It was part of their job.

She went back home and tried to lose herself in some gardening. Khar did all the complicated tasks, but Elena liked to potter among the flowers and herbs. That proved no diversion. She even went to sit upstairs in Henry's room, but it was no good either. Her thoughts kept straying back downstairs.

Finally she gave in and went to Gulzun. Her friend was never normally short of advice, but today Elena was to be disappointed.

'Look, much as I'd like to have a good chat I'm just off to pitch for work with the Franks——' Gulzun reefed up her skimpy blouse to reveal rather more than it concealed.

'I know you're busy... but I'm desperate.'

'And so am I. Have you *seen* some of these Franks?'

'Gulzun, be serious. I'm in trouble.'

Elena sat on her friend's sumptuous gold and ivory bed while Gulzun got ready to go out. The room was filled with a haze of expensive perfume and pink muslin draperies. Although to sit amid such splendour usually made Elena giggle and gasp, today was different.

Gulzun's expression became thoughtful as she fiddled with a catch on her fourth pair of earrings.

'Is it money? How much do you want?'

The Turkish girl laughed and threaded enough rings on to her fingers to finance half a dozen businesses.

'No—nothing like that. Look, I'm only telling you this because I know it won't go any further.' Elena sighed and stroked the silken coverlet. 'I'm in more trouble than I ever thought possible, Gulzun. I'm hiding a Crusader in my house.'

Gulzun stopped still, a hank of necklaces halfway to their destination. Although her almond eyes were heavy with make-up they opened wide with amazement.

'You're not serious?' She gaped, then added, 'You are serious!' Fastening her necklaces, she smirked at Elena wickedly. 'Elena Rethel! Of all the people in Constantinople, you're the very last person I would have ever suspected of playing fast and loose——'

'I'm not!'

'Oh, go on! You must be!'

'I'm not. And you're beginning to sound as evil-minded as he.'

Gulzun jumped up. Billowing a cloud of peach-coloured silk about her head and shoulders, she pulled on the flimsiest pair of gold slippers that Elena had ever seen and tugged at her friend's arm.

'Come on. I'm off to watch the celebrations at the palace. Emperor Alexius is taking lunch with the Franks. Who knows? We might both strike lucky today, since you've turned out to be such a dark horse!'

Taking Elena firmly by the arm, Gulzun started off for the palace. Elena was not very excited at the prospect of watching a herd of Franks at their meal, especially if their table manners were as invisible as Selest's had once been.

When they arrived at the palace the great hall was already busy with people. Silken ropes separated the table where the Emperor and his guests would eat from the rest of the enormous room. Anyone who chose could stand or sit in the body of the hall and watch the royal family at their meals.

Gulzun commandeered a pair of enormous soft pillows right in front of the table, where they would have a good view of what went on. While Elena gathered her tunic and veil about her and sat down gracefully, Gulzun threw herself down on to her stomach and wriggled into a pose.

The imperial guard entered in two lines and filed around the room until they had hemmed it with their imposing presence. This was the signal that the Emperor and his guests were about to arrive.

A thrill of excitement ran around the room. Everyone craned their necks to study a gilded screen which marked the entrance to the Emperor's private quarters.

A ruffle of movement and it swung aside to reveal the Emperor Alexius in all his glory. With a wide smile he entered the room and was at once engulfed in his cheering people. Stopping here and there as he progressed, he would speak to a subject or soldier in the audience. He even had a few words with Gulzun while waiting for the guards to unhook the silken rope before his table.

'What did he say? What did he say?' Elena forgot her manners and pummelled at Gulzun unmercifully.

'Professional advice,' her friend said lightly. 'If you must know, he suggested that I forget all about wasting my time on the duke. But we'll see about that. I'm not easily put off.'

The Franks entered quickly, to a rousing silence from the crowd. They were led in by the Lord Hugh of Vermandois, but his friends didn't seem too overjoyed at having him restored to the fold after so many months. Indeed, a squabble broke out between them all when he insisted on sitting beside the Emperor. Alexius settled it with his usual diplomacy and ate his meal flanked only by two imperial guardsmen, although an air of bad feeling persisted among the Franks.

Gulzun wasn't the only person after a Frank. There were several courtesans and catamites among the crowd—all, it seemed, with their hearts set on the divine Godfrey. They preened and pouted for the best part of an hour, but to no effect. Godfrey regarded each and every member of the audience with the same pale-eyed intensity. Never wavering, his gaze passed from one to another and then on.

His kinsmen were different. Knowing how hungry Selest had been, Elena guessed that it was only the free food they were shovelling down themselves that stopped them indulging in the other goods on display.

When at last desserts were brought in to end the meal, Gulzun stood up and with a wink strolled out of the side door. A moment later a young Crusader almost Godfrey's equal in looks excused himself from the table. He, too, left the room.

That was the worst thing about going anywhere with Gulzun, Elena thought. She was forever letting her work interfere.

Barely a moment later, Gulzun was back and tugging Elena away by the hand.

'I wasn't very interested, anyway,' Elena said ruefully, as though that might change anything.

'You might have warned me they're dirty,' the Turkish girl spat in disgust. 'He smelt like an old horse. I didn't get within arm's length. *Nothing's* worth that.'

Gulzun shuddered in disgust. That set all her jewellery jangling and she started to laugh.

'Is yours like that?'

'Certainly not. Ascony keeps him scrubbed down.'

The two girls walked out of the palace and towards the Mese.

'What is yours like, then?'

'Come back now and see for yourself. Take him home with you, for all I care.'

Gulzun turned dark, lascivious eyes on her friend. 'You don't mean that?'

Elena slowed down, thought, then bit her lip. 'I don't know. If it weren't for Henry then I wouldn't be so eager to get rid of him, no. He makes me laugh, he's young, strong and good-looking——'

'Sounds fun!'

'Then again, he spends all his time... well, making me feel uncomfortable...'

'That'll have a lot to do with being young, strong and good-looking. Enjoy it!'

'What about Henry?'

'Ah. There you have the real difference between men and women. If a man has an itch he scratches it without thinking twice. Women spend so long agonising over the rights and wrongs of the thing that they let the opportunity slip by. At least, some of them do,' Gulzun added with a wicked grin. 'Although I must say I never thought to see the day when you of all people would even consider such a thing!'

'I haven't considered it,' Elena lied unconvincingly. 'I'm far too busy at work.'

Gulzun sniggered. 'Eban says that you haven't been in to the shop much for days. Haven't you got a big order from the palace expected any day now?'

'Mmm,' Elena mused as they turned into her street. 'For Christmas. I want to have something really special ready, but things aren't going according to plan. It looks as if they're going to be stuck with the favourite old designs again.'

'There's your answer, then.' Gulzun rattled the door knocker to bring Ascony running. '"The more work, the less worry." Works every time. Ah, afternoon, Ascony! Where is he, then?'

Gulzun strolled into the house, draping her stole over Ascony's outstretched arm as she did so. The eunuch was more interested in news of peace talks at the palace, and cornered Elena for details. Satisfied that things were at least no worse, he went off to the kitchen to fetch tcha and cakes.

The Turkish girl had already found Selest by the time Elena got to the best guest room. She was perched on the arm of Selest's couch, and the two were in animated conversation.

Elena hated it. For once she really resented her friend's job and wished that she hadn't invited Gulzun back. Selest was sure to make a fool of them both.

He looked up and laughed as she entered his sanctuary.

'Ah, Lady Elena. How kind of you to supply me with such charming company!'

'Don't mention it, my lord. Gulzun was only too pleased to come and visit you. After all, Duke Godfrey wasn't interested and his relations were all a bit... "Frankish" for her tastes, so she had a few hours to spare.'

At once Selest looked thoughtful, then grinned at Gulzun.

'I hope you haven't come here expecting entertainment, Lady Gulzun. I'm a very poor fellow indeed, left with no money and precious few possessions.'

Although it was said in a typically light-hearted manner Elena sensed a subtle change in Selest's manner. His expression was guarded and his eyes wary as he spoke to Gulzun. He had never looked at Elena with such careful detachment. She wondered why.

When Ascony brought in the tcha tray Gulzun made herself comfortable on the couch beside Elena. The two girls chattered and laughed like two colourful exotic birds, punctuated by Milo's piping and Hamelin's raucous crow.

'You're losing weight, Milo!'

'He's wasting away before my very eyes. I told you, my lord. You're starving the poor child.'

'Better that Khar should take four clean plates back to the kitchen each day than a dozen discarded snacks. And that's another thing. If I was up and about he'd waste a lot faster. An hour in the sea before breakfast every morning——'

'Oh, you couldn't possibly take him out there!' Elena giggled. 'He can't swim, my lord. He's far too tiny!'

'Good grief, woman, he wouldn't come to any harm! What would happen if you were on a boat and he fell overboard?'

'He won't be going on any boats. I shan't let him,' Elena countered defiantly, patting her knees for Milo to crawl aboard. The child looked across at Selest and stayed where he was.

'Don't you want to come and have a cuddle, sweetheart?'

'That's for babies,' Milo said matter-of-factly. Gulzun laughed.

As Elena poured out three bowls of tcha and handed them around, the Crusader summoned Milo and Hamelin to him. Each received a sip from his bowl. Elena wondered how long her son's good manners would last, but Milo behaved and drank nicely before returning to his mother's side.

'He doesn't usually like tcha, my lord.'

'Children have no preferences until they're taught to dislike by those around them, Lady Elena.'

She looked at Gulzun for support, but her friend was laughing.

'Don't ask me! I'm not an expert in the baby end of things!'

She shook her head, making rivulets of jewellery dance with light. Elena watched Selest rake over her friend with his eyes and knew what would happen sooner or later.

'Would you paint up my hands again, Gulzun? The dye is wearing off.' She stood up and put out her hands to Milo and Hamelin. 'I'll go upstairs and get the things. The boys can help, although with their hindrance I shall probably be gone for an age.'

She hurried the children out of the room. Once in the hall with the guest room door firmly shut on Gulzun and Selest, Elena slowed her pace. There would be no hurry.

Hamelin had not seen Elena's room before. Following her to the dressing-table, he gazed at the pots and bottles and brushes and paints, all laid out in their proper places on the marble top.

'Here, sniff.' Elena took the silver top off one bottle. 'Perfume.'

Hamelin dipped his finger in the glass vial then licked it.

'No, no!' Elena laughed, shaking her head. Hamelin had already realised his mistake and was smacking his lips in disgust. 'Like this, Hamelin.'

She applied a dab of scent to each wrist then let him sniff. With a grunt of pleasure Hamelin held out his own wrists for the same treatment.

'I'll find you some.'

Leaving Milo burrowing down into her bed, Elena took Hamelin next door to the shadowy peace of Henry's room. In the dim light she chose a bottle from the display that had been frozen on Henry's washstand since the day he died. Tipping a little spirit on to her fingers, she stroked it over Hamelin's soft, smooth cheeks.

It was a mistake. At once the forest-fresh smell of Henry stole around the room, pricking Elena's eyes as well as her senses. Hamelin was upset too and grizzled, pawing at his face.

She was back in those dear lost days that would never come again. All those memories. If only she had been strong and made Ascony clear everything out. Then she wouldn't have been taunted by that fragrance. Downstairs, Gulzun and Selest were probably enjoying themselves thoroughly. All she had were memories and the thoughts of the warm male smell of Henry's closeness.

'Come on.' Thrusting the bottle back on to the washstand, Elena grabbed Hamelin and escaped, slamming the door behind them.

Back in her own room Elena washed Hamelin's face to try and rid him of the scent, but it clung to him and to her hands. In the end she had to douse them both in rosewater to try and mask the smell.

'Pooh! Hammy, you smell like a soppy girl!'

Hamelin chortled at Milo's screwed-up face and looked happily at Elena.

'Sissy! Sissy!' Milo sang in French, bouncing up and down on the bed.

'Milo, really! Did the Lord Emil teach you that word?'

Milo nodded his head in time to each bounce.

'You don't even know what it means.'

The little boy kept nodding and bouncing.

'What is it, then?'

'Somebody not tough and fierce like me.'

He threw himself face down on the bed and crawled towards Hamelin, snarling like a dog. The German boy screamed with delight and fell on his small opponent. Together they rolled over and over on the bed, wriggling and tussling until one over-violent struggle sent them and the counterpane slithering to the floor.

'Milo! Milo, are you all right?' Elena dashed forward but her son was still cavorting like a puppy. Hamelin was the one in trouble. Still tangled in the bedclothes, he was on all fours. Shaking his head, he banged it repeatedly against the bed, and with each movement gave a pitiful sob.

'Stop it, Hamelin. Stop! What is it—the noises again?' It took most of Elena's strength to haul Hamelin away from the bed. When she managed it at last he started to claw at his left ear as though he would pull it off.

'Milo, quickly! Go and fetch Ascony. You stay in the kitchen with the Khars, but he's to come straight away. Hurry!'

Alarmed at Hamelin's wails, Milo shrank back and began to cry.

'Sorry, Mummy! I'm sorry...'

'It's not your fault, sweetheart. He'll be fine as long as you fetch Ascony right now.'

Milo backed away, almost stumbling. He was gone before Elena realised she should have stopped him running in on Selest.

Fortunately Ascony arrived so quickly that Milo must have gone straight to the kitchen.

'Whatever is it, Ascony? I can't stop him——' Nearly frantic, Elena finally lost her grip on Hamelin. The child threw himself to the floor, scrubbing his head against the cold marble tiles. All the time his cries grew more shrill, tearing through the room like pain itself.

'All right, my lad.' Forging past Elena, Ascony grasped Hamelin and pulled him upright, ready to be lifted on to the bed.

Almost at once Hamelin stopped screaming. With a few flicks of his head and a great deal of snivelling, he was back to normal.

'That's amazing, Ascony! How did you do it?'

'I don't know.' The eunuch looked grave. He was as mystified as Elena.

'I don't like this. It's been coming on for a while, I think.' Elena wiped away Hamelin's tears with her kerchief and comforted him. 'If only we could risk fetching the doctor.'

Ascony watched her, stroking his chin with his hand. At last he offered a suggestion.

'Lady...could we not say that he was a common street urchin? It would not be so very far from the truth.'

'What about Selest? Dr Kelka always takes a drink with me in the best room when he comes. It would seem suspicious to change things——'

'I was thinking of taking the child to his house, lady. Hammy—Hamelin is difficult to understand, even with knowledge of the German tongue. I don't think that he could incriminate us. And it could be that what ails him needs more than the care that we can give him here.'

There was a sad note in his voice, and Elena did not want to question him further. She knew that the onset of fits—if that was what Hamelin had suffered—was a serious matter. Gulzun's little Hussein hadn't lasted long after they began.

'Will—will you take him right away?'

Ascony crouched down in front of Hamelin and to Elena's delight caressed him almost fondly.

'It might be as well, lady.'

'Then I'm coming with you.' Elena was already pulling a stole from her wardrobe.

'And another for the child, lady. We can at least disguise his Frankish colouring until we get there.'

There was no time to disturb Selest and Gulzun. Settling Milo with the Khars, Elena and Ascony set off for the doctor's house straight away.

As it was Easter Day, and with noble guests to be inspected at the palace, the streets were nearly empty. What people they did see all wanted to know about the child that Ascony carried, since it clearly wasn't Milo. Hamelin was well wrapped up, but Elena discouraged anyone from taking a look. Stressing the urgency of their business, she managed to put off the curious.

At last Elena and Ascony reached the doctor's house, and without Hamelin's true identity being discovered.

Dr Kelka was not a man to let a little thing like his afternoon nap stand in the way of a patient. Ever eager to help, he was galloping through his hall to meet them, full of smiles, before his housekeeper had time to draw breath.

Ushering them into what he laughingly called his 'workshop', Kelka unwrapped Hamelin like a long-awaited present.

'Well, well! A little Frank, isn't it?'

'Er——' Elena looked at Ascony, but Kelka was more interested in Hamelin than her excuses.

'Looked like a fit, you say? Tricky.'

He lifted Hamelin up to sit on a large wooden table. The boy thought all the attention was wonderful, grinning and jabbering happily at anyone who looked in his direction.

'Urchins don't last long, as a general rule,' the doctor said regretfully. He allowed Hamelin to inspect a horn cone before using it to listen to the boy's chest. 'They either pick up disease and die through lack of care or some accident befalls them. Hmm. Well, this little lad certainly shows signs of having had a hard life, but seems otherwise all right on first sight.'

Kelka started to search through Hamelin's hair, which the child loved. 'He's very clean for an urchin, especially a Frankish one. Are you sure that he doesn't belong to anyone, Lady Elena? From his prettiness and perfume I'd say he came in with Arabs, but there's no other sign——'

'That was me,' Elena said quickly. 'We cleaned him up a bit before we brought him.'

Kelka gave her a quick smile. 'You've done a good job. Although perhaps a little less rosewater next time!'

With Ascony as interpreter the examination moved to Hamelin's eyes.

'Nothing there, except a trace of old infection, but that's nearly healed. He follows movement well enough, don't you, bright eyes?' Kelka tweaked Hamelin's cheek, then turned to Elena. 'He was favouring the left side, you say?'

She nodded, wondering what the doctor was going to do with the small taper he had lit. Hamelin was wondering, too, and shrank away at the next approach.

Kelka tilted Hamelin's head away and, while Ascony handled the taper to put more light on the subject, the doctor peered and probed gently. After a moment he stood up and scruffed Hamelin playfully.

'You horrible child! Causing this good lady so much aggravation.' The doctor turned to Elena. 'He has something well and truly lodged down in this ear, lady. Any vigorous exercise, a fight, say, might disturb it sufficiently to create strange noises for him. Anything that's built up behind it won't help, either. That could cause pain, crackling and perhaps even trouble with balance.'

'Can you do anything?'

The doctor laughed. 'Don't look so worried, Lady Elena! It's such a common occurrence in horrible children,' he tweaked Hamelin again, 'that I've got a special little device especially for the job.'

Ascony translated for Hamelin, but the explanation took longer than the act. In an instant Hamelin was clutching his ear and looking astonished.

'Now, I'll just give both ears a quick hose down and we'll see what difference that makes, if any.'

Hamelin wasn't so keen. Chattering nervously, he clutched at Elena's hands for grim death as Kelka worked.

'He's moaning that everything is too loud now,' Ascony said, but Elena noticed that he stroked Hamelin's hair kindly enough.

'You'll soon get used to that, bright eyes. Now,' Dr Kelka moved around Hamelin and began preparations on his other ear, 'I'll do this one as well, to be on the safe——'

Hamelin collapsed as though pole-axed.

'—side. Oh, dear.' Kelka looked grave. 'That wasn't supposed to happen.'

Elena helped the spluttering Hamelin to his feet and wiped his face. He gave her an unsteady smile, but his eyes were full of tears.

'Poor little chap. Damage to the eardrum on that side, then. I can't do anything about that. Perhaps having something in his other ear protected it from a similar fate. You can hear all right on that side, can't you?'

Hamelin turned at the sound of the doctor's voice, shrinking at the unusual amount of noise. All he really wanted to do was bury his head against Elena's neck.

While Elena settled up with the doctor, Ascony rewrapped Hamelin for the journey home. Once outside in the sunshine, however, it seemed as though their caution was not needed.

Duke Godfrey had taken up a heroic stance before the city gates, his horse side-stepping and fretting gracefully. He had drawn his battle-scarred sword and the gates were beginning to open.

From outside the city walls came a great noise. It was like the rushing of a mighty tide over rocks, and it was the Crusading hordes.

They stormed up to the widening city gates, and Elena clutched at Ascony in terror. Just when it seemed that they might be trampled to death under the rampaging Franks, the Crusaders stopped, as one man. Godfrey had spoken.

'Are we invaded? Ascony, what's happening?'

Hamelin struggling with curiosity in his arms, Ascony listened to the duke's speech and translated. 'A peaceful invasion, lady. If it isn't, then the duke will deal with any trouble personally.'

'Then it's over? All the waiting and worrying about Emil and Hamelin?'

'It would seem so, lady. We can be rid of the rascals at last. Although not before gaining several thousand more first!'

All around them doors were slammed, windows bolted and shutters secured as Constantinople took cover. Still carrying Hamelin, Ascony rushed Elena back to the house as torrents of Franks jostled into the city. Once inside the house he shut the door and leaned against it thankfully.

'You can put Hamelin down now, Ascony.'

'I thought that we were in trouble for a moment there,' her servant gasped, letting Hamelin slip to the ground. At once the child skipped off to the guest room, still clutching Elena's stole about his head like an Egyptian. Only when he had disappeared did Elena remember Gulzun and Selest.

She dashed after Hamelin, but found that he hadn't been the first to disturb the happy couple. With shrieks of laughter Gulzun was teaching Milo to do handstands against the wall. Hamelin was happy, too. He was gabbling away to Selest even faster than usual.

'Lady Elena? What on earth has been going on?'

'A minor domestic crisis, I think you would call it.'

Nothing in the room had been disturbed, as far as Elena could see, but jealousy had touched her and she resented it.

'Is Hamelin making this up? Did a man really pour water into his ears?'

'A doctor, my lord. We thought that it was a real emergency. As it is Hamelin has had at least a little hearing restored.'

'Fancy that.' Selest sat back and made no complaint when Hamelin scrambled on to his lap. One arm around the child, he tried out the words that Hamelin had never been able to manage before. His greatest delight came when Hamelin took to the word 'Emil', and he hugged the child vigorously. Only as Elena started to smile did Selest shove Hamelin aside roughly.

'Ungrateful wretch. He's complaining now that even air against his ear is too noisy.'

'Dr Kelka says that will pass. We must watch Hamelin carefully for a while, in case there are any more problems, but he's very hopeful.'

Selest took her hand, which Elena realised was a gesture of thanks.

'And when can you take me to this miracle-worker?'

'Oh, the news! I completely forgot! He can come here, now. Any time. Your Frankish friends have decided to give in to Emperor Alexius.'

Selest's dark eyes flashed dangerously and he dropped her hand.

'Duke Godfrey never gives in to anyone.'

'An arrangement has been reached, then. First a party this morning, and now all the rest of the troops have come into the city——'

Elena had thought that the news would cheer him. Instead he looked away and began fiddling with a pack of cards scattered on the side-table.

'They won't linger here. I shall be left behind.'

Walking slowly to the couch, Elena sat down beside him. Gulzun would have taken the edge off his appetite, she thought. Sympathy could be given safely now.

'There are so many to embark from the port it will take a long time before they're all gone. You might make it yet. How does it feel? You haven't been putting any strain on it, have you?'

'Of course not,' he snapped. 'The only strain is on me, being stuck here while everyone goes on.'

'I wish I hadn't told you the news now.' Elena flicked her plaits aside haughtily.

There was a pause while Selest drummed his fingers on the sheet covering him. They watched Hamelin try to copy Milo and his handstands, and Gulzun's delight.

At last Selest cleared his throat uncomfortably.

'I'm sorry, Lady Elena. It's just that I'm sick to death with sitting in one place. Despite the company,' he added hurriedly.

'I'll send for Dr Kelka. He'll be able to tell you when you'll be fit enough to leave, but——' Elena looked away to study the carpet. 'You're welcome to stay here for as long as you like.'

Dr Kelka arrived early that evening in a haze of good humour. 'Just come from a birth. Easy as shelling peas,' he slurred merrily. 'The new father was so delighted, he poured most of a jug of wine into me. Not that I was complaining, you understand.'

He frowned at the sight of Selest, then looked at Hamelin. If he had realised that the two Franks must have been in residence for some time, he did not comment on the fact.

Hamelin and Milo milled around, scrambling in the sand unpacked from around Selest's foot. When the injury was exposed, Kelka called for more light. The swelling had subsided and much of the bruising was already beginning to fade. Manipulating each of Selest's toes in turn, the doctor had only the harshness of Selest's expression to use in discovering what hurt and how much.

'Funny things, ankles. They have to do so much work that often muscles tense up around quite small injuries to protect them. As the Frank is so keen to go off and be killed I can strap it up properly, which will at least get him mobile. Tell him not to do too much at first, mind. Little by little. I'll come back tomorrow and do the bandaging, if you don't mind.' He laughed in a mist of wine fumes. 'All the good will's gone to my head, you might say!'

When the doctor had gone Elena went straight up to her room. It had been a very long day, and she was ready for sleep. That evening the peace and quiet was welcome, but she did miss having Milo to settle. He was downstairs with Selest and Hamelin again. Elena had to agree that Milo was advancing in leaps and bounds, but whether it was in the right direction she wasn't sure.

To Elena's dismay Selest encouraged the boys in their tussling. Milo was learning so quickly that Elena's sympathies were soon with Hamelin. The German boy was placid by nature, but followed Selest's instructions with dog-like devotion. Unfortunately Milo was an instinctively dirty fighter and soon learned where to kick and pinch for best effect in their rough and tumbles. Hamelin would soon break free and run to Elena for protection, to the scorn of Selest and Milo.

Elena thought a lot about Hamelin that evening as she was getting ready for bed. He was so young and frail to be going with the Crusade. It wasn't right. Plenty of children had already left their bleached bones on the way through the Levant, and Elena didn't want it happening to Hamelin. She wondered if there was anything that could persuade Selest against taking the boy with him.

There was another thing worrying Elena. Selest seemed so eager to leave. The time spent alone with Gulzun appeared to have made up his mind, if there had ever been any hesitation. All he talked about was the day of his departure. Like one who watched swallows congregating to leave, Elena found herself wishing that the day would not come.

To lose him now seemed inevitable, anything else unthinkable.

Elena knew that she could not stop Selest leaving, but wondered if she could give him a reason for returning. She fell asleep considering how Selest might be persuaded to leave Hamelin behind in Constantinople while he travelled on.

As it happened, events nearly made all her plans unnecessary.

# CHAPTER EIGHT

THE doctor returned at noon next day. For a medical expert he looked decidedly under the weather, and would accept only a glass of cold lemonade.

He did not take long to strap up Selest's ankle, covering up the purple, black and green bruises. The binding evidently felt as supportive as the sand-box, but was no such handicap. Selest was eager to get up at last, and Ascony managed to find him some crutches at the market.

Selest even got as far as the dining-room for lunch. Delighted with his progress, he and Elena enjoyed a light-hearted meal. The Frank seemed so changed—compliments came instead of irritable remarks, and charm instead of snapping. Mrs Khar had altered one of Henry's old robes so that it fitted perfectly. Good food and rest had smoothed the contours of his body, and put a gloss on the dark auburn of his hair.

Only when Ascony brought in more wine did a slight cloud shadow proceedings. 'Where is Hamelin, lady?'

They all looked at the space next to Milo at the large dining table.

'I thought he must be with you out in the kitchen, Ascony—you two having been as thick as thieves lately.'

When questioned Milo said he hadn't seen Hamelin since their last fight. Giggling wickedly, he kicked at the table leg until given a firm reminder by Selest to finish his lunch.

Elena rose to go and search, but Ascony stopped her.

'I'll find the young rascal, lady. He's probably sulking somewhere.'

As Ascony melted from the room Elena pushed her wine glass aside. Selest laughed at her frown.

'Don't worry. Hamelin can look after himself for ten minutes. Have another drink.'

He poured her a large measure and topped up his own glass. Selest was picking up manners quickly, and even passing them on to the boys. Elena had despaired of ever getting Milo to sit properly at the table, but he now did so until given permission to get down. Under Selest's watchful eye he threw few, if any, tantrums now. Elena wondered how long such influence would last after the Frank left.

'As I can get about now,' Selest said casually, dabbing his mouth with a napkin as Elena always did, 'I thought that perhaps it was my turn to do some entertaining.'

'Oh, no. Not that again,' Elena muttered, but he put down his glass and pulled a face.

'On this occasion, lady, you're too eager to fear the worst. I was going to suggest that you could show me around the city, as I'm now an official guest. Then perhaps we could have a quiet dinner alone for a change. Children are all very well,' he ruffled Milo's hair, 'but it's nice to enjoy real grown-up talk now and again.'

'I know——' Elena sighed, then remembered to have misgivings. 'It wouldn't be possible, my lord. We couldn't dine alone—not the two of us together. What would the staff think?'

'They needn't know.'

'It might be rather obvious, my lord. They would be cooking, serving, clearing away and most importantly— looking after the children.'

'Oh, don't make difficulties where there are none, woman—— '

He was interrupted by Ascony arriving with news of the runaway. Grinning widely, he whispered to Elena, who rose and took her leave of Selest.

'It is quite a mess, lady, but nothing that can't be put right...'

He led the way to Elena's room, but she could barely recognise it.

A trail of discarded clothes wandered from the wardrobe to the door and back again. Cosmetics and perfume lay scattered, spilled and forgotten on floor, washstand and dressing-table. A heavy mingling of musk and flower scents lay over the ruin, seeping into everything. In the midst of everything was Hamelin.

He was curled up on her bed, fast asleep. He was decked out in one of Elena's tunics and engulfed in a pair of her leggings, and the picture was completed by the stole he had been wrapped in the day before. It was wound about his head, stained and spotted now by the rouge, kohl and glitter he had daubed all over his face.

Elena hustled Ascony out quickly before they both burst into fits of muffled laughter.

'I'm going to have to be cross with him, aren't I?' Elena said, giggling, when she could speak.

'Indeed. Most definitely, or he will be teaching young Milo the same naughtiness.'

'Oh, but he looks so adorable. It's a pity that the lord Selest can't come up and see him in all this finery!'

She put on her best cross expression and marched back into the bedroom. After only a moment's hesitation she shook Hamelin awake. He squirmed luxuriously, stretched, then opened his eyes.

'Naughty boy. Grr!' Elena pointed at the mess. She clapped her hands for emphasis then mimed his punishment. 'I'll take you downstairs and scrub your face clean. Then you can jolly well come back here and tidy up.'

Hamelin looked crestfallen and searched through his small collection of French words. 'Good! Good toys!'

'No. These are not toys. They are my things, and you're a naughty boy!' Elena said firmly, marching him off down the stairs.

As they reached the hall Selest swung himself out of the dining-room to see what the commotion was about. Once he saw the state of Hamelin he stopped, thunderstruck.

'What in the world——?'

'Don't laugh, my lord. Hamelin's in disgrace.'

'I'll say he is!' Selest growled at the child in German, and Hamelin froze. The Crusader limped nearer, putting the fear of God into his prey.

'I knew all along that this was a wicked place,' Selest muttered in an undertone. 'Now it's infected the boy. There's only one sure remedy for this.'

They were all standing by the bath house door. Surprisingly agile despite his crutches, Selest bent down and slapped Hamelin's legs, hard. Then amid a stream of German that made Ascony wince he shook the child like a puppy and, bundling him into the bath house, slammed the door shut.

Hamelin was hysterical by this time, his screams of terror muffled by the tiny room.

'Oh, my lord! Don't! It's so dark in there without a candle——'

'He stays in there until he stops making that noise.' Selest thumped on the door and roared more German in at Hamelin.

'There's no crime worth this, lord! The child is terrified! I've already scolded him for it—this is only confusing him, surely...'

'I've told the boy he'll be reported to the priest for punishment fitting his unnatural vice. Kindly arrange it for me, lady.'

'No...'

Selest moved close to her, an angry flush colouring his normally pale features.

'He has to learn that men don't wear women's things where we come from. Not the sort of men that I want anything to do with, anyway. This place is...evil. They told us that, and now I believe them. It's corrupted poor Hamelin, but it's not going to corrupt me. I would be grateful if you could return to me the clothes that I arrived in, Lady Elena. As soon as possible.'

He turned and swung back to the dining-room, leaving Elena to fling open the bath house door.

Hamelin was crouched in the furthest corner, made tiny with fear. When light fell upon him he screamed, looking frantically for an escape from further wrath. He tried to scuttle past her, but Elena caught him.

'Ssh! Hamelin... it's all right now. You've been punished enough. I won't let anyone hurt you again. Hush...'

She held him until his screams became uneven sobbing, then the tears of pure grief. It was a long time before he could speak, and then it was with renewed anguish.

'Wet... Sorry, Mummy...' Hamelin used Milo's word and pulled at the tunic slopping about him, sobbing all the time. 'Sorry, Mummy... Wet...'

'Only a little accident. You were frightened, that's all.' Elena smoothed the blond hair back from his colour-stained face and smiled. 'Emil was very cross because you were a naughty boy, but by the time you're washed and dressed properly you'll be friends again. Promise.'

Hamelin listened to her dumbly, smearing red, gold and black across his face as he wiped away tears.

'Go along with Ascony, now. He'll clean you up and give you some cake. Would you like that?'

Hamelin liked anything that meant he was spoken to kindly. Once more he slipped his hand confidingly into Elena's and let himself be led out to where Ascony was waiting.

When Elena returned to her deserted meal she had harsh words for Selest.

'You can be hateful to that poor child.'

'No more than is necessary, Lady Elena. The priests out in the camp were forever warning us that Constantinople was a place full of strange, seductive wickedness. It's my Christian duty to see that he doesn't succumb to any of it. The priests said that we had to look out for each other, as well as ourselves. It can creep up unnoticed on the unwary.'

Elena sighed. It wasn't Selest's fault. He had thought he was doing right.

'It was only a childish game, my lord. He could have picked Henry's room and dressed in clothes from there. I don't think there was any sin involved at all.'

Selest rolled wine around his glass, watching the effect of sunlight glowing through the liquid gold.

'It was only chance that he went to my room instead of Henry's. Please don't be any harder on him.'

'You still call it "Henry's room",' Selest said at last. 'Still in residence, is he?'

Elena suddenly felt very small and foolish.

'No, my lord. It is where all his things are kept.'

There was another pause. Bored with the silence, Milo clambered down from his chair and ran to Selest.

'Milo.' The Crusader put his face down close to the child. 'What have you forgotten?'

Meek as a mouse Milo ran back to his chair and pretended to sit on it again. Leaning back against the seat, he grinned at Selest.

'Please may I leave the table, Emil?'

'You may, Milo. Run along to Hamelin and tell him to bring his lunch in here. I want to talk to him. Tell him I'm not cross any more.'

When Milo had scampered off Elena and Selest sat in silence. Elena had expected him to make more clever remarks about Henry's room, but he said nothing for a long time. Instead he continued to roll his goblet stem between his fingers while sunlight played over his face and hands. He was even more uncomfortable in his Byzantine clothes now and sat rigidly upright in his jewel-encrusted finery.

'I realise that I must often seem insensitive to you.'

'You cannot help it,' Elena began. She was going to add, Because you are a Frank, but didn't. Something told her that Selest was at least making an attempt at sensitivity.

'From now on I will try to be less unforgiving, Lady Elena.' He took a slow drink, then put down his glass. 'You must find it strange to be in the company of a man from your own class after so long.'

Elena finished her wine with a smile.

'Yes and no, my lord. It's true that I never normally entertain gentlemen on a purely social basis, but then these are not normal times. Then again, we are hardly of the same social class, you and I.'

'You snob!' He laughed.

'Oh, no, my lord. I came from the very humblest of beginnings. Like all Franks you must have land and fame to spare back in your own country.'

Selest shook his head. Leaning forward, he trapped her with a gaze, dark eyes soft and shadowed.

'My mother produced a baby every year from her marriage at fourteen to her death before she was thirty. Nine of us survived to share a room a fraction this size with father and all our animals. My home has mud walls, a turf roof and a floor of beaten earth. Father has only three acres of land to keep us all, which was bad enough. Then the rent went up. Our lord was taking more than half our produce in rent. In '95 the crops failed, and by December we had only five sacks of corn and a few onions left to last the winter. We were at least able to scratch for roots in the forest until the really bad weather set in. And then our lord decided he would have a banquet to celebrate the new year. He took our breeding sow. The only bit of our stock that we hadn't been forced to eat.'

'Surely you could have refused to give it to him?'

Selest snorted in derision. 'What could we do? Life is very cheap at home, Lady Elena. Others were in the same position, too. Our entire village was starving. The weather was so hard that the lord's deer came out of the forest to strip bark from the village fruit trees, killing them. There wasn't a thing that anybody could do to stop it. Our masters are very fond of their deer. No one is allowed to harm them, while they can do what they like to ruin us. I've even seen children murdered for eating hay put out for the lord's deer.'

Elena realised then why Milo's chubbiness offended Selest.

Her guest continued his tale.

'We struggled through winter somehow. Last spring we all worked the land for Father, who was too weak, but our parcel of land couldn't support the whole family. I and two younger brothers walked ten miles to the nearest town in search of work. We were going to get good jobs and send all the money home. That was the plan. When we got there we found that you can't get a decent job without being in a guild, and you can't enter a guild without being in a decent job. It's hopeless.'

He stopped, and Elena realised how painful the memories must be. Selest bit his lip and studied the decanter until she could stand it no longer.

'What happened?'

'We lived rough in the woods, begging through the town by day. Towards the end of summer we scavenged wood through the forest, selling it to those in the town who were too weak or lazy to collect their own. We made enough money to buy my brother Hans an apprenticeship with a baker. A steady job with all the stale and mouldy stock that he could eat. A triumph—we could send food as well as money home! A lot more wooding and I could afford to get Emmich a butchery apprenticeship on the same terms. Bread and meat for the family once a month—we couldn't believe it.'

Elena was beside herself with indignation. 'You mean to say that Franks can only get a job if they can afford to buy their way into a trade? That's awful! Here in Constantinople apprentices are taken on because they want to earn money, not give it away. That is the way of things here—we all look after each other. Don't Franks care for their own?'

Selest poured a thin stream of wine into his glass, making bubbles dance across the surface.

'Of course. But the rich protect each other, the clergy band together and the poor likewise. Unfortunately it is the rich and religious who have all the money. All the family ties in the world can't compensate our poor for that.'

'Let me send some money to them,' Elena said without hesitation. 'How much would your family need?'

Laughing, Selest reached out and took her hand.

'More than you could ever provide, Lady Elena. In my land wealth doesn't endure as it seems to here. It is our system that needs changing.'

With her small hand enclosed in his strong, work-worn fingers Elena felt the strength of purpose that had brought him so far.

'When the priests preached that we should all go East for Christ, I saw an opportunity. Everyone at home knows that the lands of the Levant run with milk and honey. No man could ever be poor or hungry in the lands where Christ once walked, or so the story goes. I set out to find my fortune, in the company of thousands of others. When I got to the Holy Land I was going to get a good big plot of land, stock it with animals and then send for all my family. Bella, Annie, Lise, Tild and Gerda would all marry rich Christian princes. Father and I would work the land while Peter got an education. And of course Hans and Emmich would be in charge of the food.'

Elena listened to the great plan in silence. Selest had been animated by his memories and now land, Selest land, lay before his eyes. Sunlight rippled over his auburn curls and set the amber glints in his eyes gleaming. Elena clasped his hand with her own.

'Our lands have pleased you, then, my lord.'

Eyes dulled, he turned to her. Enthusiasm had fled from his features.

'People in the villages here are as poor as they are at home.'

'I don't think that there's a country in the world that doesn't know poverty, my lord.'

The touch of his skin against hers ignited Elena and she squeezed his hand more firmly. In reply he set his features with more determination.

'Things will be different when we get to the Holy Land. That must be where the riches are.'

'The Bible stories are full of paupers, Emil.'

He looked at her in afternoon sun so gentle that it even managed to coax beauty from his bitter expression.

'That's as maybe. I shan't see it now. I'll be left behind here to rot.' He pulled his hand away from her almost savagely. 'You think I'm stupid. You think that my ideas are so much hot air, don't you?'

'Don't get angry, my lord. Everyone needs hopes and dreams.'

'At least we'd be willing to work for our living. We wouldn't dip ourselves in paints and perfumes and sit about being waited on.'

'Constantinople isn't all like that, my lord,' Elena said evenly. 'You haven't seen it properly yet. Most people here work very hard indeed. If you weren't so keen on playing the injured innocent you could come out tomorrow and meet some of my workmen. I shall be taking Hamelin. I think he might find it interesting.'

Selest laughed, but it was without mirth. 'Going to find him a job, are you?'

That had been Elena's idea. She had felt too nervous to suggest it, but for Selest to mention the matter even in jest gave her confidence.

'There might be that possibility, yes.'

At once the Frank lost the angry set of his jaw and looked at Elena searchingly.

'I've looked after him this long. We're travelling on together.' His voice had none of the conviction that the words might have suggested. This gave Elena the courage to carry on.

'He's awfully small to be a soldier, my lord. Don't you think he'd hold you back——?'

'We'll travel at his pace. There are plenty smaller than Hamelin travelling with the Crusade,' Selest blustered. 'We'll manage—I've looked after him so far, and I won't desert him now.'

'You wouldn't *be* deserting him, my lord,' Elena continued gently. 'There would be a bed for him in the apprentices' room with the others. They're good boys, but as ready for a rough and tumble as you might like. Hamelin would learn a trade while being well fed and housed. He'd never have to sleep on the bare ground again, or go hungry. And when you've made your fortune and come back to collect your family, he'll be waiting here for you.'

Selest rubbed his thumb thoughtfully across his lips. 'I'll have to think about it. What if he can't manage the work?'

'Come on, my lord. You've said yourself that he's turning out to be as bright as a button now that he can hear a little better.'

'He's German, for heaven's sake. He won't understand anything——'

'Now you're scraping the barrel for excuses. He's picking up Greek words all the time from Milo. We aren't ogres, my lord! We'll teach him, and take time to explain. And, of course, Ascony can't be the only person in the city who can speak German.'

Selest slumped back in his seat. Something told Elena that her arguments had been convincing enough, but she knew that Selest wasn't the sort of man to back down easily. He would take that as a sign of weakness.

'The quicker that I'm up and about properly, the faster I'll be fit enough to follow the gang. I think I'll join you in your visit tomorrow, Lady Elena. If that would be all right?'

Milo and Hamelin burst out of the house in a riot of energy. They racketed up and down the quiet street, causing blinds to twitch and shutters to slam.

'Ssh!' Elena scolded without result. It was bad enough helping a lame Crusader out of her front door without all the noise.

Relaxed now that he had his own cleaned and repaired clothes to wear, Selest was in a cheerful mood. 'They've been cooped up inside for too long, Lady Elena. Let them work it off.'

'But we don't like noise here. This is a respectable area!'

'Very well, then. Let's take them to a disreputable area. Where does your friend Gulzun live?'

At once jealousy put Elena on the defensive. 'Don't think her neighbours would put up with this rowdy behaviour, my lord. They're——'

'Respectable?' Selest leaned into his crutches and swung himself off towards the Mese. Cackling and cavorting, the boys galloped around him while Elena had to hurry to catch up.

'Careful, my lord! You'll fall, and then what would you do?'

'Get up again!' Selest replied with a grin. 'Ah, this is more like it!'

They had reached the Mese and he paused to take in the scene. Subdued at first by the arrival of the Crusaders, this end of the Mese had come back to life now that the strangers had moved on. Tradesmen cried their wares once more and people laughed in the sunshine. Lop-eared goats bobbed and bleated along, followed by barefoot, brown-baked country children. Milo and Hamelin immediately ran forward, but stopped when they realised that they were being sized up as opponents by the urchins. At a whistle from Selest the two lads ran back to him, honour satisfied with a few snarls over their shoulders at the goatherds.

'Good boys. No fighting out here. This is a respectable area!' He winked at Elena, but she pretended to ignore him.

They stepped out from the shadowy protection of the houses and into the sunny stridency of the Mese. Many people were frightened of coming across Franks, so the highway was not as busy as usual. Even so, Levantines, Greeks, Turks and many other nationalities chatted together in doorways or strolled in the spring sunshine. Tradesmen swept their areas among the collonades of the Mese while their wives scrubbed down the marble columns dividing individual pitches. A covered nightsoil cart moved down the highway, furtively removing all trace of revelling Crusaders and their horses. The only thing that Constantinople ever smelled of was money, and the Byzantines were determined to keep it that way with sawdust, brushes and hot soapy water.

'Good grief!' Selest stopped and touched Elena's arm. 'Would you look at that?'

Elena looked, but could see nothing that might have amused Selest so much.

'There—that swarthy chap leading something like a horse!'

A high-stepping, highly bred stallion was strutting towards them, accompanied by its loving owner. Neck arched and tail carried high as a banner, the horse flounced down the street, dipping its neat head now and then as though acknowledging the homage of its people.

'It's legs are so thin it's a wonder they don't snap!' Selest laughed. 'What sort of a nag is that for a man to lead around?'

'That's no ordinary horse, my lord, or any ordinary man. They are cataphract—man and horse named alike, because they live and work as one unit. Each would die for the other, and they are so fast and such fearsome fighting machines that it's said they sweat blood in battle.'

'The Byzantines must be mad if they put their faith in monstrosities like that! How could that thing stand up to a full day in the field carrying a knight in armour?'

Elena considered this. Something had already occurred to her about the Frankish horses that she had seen, and now her worse fears surfaced.

'Then...the animals that Duke Godfrey and his men ride are the only sort you have?'

'Good sturdy animals. Steady and dependable,' Selest said proudly.

'Oh, dear.' They watched the cataphract strut nearer, and Elena sighed. 'Then I'm afraid, my lord, that the Seljuk will run rings around you. They all ride horses of this sort. Fast and wiry.'

'Pah! They'll never get the better of us. We've got skill at arms, and more importantly we are on the Lord's side.'

'I believe the Seljuk have been heard saying exactly the same thing, my lord,' Elena said quietly. She picked Milo up as Selest hailed the cataphract.

'Will you interpret for us, Lady Elena?' Selest called over his shoulder as he limped towards the horseman and his charge.

Elena followed him with the children. While Hamelin was quite happy to watch his friend's detailed examination of the prancing animal, Milo was frightened and hid his face. It took all Elena's wits to avoid being strangled by her son, translate Selest's many questions and still keep clear of the dancing hoofs.

Suddenly the stallion stood stock-still, nostrils flaring. Used to the moods of his charge, the horseman took a firm grip on its halter and brandished a long thin crop. Selest moved back with a laugh.

'Watch out for some fun now, Elena. Look over there!'

She followed the stallion's white-rimmed gaze and saw a second cataphract, the animal part of that combination a beautiful mare. The horse beside them whiffled a sigh of longing and started to strut.

'I don't like it, Mummy!' Milo cried as the stallion shook off its owner's hand and reared. Manoeuvring to a safe distance, Selest watched with amusement as the man flicked his horse. It was no use. The stallion had other things in mind.

Women screamed with laughter and men cheered at the struggle to maintain a dignified partnership. Only when urchins eager for cash threw themselves into the fray was the horse brought under control. To a round of applause the cataphracts were able to meet and discuss a deal.

Elena pulled Milo's head further into her neck, trying to cover his ears. Selest was delighted.

'What are you doing, Lady Elena?'

'Only protecting my child, lord.'

'What from? He must have seen it all a hundred times before.'

'Not at all. To see this in the street is an unusual occurrence. What do you think we are?'

Selest raised his eyebrows in amusement. 'You'll only make him ten times more curious, lady, if you make a secret of the business. Look at Hamelin.'

After laughing and cheering with the crowd Hamelin had lost interest in proceedings. He had discovered an ants' nest and now squatted in the gutter, poking it with a stick. In contrast Milo was squirming with curiosity, dying to escape from his mother's clutches and see what all the fuss was about.

'He'll get a good view from up there, anyway, Elena.'

Elena turned her back on the street scene and put the child down. Holding Milo close to her, she tried to stop him wriggling, but it was a difficult task.

'Here.' Selest balanced on one crutch and held out his hand. 'Send him over to me.'

She hesitated, still gripping the squealing Milo.

'Do you want to have to hold on to him every single time this goes on, until he gets married? Or would you rather he took no notice, like Hamelin?'

At the mention of his name Hamelin looked up and beamed, uncaring of the noisy courtship being conducted behind him. With regret Elena let go of Milo, who dashed to Selest.

'Look, Milo. Look!'

The Frank pointed across at the pair of cataphracts. The stallion was showing off to the mare, prancing and strutting before her.

'What are they called, Milo?'

Beaming widely, Milo was only too keen to show off his French. 'Horses!'

'Good boy.' Selest patted him, but at that point Milo began to get agitated. If he hadn't been so eager to be seen as a brave boy he would have put his arms around

Selest for comfort. Instead he clutched the Crusader's hand and called out to Elena.

'He says he doesn't like it when the horses fight, my lord,' Elena said with satisfaction.

'You interpret for me, then, Lady Elena, while I tell him what's going on.'

'Oh, no! I couldn't!'

'Tell him what I say. Word for word.'

Selest bent down and ruffled Milo's hair. 'They're not fighting, Podge. Look.'

Elena translated, but used 'Milo' instead of the hated 'Podge'.

'They are fighting, Mummy. That one's biting.' Milo pointed accusingly, then suddenly noticed something else.

'Mummy, look! What's it doing now?'

He spoke in a loud, clear voice that Elena knew must have carried half the length of the city. She blushed to the roots of her hair. Had Selest not managed to stop laughing for long enough to catch her by the arm, Elena would have melted away in shame.

'Say this, Lady Elena. He's giving the mummy horse a foal to look after until it's big enough to be born.'

Elena stammered through the words, much to Milo's delight.

'Can I see it? Can I have the foal? Mummy, you said I could have a horse when I was bigger. I'm bigger now, Mummy! Can I have a horse? Ple-ease...'

'Now look what you've done,' Elena muttered. 'He won't shut up until I buy him a horse of his own, now.'

'Nothing to it, Lady Elena.' Selest laughed. 'Look, he's already forgotten about what they're up to over there. Just say, "Not even Emil is big enough to have a horse yet. When you're bigger than he is, then you might be able to get a horse for yourself." That's all. Then change the subject—say, "Emil can't wait to see what's going on at the shop," or some such.'

To Elena's surprise Milo really did forget his whining and the cavorting horses. All he could think of was leading Selest off to the shop. Anxious that Hamelin should not hold them up, he grabbed the German boy's anting stick and threw it down before marching off down the street.

'I'm surprised at you, Lady Elena!' Selest said archly as the children scampered ahead. 'If your family was as poor as mine, life should hold no embarrassments for you!'

'We were never so poor that we couldn't afford a bit of curtain for privacy, my lord,' Elena countered. 'Besides, I want better for Milo. He's going to be brought up as a gentleman.'

Selest gave a stifled laugh. 'They're the worst, my lady!'

Despite his light-hearted scorn Elena drew closer to him. Three Frankish youths, blond and bristle-headed, were rollicking about in the fountain just outside Elena's shop.

Calling the children back, she caught hold of their hands.

Soaked to the skin and very drunk, the louts were singing at the tops of their voices. Shopkeepers and merchants were looking on in horror as great heavy boots clumped about tasteful municipal stonework. What would be next? Their shops?

Selest looked from the louts to the nervous crowd.

'Lady Elena—would you be so kind as to buy me a bag of figs from that stall? The owner seems to have little else to do but sigh and shake his head.'

'We have plenty of figs at home, my lord——'

'It's for our brave boys over there.' He gestured towards the yelling group of Frankish youths. 'You and the others do want them out of the fountain, I suppose?'

'Lumps of raw meat might be better as bait, my lord...'

'Do as I say, Elena.'

She went away, returning a little while later with a tiny frail of figs for him. Thanking her, Selest took them and the faithful Hamelin over to the fountain. Ignoring the young Franks, he sat down on the marble steps. Together he and Hamelin started to enjoy their figs.

Catcalls from the louts brought only the sunniest replies from Selest, who carried on regardless. This intrigued the Franks, who stopped splashing. All three peered at him, gargoyles leering over the fountain's lip.

Selest spoke to them in German for a moment then offered up the frail of figs. One by one they accepted, then at Selest's words they all looked at Elena and cackled lustily. After a brief exchange with Hamelin and Selest they climbed out of the fountain and dripped down the steps. They sat down.

Although she could not understand their rough speech, Elena did not like the way that they all kept looking her up and down. She kept a tight hold on Milo, and hoped that Hamelin would be all right. The louts were all so big beside him.

When the figs were finished, all five Franks sat talking together. Then without any fuss the three youths got up and strolled down the Mese, looking back every so often to wave unsteadily to Selest and Hamelin. The citizens breathed sighs of relief, glad to have shops left to return to.

Selest sat on the steps until Elena went over to him.

'Excitement over.' He smiled at the crowds, who were looking at him with shy regard. 'Having won my spurs in the eyes of the Byzantines, all I need now is the help of a nice young lady to get me up.'

Elena was not convinced that he was stuck, but gave him a helping hand anyway.

'What were you saying about me?'

'Oh, nothing much.' Selest adjusted his crutches and started on down the Mese, knowing that Elena was bursting with indignant curiosity. After a finely judged pause he continued, 'Only that if they played their cards right they might be able to find a pretty little landlady who would buy them figs.'

Elena nearly exploded. 'You didn't invite them home?'

'Of course not. They've got no rent for a billet, having spent it all on drink, so I sent them off to find Duke Godfrey.'

'I can't see a decent man like him wanting to be bothered with the likes of them.'

'Oh, he'll bother with them, Lady Elena. He'll either help them himself or find someone who can.'

Selest had held on to her for a few minutes longer than was necessary when she helped him up. Elena wondered what might happen next, but the moment passed. She wondered whether it hadn't been her own wishful thinking that had thought him forward in the first place.

He had been slowing down, but refused her offer of help over the last few yards towards the shop. Eban offered him a seat right away, having seen the business with the lads. Selest accepted gratefully.

'Another Turk?' he whispered to Elena with resignation.

'Yes, my lord. Don't worry—there are plenty about!'

Milo took Hamelin off to play in the sand-box that Eban had made for him. While Selest pinched life back into skin rubbed numb by the crutches, Elena told him about the business.

It was in three parts. At the front, where they sat now, was the shop. This faced on to the Mese in a prime position. Here, glass goods of all descriptions were displayed and sold. With light flickering across shelves and shelves of delicate glassware in shades from earth to sky, Selest could see the attraction.

A small office lay at the back of the shop, with steps up to the apprentices' room and stores. Beyond this room were the workshop and furnaces. They were separated from the office by an iron gate, so Milo could be left there in safety while his mother was busy.

'You don't mean to say that you actually work here?'

'Of course, my lord,' Elena said over the clatter and whistling of the workers outside. 'I can't expect Eban to work here all day every day without a break.'

'But you're a girl! I would have thought that somebody with all your money could afford to pay someone else——'

'Any business-person worth the name will tell you that money alone doesn't stop them working. Besides, I like coming here,' she said softly, looking around the light, bright shelves.

'No woman of mine would work. Except in the house,' Selest said darkly.

'Then it's as well that you don't live here permanently, my lord. All but the very lowliest in the city employ staff of some sort. In that case any "woman" of yours, as you so charmingly call her, would have no work to do in the house. I'm sure she'd soon die of boredom!'

'Children keep a woman occupied well enough.'

Elena threw up her hands in disbelief, her bracelets tinkling like bells.

'I like that! Every time I show poor Milo any scrap of affection you jump down my throat! And I would have thought,' she said accusingly, 'that someone who had seen his mother ground down by having so many children would have been a bit more understanding.'

'Leave my mother out of this,' Selest muttered, putting his crutches down carefully. With every movement glassware all around them shivered in chorus. 'She was never very strong.'

'I shouldn't think she was, struggling with so many children.'

Elena realised that she had gone too far. She had already learned from experience that when his jaw was set in that determined line it was time to change the subject.

She picked up his crutches again and handed them back to him. 'Don't make the place look untidy, my lord!' she said sweetly. 'You're here for a reason, remember. Come out and see the workshop. I want you to meet the apprentices, and decide whether they're likely to be suitable company for young Hamelin.'

# CHAPTER NINE

WHEN Selest followed Elena out into the office his movements were already a little slower. Hemmed in by packing cases, the boys were happy playing sand-castles and barely noticed them pass.

The workshop was well ventilated by windows and large double doors, for good reason. Great furnaces roared along the length of one wall. Each one was shaped like a flask, its neck acting as a chimney for the fire that burned within. Just above waist-height a small hatch was cut into each furnace. Into these the glass blowers dipped their rods, heating and manipulating molten glass at arm's length as easily as if it were putty in their hands.

Then the long rods magnified their movements so that a barely perceptible twitch of finger and thumb moulded steady breath into a flawless shape.

Each specialist had a table beside his own furnace. This held his collection of rods and short lengths of sharpened stick.

'This is Joshua,' Elena said as they reached the first table. Joshua looked up from his work and smiled at Selest with liquid dark eyes.

'He's Jewish, isn't he?' the Frank said warily.

'Oh, for heaven's sake, my lord, what does it matter?'

'We've been told to look out for them,' he said, but there was uncertainty in his voice as though priestly rantings were already half forgotten. 'If we're going to free the Holy City then we must be able to recognise all the different sorts of infidel——'

Elena kicked his good ankle savagely, but fortunately Joshua did not understand what was being said. Smiling still, he carried on with his work, making a cheerful comment as he did so. At once Elena turned on her employee with an angry reply. Joshua looked suitably crestfallen, to Selest's curiosity.

'What did he say?'

'Nothing. It doesn't matter.'

'It must do. You certainly took the wind out of his sails for him.'

Elena pretended to be interested in the work that was going on about them, but Selest wouldn't let the matter drop.

'All right. If you must know,' she sidled between Selest and the industrious Joshua, 'he said he was surprised that Franks are allowed to walk the streets unmuzzled.'

Selest wasn't immediately stung to anger, as she had expected. Instead he regarded Joshua for some time until the young workman looked to Elena for reassurance.

'Is it true,' Selest said at last, 'that Jews marry their own brothers and sisters? Ask him.'

'I've never heard so much rubbish in my life!'

'That's what the priests tell us.' Selest swung his left leg, still staring at Joshua. 'Humour me, Lady Elena. Ask him.'

Elena phrased the question as delicately as she could, but Joshua was delighted. He grinned widely at Selest and replied with much evident amusement.

'He says,' Elena folded her arms as though defying Selest to lose his temper, 'that Jews marry their sisters about as frequently as Franks eat babies.'

Selest pursed his lips and thought about this. 'Is that what they're told about us?'

Elena shrugged and asked her worker. His answer was good-natured, but it was easy to see that he was observing Selest closely.

'He says that there are always stories told about any strangers. It's hard to know what to believe. They are told that Christians drink blood, burn synagogues and torture Jews. On the other hand, my lord, you might take consolation from the fact that Joshua doesn't think you look like someone who would do that sort of thing.'

Selest was watching Joshua as intently as he was being watched in turn. The young workman had reached a break in production so both could study the other.

'We're told that Jews live off money extorted from innocents, and never do a day's work for themselves,' Selest said slowly, then looked at the finished work that an apprentice was removing from Joshua's table. 'But this Joshua of yours seems to earn his keep.'

With great care, Selest moved both his crutches to one side. He wiped his right hand down his breeches then looked at Joshua warily. After a hesitation he put out his hand to the Jew. With equal caution Joshua considered, then both men shook hands in a gesture that was as embarrassed as it was sudden.

Joshua turned back to his work and Elena led Selest away quickly to prevent further discomfort. One small step at a time might be as well to begin with.

'He wears earrings!' the Crusader hissed as they watched Joshua from a diplomatic distance.

'So do I,' Elena countered.

After that Selest was content to watch the work in progress. Joshua worked methodically and with unhurried movements. Soon a molten blob of nothing was a nearly recognisable shape. At this point Joshua took the rod and its rudimentary vase back to the table. Here an apprentice was ready to hand him wooden dowels of appropriate size to shape the glass.

With one hand Joshua rolled the rod along the table's edge to keep the soft glass from dripping to the ground. With the other he moulded a neck and lip of perfect proportions, using a succession of sticks as they flared and charred on the molten surface.

'That's amazing,' Selest whispered. 'Can I have a go?'

'We have no guilds here, my lord, but we do have apprentices. They might be upset to see you doing at once what they have waited a long time to attempt.'

He nodded his understanding. 'Do you think that Hamelin could ever turn out work like that?'

'He would be given every chance to learn, after a suitable apprenticeship.'

Selest bit his lip and gave the matter some hard thought. After he had been through a ritual of pulling one ear and sighing heavily he turned to face her directly.

'You know better than anyone that I haven't got a bean. I couldn't possibly pay for an apprenticeship for Hamelin until I returned from the Holy Land—always supposing I live long enough to return. And then I couldn't guarantee that I would have made my fortune, or indeed any money at all...'

'My lord, you must have a very short memory. I've told you before. You don't need to buy him a place— he would be quite welcome as it is. He'd get paid—oh, not much to begin with, but then he'd only be sweeping up and running errands—but his money would be his own. After a little has been deducted for his board and lodgings here, and savings——'

'What on earth would Hamelin want to save for?'

'Don't laugh at thrift, my lord. One day when he's a master craftsman he might want to set up his own little business. Or get married, or look after you in your old age if you come back to him...'

'I haven't decided if I'm going to leave him, yet,' Selest muttered, limping towards one of the tables of finished vases.

'These are pretty.'

'Seconds, I'm afraid. They're to be scrapped.'

Selest gasped. 'Let me take one, then. It seems such a waste to throw them away. You said that glass is so very expensive!'

'They won't be thrown away, my lord. Nothing is ever wasted here. Mistakes spotted when the glass is still warm go back in for reshaping. If a flaw is found in the finished item then they're smashed and the fragments sorted by colour and size. Henry used to give them free of charge to an icon-maker, but I've got my own team working here now. We sell icons direct, and also mosaic tiles. Abstracts for the Muslims and actual pictures for everyone else. Some of the sand that we receive still has shells in, so they're salvaged and made into jewellery. At the moment I'm trying to discover how to make better cosmetics than I can buy. We use shades of ochre and extracts here that are much prettier than I've seen in any make-up. I'm sure I could find a market there, too, if——'

'Good grief!' Selest was looking at her with new eyes. The gaze was not altogether complimentary. 'What sort of a woman are you?'

'A businesswoman,' Elena said sharply.

It took them an age to get home from the shop. Elena thought that Selest must be tired, but when they reached his couch in the guest room he flung his crutches the length of the room.

'Those—instruments of torture—have rubbed me raw,' he spat with fury.

'Why ever didn't you say, my lord? I could have sent the boys to fetch Ascony. He could have carried you home.'

'I'm not a child, lady.'

'But you are in pain. Let me see.'

He unlaced the collar of his old shirt to display brownish red welts beneath each arm.

'Arnich water will cool that. I'll have Ascony fetch some from the Egyptians.'

'And while he's out there, tell—I mean ask—him to fetch Gulzun for me, would you? I need to see her.'

Elena was miffed, and showed it.

'Gulzun will be on holiday at any time now. She won't want to be bothered with you, or anybody else for that matter.'

'On holiday? Better and better. Just what I wanted to hear.'

He settled himself into his seat with much puffing and blowing at the bruising. Elena clasped her hands uncomfortably and wondered how to explain.

'Holidays have a rather different meaning to a girl in Gulzun's profession, my lord. She takes them because she cannot work, not because she wants a rest.'

'I know what I want, Lady Elena, and that means the Lady Gulzun. Please arrange for her to visit me here.'

He finished with a tone so forceful that Elena left at once to find Ascony. The eunuch agreed to fetch the arnich water, but shared Elena's opinion that Gulzun should not be worried by the Frank's unnatural request.

Unfortunately neither had bargained for Ascony's love of gossip. With such a succulent item to barter with he came home with a lot of trivial stories, and Gulzun herself arrived shortly before supper.

'If you want anything broadcast the length and breadth of the city, tell Ascony,' she said languidly, arranging herself on a couch beside the supper table. 'Fortunately I was able to put several people right about the matter.'

Elena sipped her tcha primly and handed almond wafers. 'You needn't think that I'm going to allow anything of that sort to go on under my roof——'

'This is a respectable neighbourhood, after all,' Selest said, mocking her serious tone. 'Well, Lady Elena. Respectable young ladies should know when to keep their curiosity out of other people's business, so you'll be giving us a few minutes alone after supper, I hope?'

'Oh, go on, Elena. Don't be mean...'

'You're encouraging him? Gulzun, I'm surprised at you!'

'As the gentleman said, Elena. It's other people's business, not yours,' Gulzun said with a tilt of her chin.

Elena considered herself outflanked. As soon as supper was over she left Gulzun and Selest to their own devices, taking the children out into the dusky garden.

They hadn't been playing on the swing for long when Gulzun strolled out to join them, a smirk of satisfaction on her face. To begin with Elena tried to ignore her, but the girls had been friends for too long. She gave Gulzun a long-suffering shrug, and Gulzun giggled.

'You're jealous, aren't you, Elena? Own up!'

Elena pushed Milo and Hamelin into more laughter on the swing.

'I don't know.'

'You *do* know!'

Gulzun threw her veil back over one shoulder and hopped up on to the swing, one tiny foot jammed each side of Hamelin as the German boy held Milo on his lap.

'Come on, boys, let's see how high we can get!'

The wooden framework creaked and groaned, but Ascony and Khar were good joiners. Their work held, much to Elena's relief and the children's delight.

'You've got no worries with Emil, Elena,' Gulzun called as she kicked the swing higher. 'Just you make sure that you treat him properly!'

Next morning, Elena woke to grievous bodily harm amid the rattle of crockery. Hamelin and Milo were crawling all over her to find the warmest spots in the bed while Ascony stood aloof, bearing a breakfast tray.

'Ascony? What time is it? What's wrong?'

'Hurry up, Mummy! We're going out!'

As he chirrupped, Milo worked his small feet against her thigh. They were chilly as fish, and as Elena jerked away in surprise Hamelin's knees connected with the small of her back. Both boys shrieked with laughter at her groans.

'They have given me no peace since before cock crow, lady. Perhaps it is your turn to suffer now.' Ascony sighed.

Elena dragged herself into a sitting position, still trying to shake sleep from her mind. Things had begun to register slowly.

'Going out, Milo? Where?'

'To the sea!'

Ascony thrust the tray at Elena and at once the children pounced like hungry nestlings.

'The Frank wishes it, lady. He says that you are to show him more of the city.'

'Don't speak of him like that, Ascony. He does have a name.'

'Indeed, lady, and the household staff have employment here, too, but for how much longer I would not like to guess.'

'We made breakfast for you, Mummy. I poured the kefir and Hammy did the bread and butter.'

'It was very clever of you both.'

Elena lifted up her glass of kefir. Half the contents were already swimming about on the tray and what was in the glass had a thick powdering of crust crumbs. Various lumpy combinations of bread, butter and soot lurked on a plate while a suspiciously neat arrangement of meat slices completed the meal.

'I took charge of the meat, lady,' Ascony whispered quietly. 'That at least should be safe.'

'How does the kitchen look?'

'As though it has been invaded by rampaging Crusaders. As indeed it has been,' Ascony finished, grimly trying to maintain a little dignity in the midst of chaos.

'Hurry up, Mummy!'

Bouncing up and down, Milo clapped his hands, catapulting most of Elena's remaining kefir over her meat. Meanwhile Hamelin had got out of bed and was heading for her cupboard. Elena was about to call him back when he turned to Ascony, still pointing at the wardrobe.

'Pink... Pink for Mummy...'

Ascony smiled indulgently at Hamelin and reassured him before speaking to Elena.

'It was especially requested that you wear the apricot-blush silk today, lady. The Fra—my lord Selest also mentioned that you were not to stay your hand with regard to make-up on his account. He realises now that all the Byzantine women are decorated alike, and that you felt uncomfortable unpainted yesterday. I thought the wretch must be showing some sensitivity at last, but he then urged that you should not take too long about the preparations, lady.'

'My lord Selest is already up, then?'

'Indeed, lady, and ready to go,' Ascony said with a supercilious sneer.

Elena sighed and got on with her breakfast. When she had finished, Ascony removed the tray from her lap in one easy movement and the children in several more difficult ones.

Left alone to wash and dress, Elena took great care. She wasn't going to hurry, for Selest or anybody else. Oil and perfume took time to apply. Make-up did too, and Elena had decided to take Selest at his word, painting up for the occasion. It would be the first time that she had felt properly dressed for days.

A base of white powder gave Elena a pale canvas of face, neck and breast to begin work upon. First she used dustings of rouge to highlight cheekbones and cleavage. Then gold glitter powdered the gentle curves of cheek, breast and ear. Henry had always been very interested in ears. Frankish women evidently kept them well covered, and the novelty had given him great enjoyment.

Then it was time to paint up her eyes. Elena laid the slim handle of a rouge brush against the right side of her nose. She made a tiny mark where her eyebrow began—or would have begun had they been in fashion. Pivoting the end of the brush to the corner of the same eye, she made a second mark, so plotting the extent of one technically perfect eyebrow. All that remained was to repeat the process for her left eye, then join up each set of dots in a pretty colour.

Elena picked up a red eyebrow crayon to match the colour that her lips would be, then put it down again. 'Hazel Tan' would be good enough for Selest.

Her brows drawn in, Elena mixed pink ochre and gold dust, applying a heavy coat to each lid. Between the crease and her new eyebrows she painted on glitter mixed with a speck of oil for extra shimmer. Kohl lined her lids and swept up from the corner of each eye to join the Hazel Tan eyebrows.

Red lip-colour protected and polished by a slick of grease completed the picture. Elena stood back from her mirror to survey the whole. There was nothing natural about her looks today at all. Good.

Next her hair was released from its single night-time plait. She brushed it thoroughly then glossed it with rose oil. Six plaits today, she thought, even though Selest and the boys were already moving about in the hall below.

Elena worked quickly, braiding in gold cords to provide a net covering the crown of her head and tassels at the end of each plait.

The last chores were to scratch across a block of soft wax, lodging colour beneath the tip of each nail, and dot the designs on the backs of her hands with similar colour.

Despite calls from downstairs, Elena didn't hurry over choosing her jewellery, either. When she had finished a line of stars rimmed each ear, while three large hoops of gold wire hung from each lobe. Her necklaces were of gold, too. Iridescent gossamer, the ten together were barely the weight of a baby's breath. If she must be thought of as a Crusader's landlady then let no one think it was because she needed the money.

Elena piled on rings until her fingers were stiff with them, and added more glittering bangles to the marriage bracelets that she wore night and day.

Finally came the time to put on her clothes. She wondered why Selest had chosen the apricot blush in particular. Of all her clothes, the outfit that he had seen her in first was perhaps the most revealing that she had.

Instead of blouse, long overtunic and leggings the apricot-blush silk was of very different style. The tunic was long-sleeved, but left her midriff bare. Matching trousers were generously cut and all was translucent. It was so thoroughly Byzantine that Elena loved it to death.

Over all she laid an enveloping hazy veil of pale gossamer, set with hundreds of tiny gold spangles. A pair of simple rose and gold sandals, and Elena was ready.

Selest didn't say anything as she emerged from her room and walked along the landing. Surrounded in a mist of rose oil perfume and whispering silk, Elena rustled down the stairs. The boys ran towards her, chattering with delight.

'Hamelin says that you must be a fairy, Lady Elena,' Selest said with a smirk. 'Are you indeed equipped to work magic charms?'

She looked up, laughing with the children. Then she saw that amusement had been replaced by some other look in his eyes. 'No, my lord.' Elena looked away, flustered. A pause hung between them.

'We may put that to the test yet, Lady Elena.'

His crutches had been newly padded with wads of cotton cloth. Elena had noticed that he was not leaning so heavily on them this morning, and used this as a desperate attempt to change the subject.

'I—I trust that the arnich water soothed your skin, my lord.'

'Well enough.'

He started for the door. Elena was glad to see that the plainer of Henry's gowns had been reshaped into a shirt for Selest, so he now had two shirts, if only one pair of breeches. That could soon be remedied.

Selest was moving with more ease than he had done the day before. He soon stopped staring at Elena, too, when he saw the increase in people out on the Mese. The Byzantines were losing their fear of lurking Franks and were now out in force. Elena's make-up and dress were as nothing compared to some of them.

'Do all these people know about me, then?' he whispered as they reached the golden gates of the city. 'Dozens have said good morning, and half of them have stopped to talk.'

'We all like to chat,' Elena said simply. 'All you Franks are strangers, and might have something exciting to say. For a Byzantine, conversation is adventure. And as for conversations about religion—well, they'll stand in one spot until nightfall.'

'They don't even seem to mind that I don't speak their language,' he marvelled.

'It's probably an advantage to them. A captive audience, with no interruptions.'

Wandering on slowly to the seashore, they found a large rock that served both as seat and sun-trap.

'Your Ascony was saying that sea water is a good cure for injuries. I'm going in. It's about time Milo had his first swimming lesson, too.'

'Oh, but I didn't think to bring any towels——'

'The sun will be hot against this rock by the time we get out. They can run about to keep warm, too.'

'—or anything for them to wear...'

'What on earth would they wear for swimming? Clothes pull you down!'

Elena had never been swimming, so she didn't know. The only standing water in her own village had been a brackish pond, fouled by oxen and rats. Nobody had ever risked going into that, clothed or not.

Gulls wheeled and screeched over bobbing boats while larger birds, black and shiny as wet rocks, perched here and there hanging their wings out to dry.

The boys were in their element. They were already making scrapes on the foreshore, shrieking with delight as wavelets hurried in. Sea water soaked upward from the hems of their gowns, darkening the fabric with an irregular tidemark.

'No sense in getting good clothes wet,' Selest said mildly and pulled out his shirt. As he unlaced collar and cuffs Elena began to get uneasy, but nothing would make her admit it. Sitting on the rock beside where he leaned, she tucked up her feet and arranged her veil over them neatly.

'Do you need any help, my lord?' she offered gingerly, hoping that he would say no.

'I think I can manage, Lady Elena.'

She stared resolutely out to sea. He was struggling now, she supposed, to remove his breeches without putting his injured foot to the ground. She dared not look to find out.

Then all was quiet. Elena still did not look around in case he was expecting her to. After a pause he gave a soft laugh then whistled up the boys.

At the thought of going into the sea Hamelin and Milo tore off their gowns at once, but Elena was nervous.

'Don't let Hamelin get water in his ears. You know what the doctor said—he might pass out, and then you'd end up drowning him. And don't go out too far...don't take your eyes off Milo—he's too small to swim——'

'Any more instructions?'

'I don't know why I'm letting you take them. It's madness.'

She risked a glance at Selest. He was bent over unbandaging his ankle and she saw only the smooth curve of his spine.

'They'll love it, Elena. We'll come out here every morning from now on. Fresh air and exercise. Nothing like it.'

He sat up, making Elena look away sharply. She could hear the smile in his voice as he persuaded Milo to scramble on to his shoulders, and knew that it was directed at her.

Milo squeaked with excitement as Selest stood up, and Elena could bear it no longer. She had to look round.

'He'll fall!'

'You won't, will you, Podge? Hang on tight!' Selest ducked, throwing the squealing Milo forward. Elena shut her eyes in horror.

'You mad fool! You'll kill him!'

Selest bounced his little burden up and down. Milo was hiccupping with laughter.

'Elena, the worst thing that can happen is that Podger here will pull out even more of my hair with his iron grip, or he'll christen me with excitement. I think we'd better go before he does either, don't you?'

With the help of Hamelin and one crutch, Selest made his way into the water. When they were in up to Hamelin's chest he sent the boy back to drop the single crutch on the shore.

Elena could hardly bear to watch, and her fears seemed justified. As soon as Hamelin had hurled himself back into the fray, Selest tumbled his little friend off balance and beneath the surface. Before Elena had time to cry out Selest was heaving Hamelin up. Gasping and pawing, Hamelin spluttered, yelling heartily until the Frank gathered him in his arms. What followed Elena would have thought of as hugs and kisses had Selest been that sort of a chap.

She noticed that Milo seemed to have gone very still and quiet while all this was going on. His turn was to come. When Hamelin was recovered, Selest lifted Milo down and put him gently into the water. Elena immediately jumped up and ran to the water's edge.

'Don't you dare let go of him!'

In reply Selest waved with both hands while Milo hung on around his neck like a limpet. The little boy's eyes were tightly shut and his face screwed up.

Elena dashed backwards and forwards in her distress. 'Bring him back! He's frightened!'

'Rubbish. He's loving every minute of it!' Selest yelled back, quite unconcerned. While Hamelin splashed about with head held high, Selest looked down for a few words with Milo. Unhooking the little boy from his neck, Selest supported him and tried to make him kick. Milo was having none of it. He lay rigid. Elena was beside herself.

'What have you done, you monster? What have you done to him?'

Selest and Hamelin were having a wonderful time. Despite their encouragement Milo still lay motionless, only thin wails escaping from him.

'What's wrong? What is it? Tell me!'

'Nothing, Elena. You've brought him up too well, that's all!'

With a laugh he started to tow Milo towards the shallows, giving him to Hamelin when the water grew too shallow for support. Elena rushed towards them as they came on to the shore, but Milo had more important things on his mind than cuddles. Hamelin dragged him behind a nearby boulder. Elena followed, but soon Hamelin came back to meet her with a worried expression.

'Mummy—come to Milo?' He caught her hand. 'Come quick!'

Milo was standing behind the rock, wriggling frantically and hopping from foot to foot. At the sight of Elena he squealed and burst into tears.

'Wasn't me, Mummy! I wasn't naughty! Don't be cross...'

He trembled with tears. Elena looked from her son, to the puzzled Hamelin and then to a dark splash of moisture staining the rock. After what seemed like a lifetime of teaching Milo not to go where he thought he would, this was going to take some explaining. With a sigh Elena knelt down beside her son.

'Did you see how that got there, Milo?'

'Wasn't me, Mummy! It was Hammy! He was naughty!' Milo paused in mid-wriggle to point accusingly. Not understanding what he was supposed to have done wrong, Hamelin frowned and took a step back.

'Hamelin wasn't naughty this time, sweetheart. Outside is special, not like inside houses. This is a special place where nobody can see. It's all right here, but not anywhere else. Not at home.'

Milo took some persuading, but when Elena flatly refused to take him all the way home then back out to the sea, desperation overcame him. He eventually managed to copy what Hamelin had done, but kept an eye on Elena all the time—just in case.

Before Elena had a chance to lavish praise upon him Milo had grabbed Hamelin's hand and the two scampered back to the sea. She watched them go with more than a little regret. Of all the useful things that Milo might have picked up from his friend, how to dampen rocks was not one to be proud of.

Once back in the water the two boys fooled about with Selest for quite some time. Milo grew bolder every minute. Towards the end he was splashing about supported only by Selest's cupped hand beneath his chin. When the time came to leave the water he thought of throwing a tantrum, but Selest soon nipped that in the bud.

When they had taken Selest his crutches he sent them off on a race to warm up. Elena took the opportunity to confront the Crusader with her complaints.

'I told you to mind Hamelin's ears, and what's the first thing you do? Push him under!'

'Only to show him what would happen. I could have told him to be careful a score of times, but until he knew why he might have forgotten. Where would that leave him if he ever went off for a swim on his own? He'll be able to look out for himself, now.'

Selest reached their rock and pulled himself on to a sun-warmed ledge. After scrubbing himself roughly with his shirt he lay flat, soaking up the sun. When he had caught his breath he said quietly, 'I wonder, Lady Elena...would you be kind enough to bind my ankle up again? I was going to do without, that's why I removed the bandage, but it is nagging a bit now...'

Wordlessly Elena took up the length of discarded cloth. Dabbing droplets of sea water from between his toes with her kerchief, she bound his ankle firmly in the way that she had seen Dr Kelka do it. She tried to keep her eyes on her work, but was painfully aware of Selest's body curving away above her like some sleek, lean predator.

The pale gold of his skin, lighter where clothing had hidden it from the weather, was the Frankish colouring that Elena remembered so well. She found herself looking up at him cautiously. Selest seemed to have his eyes closed, and Elena thought that he could not see her.

'Your hair...goes straight when it is wet...'

He lifted one hand with easy languor to wipe salt spray from his brow. 'Finished bandaging yet?'

'Yes, my lord.'

His response was to extend one hand towards her, across the line of his body. In accepting it she was drawn up in silence to rest beside him on the ledge. Sounds of seagulls and sealife, children and chatter were lost to Elena in that moment.

He had brought her here, yet he was still lying with eyes closed. Damp darkened his lashes, making them seem even thicker and longer.

Without hurry he opened his eyes and looked at her, the curve of his brow softened by rapidly drying curls. The line of his nose and a glimpse of white teeth between slightly parted lips—all this Elena took in.

In turn she was being studied, too. His deep hazel eyes moved slowly, taking in every detail. With equal care his hand moved to net his fingers with hers. They brought her hand to his lips and he kissed it gently.

Elena felt like a moth that was attracted to a deadly flame. They were barely inches apart now, and Elena felt herself thinking not of the danger to herself, but of the horrors that he had suffered at home and on the road. Starvation and anguish...pain and deprivation, yet in that moment he seemed as pure as a new-minted coin.

'It's all right, Elena. It's all right. You can...I won't stop you...' he whispered as softly as a breath.

Elena could resist no more. She kissed him. It began as a light, gentle kiss of pity and friendship, but longing was not slow to surface. He tasted it and no longer lay still in her arms but responded, drawing her body closer to cover his own.

'Mummy? Mummy, what's the matter?'

A querulous little voice woke Elena as though from a deep sleep. Selest sighed in simple enjoyment as they slipped apart.

'Nothing's the matter, sweetheart. Run around again.'

There came no sound of little feet running away.

'Emil?' Milo called doubtfully.

'The Lord Selest is tired, sweetheart. He wants a rest.'

'I don't, I don't!' Selest moaned quietly, grinning up at her.

'Are you tired too, Mummy?'

'No, Podge. Your Mummy's getting up now.' Selest raised himself up on one elbow as Elena moved away. 'We're all going home to enjoy that great big breakfast I promised you. How's that?'

Milo jumped up and down with excitement.

'Go and fetch Hamelin, then, Podge. And don't run!'

Selest watched the little boy run off. He lay still for a moment, running his fingers up and down Elena's back. When he looked at her again it was with a laugh.

'Poor Milo. Sent as a spy because Hamelin wouldn't risk coming to find out for himself!'

'He's certainly watching us.' Elena sat up and re-arranged her veil. 'Why should he be frightened?'

When Selest did not answer at once she looked down to see that the fearless Crusader had coloured slightly.

'We were camped out here for a very long time, Elena. Hamelin and I had only a small shelter to share. There was barely room for just two, and—well, I admit that sometimes I sent Hamelin out for a walk while I..."entertained"...'

He mistook her blank expression for shock.

'Only once or twice...now and again...' He was floundering. 'With soldiers packed shoulder to shoulder out here the girls found it a happy hunting ground. We were never short of opportunity...'

Elena realised at last what he was confessing.

'Oh...you mean girls like Gulzun?'

'Not half as pretty. Or half as charming,' he said loyally. 'Once or twice Hamelin came back a bit too early and I had to send him away with a flea in his ear.'

'No wonder he's wary.' Elena stood up and beckoned to Hamelin. He ran forward happily to meet Milo and race him back to the rock.

While Elena dressed the children Selest pulled on his breeches then used his shirt to rub the children's hair dry.

Speech seemed to have become easier between Elena and Selest. Although Elena tried her hardest to feel shame about the stolen kiss, all she seemed able to think about for the moment was Selest himself.

Her feelings were increased as they walked back to the house. He carried his shirt tied around his waist, rather than wearing it in the strong sunshine. Each movement with the crutches made the muscles of his arms and shoulders stand out and ripple like sunlight on water. He saw her watching, and smiled.

The house was deserted. If Elena hadn't been surprised before, she was now.

'Where is everybody?'

'The Khars have gone visiting their son——'

'But they never said! He lives donkey's miles away!'

Selest held up his hands for silence. 'They'll be back the day after tomorrow. Oh, and Ascony said he'd like a trip out of the city, too. He went with them.'

'And they said nothing to me? I don't believe you, my lord! You're making it all up!'

'Every word is true, Elena. I arranged it all, as I arranged with Gulzun that we would have lunch with her today. That's why I wanted to speak to her yesterday—there was nothing suspicious about our meeting at all. I don't know what you were all getting so excited about.'

Elena fumed, but the fact that he had thought to arrange lunch with Gulzun had mollified her a little.

She got down the big black frying-pan from its hook on the kitchen wall while the boys hunted out meat, bread and eggs.

'I don't like this. You shouldn't have gone sneaking around behind my back. I don't like not knowing——'

'Think of this as a great big adventure, Elena. A holiday. A surprise—yes, that's it! You like surprises, don't you?'

'No, I don't,' she snapped.

'You do. I was a surprise, wasn't I?'

Elena looked up to scowl at him, but it was impossible. He was looking down at her so merrily, his hair all tufting into elf locks as it dried.

'I thought you were cutting down on Milo's food.' She tried to sound disapproving as Selest excited the boys with promises of bacon, egg, sausages and fried bread.

'He's used up a lot of energy this morning. Gulzun's only arranging a light lunch.'

'I'm surprised you left her any choice in the matter. Is there anything else that you haven't arranged, my lord? You tell me what to wear and who I am to lunch with. Is there anything else that I should be doing?'

'You could start calling me Emil again.'

He pulled himself across the kitchen to the range while Elena was left speechless. She soon found her tongue as he scooped a spoonful of dripping into the frying-pan.

'And what are we going to do about dinner with the Khars away? We can't live on bacon and eggs! A fine holiday this will be for me if I have to do all the——'

Selest had opened the oven door to display a casserole sitting fatly inside.

'I never told you that I can conjure up something from nothing, did I? You don't know how much easier it is when you can lay your hands on something worth cooking.'

Elena was suspicious. 'What is it?'

'Frog's legs and dog chops in pony juice.'

'We usually have a roast on——' Elena began carefully, then realised that it was another joke at her expense. 'What is it really?'

'You'll just have to wait until this evening, won't you? It takes all day to cook. While we're out enjoying ourselves it will be quietly getting itself ready.'

He spooned hot fat over chuckling eggs and fried bread for himself and the boys. Elena watched him, and wondered. Things were taking a very sinister turn. The staff out of the way... a secret dinner... As Ascony had said, no good could possibly come of this. No good at all.

# CHAPTER TEN

ELENA started the day on edge, but fun soon blunted her nervousness.

When the three swimmers had finished their breakfast and were rested they set off for a walk through the city. Even though Selest had been out and about before, the richness and style of Constantinople still astonished him.

'Every house is like a church, and every church is like...'

They were standing in front of the church of St Sophia. Selest shook his head in wonder as sunlight played over dome after dome on the roof then cascaded down the lemon and grey stone walls like streams over a rocky waterfall.

Elena had brought two bags of crumbs for the palace pigeons and while Milo and Hamelin fed the birds she sat in the square with Selest.

There was a more relaxed air between them now. Elena had risked pleasing herself for once, and he had not taken advantage. He did not refer to the matter, which made Elena like him more. It was as though he sensed that she still had reservations about this new side to their relationship.

The pigeons rose in a fluttering sheaf as a great shout came from over at the quay. For the first time Elena noticed the tall masts of ships that pierced the hard blue sky between dockside houses.

'Oh, no, my lord—Emil...look! They're going without you!'

Selest cast a glance to where she pointed, then looked back at Elena.

'You almost sound sorry, Elena.'

'Only because I know how eager you were to go with them ... Emil.'

'They aren't going far.' He gave a secretive wink. 'I might catch them up yet. Gulzun's been busy—she heard that a holding camp has been arranged just the other side of the Bosphorous. More Crusaders from the north are expected any day now, and your Emperor Alexius wants to keep the Franks moving through. A camp over there will keep them out of his way while they gather their strength. That gives me a few more days here, at least.'

An inner glow was growing within him, as she had seen it flare in Godfrey. Elena didn't like it and took Emil's arm. She could only hope that a few hours in Gulzun's company would turn his mind away from higher things.

Surprises weren't over for Selest. Gulzun lived in such a nice part of the city that he wondered whether her neighbours knew of her work. He was even more astonished when Elena told him that several other houses in the refined avenue were owned by working girls, too.

Quiet, and close to the palace, Gulzun's street was studded with fountains and lush with flowering trees. When they knocked at the door of a beautiful white marble town house Selest's amazement knew no bounds.

'I don't think Frankish street girls live anywhere. This is——'

He stopped as a servant opened the door and ushered them in. The children tore into the house, with Milo yelling for Gulzun at the top of his voice. The servant led Selest and Elena in at a more dignified pace.

'Another eunuch?' Selest mouthed at Elena behind the servant's back. She nodded, then laughed at his expression. Gulzun's eunuch was twice the size of Ascony in all directions and four times as haughty in bearing, if that were possible.

'They're as variable as anyone else, Emil. It takes all sorts to make a world.'

The eunuch led them to a cool green quadrangle where Gulzun was waiting. Her house was like Elena's, but was decorated very differently. Where Elena had one or two tastefully artistic works of art around the place, Gulzun's selection was rather more exotic. Elena was relieved to find that some of the more carefree sculptures had been swathed in muslin robes for their visit.

Gulzun was full of news. Sending Milo and Hamelin off with the servant to visit her menagerie, she poured lemonade for Elena and Selest, beside herself with delight. Drawing her chair up close to Elena and Selest, she bent forward eagerly.

'*He's* been here!'

Selest and Elena looked at each other for clues, but it was hopeless.

'Who?' They chorused.

Gulzun shook her head in disgust, making her veil ornaments and earrings rattle with scorn.

'Godfrey, of course. The duke!'

Selest threw himself out of his seat. 'I don't want to hear this.'

'Oh, come and sit down. You don't know what I'm going to say, yet!'

When Selest sat down again Gulzun added as an aside to Elena, 'Is your friend always like this?'

'No. Sometimes he's worse.'

Gulzun flicked out her translucent tunic over her equally translucent leggings.

'Well, to cut a long story short I'd been working on him like mad, inviting myself on their tours around the city, that sort of thing…' Her dark eyes went quite dewy. 'I think Godfrey is the most perfect, delicious-looking——'

'I'm not listening,' Selest snapped viciously.

Elena sipped her lemonade and moved closer to Gulzun. 'He's only jealous. Take no notice—tell me!'

'Anyway, yesterday there was this great gang of them sat in the park—Godfrey in pride of place, of course.

Well, I happened to be strolling past—quite accidentally, you understand—when all of a sudden I knew. You can always tell. He got up and started towards the palace, where he's staying, and I really thought that I'd cracked it. I followed and lo and behold as soon as I reached a quiet spot, he was waiting. Oh, those eyes...and all those muscles...'

'Get on with it!' Elena laughed.

'Well, all he wanted at that stage was my address. Sister, he called me...' Her voice trailed away, and she shivered at the delight of it. 'So I went straight home and spent the rest of the day getting ready. He was due at nine, and by then this place was immaculate. You've never seen it so classy—or me! At exactly nine o'clock he arrived. I had draped myself artistically along a couch, but imagine my surprise when I realised that he hadn't come alone!'

She rolled her eyes for emphasis. Selest snorted in disgust and, leaping up, limped off for a few yards.

'He'd only brought his priests with him!' Gulzun shrieked with laughter. 'They set up, here, in my lounge! Prayers, communion, the whole lot. Then Godfrey himself came and took my hands—oh, beautiful hands, he's got: harsh, but no scars. And he spoke to me...' She sighed and paused for a drink before asking innocently, 'Where is Babylon?'

Selest had been pretending not to listen, but at this he turned round and started to laugh.

'It's a very wicked place,' Elena said primly, 'in the Bible.'

'Oh.' Gulzun sighed with regret. 'In that case I don't think he's very keen on Constantinople. He kept calling it, "This new Babylon." I'm all right though—I've been saved.'

Elena's eyes opened wide in amazement, but Gulzun gave another shriek of laughter. 'It's true—I must be! Godfrey told me so. He crossed himself, cut a notch in the hilt of his sword and then they were all carried away in a cloud of incense! I tell you, my lord Emil, I've seen some things in my time, but your Duke of Lorraine takes the biscuit!'

Both Elena and Selest were laughing by this time. Like a true hero-worshipper Gulzun had only been slightly put off by Godfrey's behaviour. She was willing to forgive him anything and spent the next ten minutes describing his face and hands and hair in the minutest of minute detail. Her guests were only rescued by the return of her servant and the boys to announce that lunch was ready.

Elena's house was expensively furnished, but Gulzun's was sumptuous. All the senses were pleasured in every inch of the house, for as Gulzun said there was no accounting for taste.

The dining-room was a revelation to Selest. Elena no longer took any notice, but he stood still on the threshold in sheer wonder.

In the centre of the ceiling was a carved golden boss. From this flowed midnight-blue material flecked with silver, forming a canopy as romantic as a summer night with stars. The fabric was caught behind golden poles at the cornice then drifted on down to cover the walls. Where windows perforated the room golden ropes held the material aside in graceful swags.

There was no dining table and chairs as there were in Elena's house. Instead, guests reclined as they pleased on piles of huge soft cushions. These formed a circle around an area of mosaic floor bare of the usual rugs.

At one end of the room two young boys strummed softly on stringed instruments as a gentle accompaniment to conversation.

Scent-warmers, candles burning beneath dishes of liquid, were set at intervals about the room. These sent drifts of flower perfume over the diners in waves of luxury.

While the boys bounced and tussled amid the pillows, Elena and Gulzun laughed at Selest's expression.

'I've never, ever, seen the like,' he whispered, still gazing about him.

Gulzun was more practical. 'If you're rich, my lord, tell your friends. If you're poor, keep it quiet. I don't do charity work!'

'How many girls work here?'

'Only me,' Gulzun winked, 'although I haven't always lived in such a lap of luxury. I've had to work very hard for all this, you know!'

'Don't some of the neighbours ever complain?'

'Certainly not!' Elena was quick to defend her friend. 'Gulzun never invites anyone here unless they are the Right Sort. They must have shining references.'

'Oh.' Selest looked down at his patched, salt-dried shirt and old breeches.

'Don't worry, my lord. Everybody knows about you.'

He scowled until he saw that it wasn't meant unkindly.

'It's so hard to tell what you two are thinking behind all that paint,' he said, laughing.

'Perhaps that's why we wear it, Emil.'

'Elena Rethel! I do believe you're beginning to flirt with him!'

'Oh...no—I didn't mean... That is——'

Gulzun laughed at her friend, but Selest merely smiled. Only when staff arrived with trays and salvers of lunch could Elena escape their attention by chivvying the boys to order.

They feasted on fresh fish and fruits, washed down by lemonade or orange juice. When at last they all flopped back on their pillows to relax, staff whipped away the remains of lunch with expert speed. In a flash they returned with a large silver goblet, bowls of warm water and a number of delicate, long-stemmed spoons of silver.

Milo sat up at once. 'Mummy? Some goo?'

'No. You know how sticky you got last time.'

Gulzun cackled with laughter. 'Oh, go on! You feed him with it, and tell him to keep his hands off the spoon.

Let him have a bit. He can't possibly make as much mess again!'

'Goo.' Picking up the word from Milo, Hamelin crawled forward and peered into the goblet. Having done so, he pulled a face then spoke quickly to Selest.

'He says it smells like the herbs that pigs eat when they're sick.'

Milo had no such misgivings. He went forward too and knelt beside his mother, mouth open like a baby bird.

'Oh, all right.' Elena scrambled around to reach one of the spoons and dip it into the goblet.

'If you once say no then you should stick to it, Elena. The child wins with you every time,' Selest whispered quietly.

Elena ignored him, twisting her spoon to wind up the long strands of sticky sweetmeat dropping from it. With a few words of warning to Milo she posted the spoonful into his open mouth. Immediately the little boy's hands went up to grasp the sticky handle. Selest anticipated him and tapped him on the back of one podgy hand.

'Ow!'

'Don't put your hands on the spoon, then.'

Astonished, Milo opened his mouth to start wailing properly. After a warning from Selest all that escaped him was a dribble of sweetmeat. It ran down his chin, out of reach of his tongue.

'Now look what you've done! He wouldn't be in that mess but for you!'

'No, but he would have had two sticky paws at large in Gulzun's beautiful room.'

'I tell you what, Elena. Let our friend the brave Crusader feed the boys his way. You and I can go upstairs. Girls' talk.' Gulzun flicked her plaits at Selest cheekily.

'At least Emil seems to have taken your mind off that wretched Godfrey,' Elena said as the girls retouched their make-up in Gulzun's room.

'I'm all right,' Gulzun said with a shrug, then laughed. 'But what about you? How are you managing about temptation with you and a good-looking chap like Selest under the same roof?'

Elena tweaked her kohl brush into an even finer point. 'There's no use in even thinking about it. As soon as he's recovered he'll be off with the rest of them.'

'All the more reason to have a bit of fun now.' Gulzun massaged jasmine oil into her palms then used them to gloss her plaits. 'No ties, no tears. Just be careful there's no evidence.'

Elena looked at her friend quizzically.

'You know!'

'I don't...' Elena said in bewilderment. One look at her friend told Gulzun it was more than simple advice that her friend needed.

'Look, how long after you and Henry became man and wife properly did you fall for little Milo?'

'Not long...a few months?'

'There you are, then.' Gulzun bent down to a cupboard beneath her dressing-table and brought out a small china pot, complete with lid. 'That will take care of you, in the unlikely event that he doesn't. And before you ask, no, you don't eat them. Use your imagination!'

Make-up complete again, Gulzun prodded her friend off towards the door.

'But—I can't...Gulzun, what about Henry? Whatever would he think?'

'He's got nothing to be proud of, Elena, although I shouldn't speak ill of the dead.'

Elena stopped and caught her friend by the arm. 'Henry was a good man. He told me that I was the only girl he—ever—well, you know...'

Gulzun put her arm about her friend's shoulders and led her to the head of the stairs.

'This is going to come as a nasty surprise to you, Elena. When you and I were kids, Henry didn't leave you to play with me so that he could talk politics with my mum.

And all those business meetings of his? How is it that your shop is doing so well when you never attend any?'

Elena clasped the china pot to her. She was too stunned to think properly for the present. Her mind was too full of the past.

'But—he was kind, and he said he loved me...'

'He did!' Gulzun squeezed her arm comfortingly. 'Men are different. They see things differently. They love affection, a settled home life and regular meals. Girls like me they treat just as—well, snacks! A sneaky pinch of pleasure on the way.'

Elena felt numb. Henry had been her whole life for so long. She had been beside herself with grief when he had died. And all the time everyone must have been laughing at her—laughing, or pitying her. Gulzun, Ascony, the Khars...everybody had known, except her.

'G-Gulzun?' she said with growing horror, but the Turkish girl anticipated her question.

'Never. Cross my heart and spit on it. Henry never once asked, and I certainly never offered. He was a good man, Elena. Girls like me, our lives are full of good men belonging to good women. There's nothing rare or horrible about it.' She smiled kindly. 'Good grief, I'd better take that pot back. Franks are notorious for playing around. If just the thought of it does this to you, don't touch Selest with a yard broom!'

Elena did not hand over the little pot, but neither did she look at Gulzun.

'I know what Emil is like,' she said evenly, eyes downcast. 'He's told me. I would expect it from him. But Henry...'

'Put it out of your mind. Don't think about it. Look, I shouldn't be trying to force your hand, but I reckon this Selest is something really special. Go home, enjoy yourself, then let him go. Love is the best cure for everybody and everything.'

They had reached the foot of the stairs and Elena hesitated before following Gulzun towards the dining-room.

'I'd certainly hide that pot, if you're going to take it.' Gulzun smiled. 'If your boys see it they'll think that it's something else to eat!'

Hamelin and Milo ran to the door as soon as it was opened. There was a pause while they scuffled about looking up at Elena, then Milo couldn't stand it any more. He pinched Hamelin hard, and his whispering was hardly private.

'Go on, Hammy! Ask Mummy, quick! Hurry up!'

'Please——?' Hamelin began unsteadily. 'Please can we stay...?' Searching for the words, he looked at Gulzun, then stabbed a finger towards the floor.

'You would like to stay here with Gulzun?'

Hamelin beamed and nodded. 'Yes, Mummy.' Now that his hearing had improved his voice was clearer, and he never had any hesitation in using it given the chance. 'We can swim in the baths, and eat cakes and——'

'Please, Mummy, can we?' Milo was jumping up and down in impatience.

'I've just thought, Elena.' Gulzun looked at her friend innocently. 'That would give you two a chance to go back to an empty house together!'

Elena looked over towards Selest. He was lounging on the floor cushions and grinning at her.

'This is your doing, isn't it?'

'Guilty, I'm afraid.' He beckoned her while Gulzun distracted the children. 'I want some time alone with you, Elena. No, don't back away. If it were purely for reckless reasons, then of course I would be content with a girl of Gulzun's profession. It's just that I think you deserve a holiday from all the worries of staff and children. Let me show you how we treat women at home.'

'I can't.' Elena spoke softly. It was regret and not dismay that coloured her voice now. She fiddled with the small pot held within the folds of her veil. 'I'm— frightened...'

'Why?' He held out his hand, but Elena shook her head. 'Oh, Elena, come on. You took my hand this morning, when we were together on the rock. Did I do anything to frighten you then?'

When she did not reply he took her hand himself. She looked up. His hand was very comforting, his eyes very soft and dark.

'I know I've been a bit rough in the past, but did I frighten you today?'

'No, my lord.'

'It's Emil now, remember?' He touched her cheek with one finger. 'Gulzun has told me a lot about you in our chats together, Elena. It's about time you gave a thought for your own happiness. Leave the children here. Come and enjoy a holiday.'

Her hand had been lying lifeless in his grip but now her fingers closed around his as trustingly as Hamelin might have held her hand.

'Come on, then,' Selest said softly. 'Let's go home.'

They did not hurry. Elena had expected him to dash back, eager to claim his prize. Selest did no such thing. First they went down to the quay and watched one of the ships loading. Several hundred Crusaders, fighting spirits topped up by more alcoholic ones, set off for the holding camp across the channel. The shouting and laughter was terrific, but Elena saw that Selest did not join in the celebrations. He watched the ship move away from the quay with a distant, melancholy expression in his dark eyes. Then he turned his back on the waterfront scene and started slowly away.

They pottered about the shops for a long time. Elena thought that the ship's departure must have upset him far more than he admitted, for he was unnaturally quiet. Forgetting her own worries, she tried to cheer him up. They strolled all the way around the large square of the Augusteum, as Elena knew he liked looking at the magnificent buildings that surrounded it. The tour did seem to cheer him up, but she was a little disappointed when he showed more interest in the Hippodrome than the Senate House.

The journey home was slow. Selest had to take frequent rests when the crutches started to bite into his arms, and they could only travel a few hundred yards at a time.

When they entered the house at last it was cool and very quiet after the sunny excitement of the streets. Selest went slowly into the kitchen to check on the progress of the casserole.

'It will be quite a while yet,' he said, looking hot and tired after the day's exercise. 'It's a shame to waste the end of a nice afternoon. Bring some wine and we'll find some shade in the garden.'

They sat in the arbour, and talked about nothing of consequence. Sheltered from any chill spring breeze, the arbour was a pleasant place to sit and watch the fish in their marble waterways.

New flowers were coming into bloom with each passing day. Before long the exotic red turban flowers would be pushing up, heralding the start of summer. Henry had brought her those from—from——

'Elena? What is it? Oh, don't cry. Look, you're making your paint all smudgy. Nothing's worth that!'

'Henry—Henry used to bring me plants. Every time he came home, there was something for me. I thought he'd been away on—on business, when all the time he'd been with—with other girls...'

'Oh, Elena...' Selest gathered her in his arms and held her close. 'There, now—don't cry! You really must still love him, like everybody says. You didn't cry when I told you about my little sins, did you?'

Elena could only shake her head. She was unable to speak. Large tears of kohl and gold shimmer dripped on to Selest's sleeve, but he didn't seem to mind. He still held her close. In his warm embrace Elena was calmed by the steady beat of his heart and felt the gentle voice welling up from deep within him.

'It seems to me that Milo has been getting all the attention around here, while it's his mother that needs it.'

A kiss light as thistledown brushed the crown of Elena's head. For the first time in years she could stop struggling against everything and everybody. She lay limp in his arms and, when she could speak for tears, began to tell him everything.

She spoke for a long time, and Selest did not interrupt. All the worries and fears that she had endured in silence since Henry died were spilled and blown away. Selest only listened.

'...and then this morning you were there and I felt so sorry for you, and for myself, and that's why I kissed you and now——'

'Perhaps you ought to stop feeling sorry, Elena, and start feeling fond.'

'But I couldn't let myself feel fond of you!' She sniffed hopelessly. 'You'll go off with the other Franks, and where will that leave me? As Gulzun said, I've got to let you go...'

She felt Selest move to speak to her, but there was a brief pause before his words came.

'Quite right. Plenty more fish in the sea, that's what I always say.'

It wasn't what Elena said to herself at all. She felt herself dissolving again but Selest sighed heavily and prepared to get up.

'I'll go and check on supper while you do whatever it is to get rid of all that gilding. There's time enough for you to have a bath and wash your hair before the meal.'

'Without Ascony?'

'He never baths you, too?'

'Of course.' Elena was still smearing the tears from her eyes, but managed a watery smile as she saw Selest's face. 'Don't look like that! It's the same in every household without a ladies' maid. I wouldn't fancy having a woman bathing me. Oh, no. Ascony might comment, but he would never compare as a woman would.'

Selest was intrigued and even forgot about her sadly slipped make-up. 'Don't you find it embarrassing? What on earth do you do while he's working on you?'

'Nothing! Don't forget, one body is much the same as any other to Ascony. He might say that I'm putting on weight, or losing it, that sort of thing. Every eunuch likes to be as accurate as a spring balance in pointless matters like that. It makes them feel superior.'

A little recovered, Elena got up and Selest followed her as she started back towards the dining-room doors.

'Will you be able to manage without him?' he began uncertainly. 'I was hoping that you'd take off all that paint and powder for dinner, and just come as yourself...'

'Why?'

He shrugged, and could not meet her steady gaze. 'Perhaps—because you have told me everything, now. There should be no need for you to hide behind a mask.'

Having said his piece, Selest went past her and into the house. Elena was left alone with only broken reflections in the watercourses for company.

She bathed, then washed the scented oils from her hair. When supper was ready she entered the dining-room in a simple white robe, her dark hair loose and fluffy about her shoulders.

Selest kept her wine glass well filled during dinner. Elena took no notice until she found herself laughing a little too freely at one of his jokes. At once she covered her face with her hands, but he moved forward and topped up her glass again.

'Oh, no—I couldn't!'

'Get it down you, girl. You're looking better every minute!'

Elena giggled and looked at him shyly. He had bathed and shaved while she had been up in her room getting ready, and looked quite unlike the ruffian she had first met in the garden. Only a few days of good food and rest had filled out the wasted muscles and starvation-pinched face. Slanting rays of evening sun warmed the depths of his hair to auburn gold and threw a strong-profiled shadow on to the dining-room wall.

Feeling her glance at him, he looked across at her.

'You're looking at me again!'

'I'm not!'

'You are, too. Anybody would think that I was nothing but a rich woman's plaything, and not a brilliant young schemer with a plot to solve all your business problems!'

Elena collapsed in another fit of the giggles. 'If your plans are as good as your cooking, I can't wait to hear them!'

Flushed with the success of his chicken and herb casserole, Selest refilled his wine glass and did the same for Elena.

'This plan is even better than my cooking. It's about that idea you've got for the palace's Christmas order.'

Elena's brow wrinkled at the very thought.

'You're trying to copy those cameo things that Henry told you about, right? Coating your vases in a second colour, then carving it away to show the original glass underneath?'

'We're going to have to give it up as a bad job. It's not working.'

'No, and I've worked out why. Who has actually seen any of these famous cameo vases?'

'Henry... nobody else, as far as I know... He used to tell Eban all about the work he had seen in Italy, on the way over here...'

Selest put on his lecturing tone. 'What you're doing is trying to pretty up your own stuff, which is proving too delicate to stand it. Make the original vessel thicker and so stronger, instead of struggling on as you are now and failing. That way you'll save time, effort and, more importantly as far as you're concerned—money.'

'Then the vases would be all thick and horrible. I like them as thin as bubbles.' The wine within Elena made her pout at him quite unselfconsciously.

'I would have thought that a businesswoman like yourself would have realised. It isn't what you like, Elena. It's what sells. If nobody has seen these cameo vases, and you're the only producers, you determine what they look like. Think of it as a totally new product.'

'Thinking is too much like hard work tonight.' Elena frowned through a happy haze of wine. 'And I shall have to think about this. Tell me again tomorrow.'

'Right.' Selest added a little more wine to his own glass, then placed the decanter at the far end of the table.

'I'll have some more wine, too.' Elena sighed happily and held out her empty glass. 'Oh, no—I forgot. That isn't the right way to ask. "More wine, please, Emil."' She mimicked the children's sing-song voices, but Selest shook his head.

'No. You've had enough, and will regret it in the morning, if not before.'

Elena's face struggled through dismay and disappointment, but stopped when it reached confusion.

'Why?'

'I can see where Milo gets it from now.'

'Stop laughing at me!' Elena aimed a blow at him but it was wide of the mark and he caught her hand, laughing.

Elena did not laugh. Instead she let her arm go limp, and Selest took her hand to his lips for a kiss without meeting any resistance.

'I'm wicked,' she said suddenly.

Selest squeezed her hand and kissed it again softly. 'Never. Not you.'

'I am.' Her lower lip began to tremble, but she recovered quickly enough. 'This morning—on the rock...I wasn't thinking of Henry when I kissed you...'

'I should hope not!'

Elena looked at him and frowned. 'Don't laugh at me. You're always laughing at me, you are.'

'I'm not!' Selest laughed, which did not improve her temper one little bit. When she fumed at him he pulled at her hand, trying to draw her from her seat.

'Come here, you silly child!'

'Don't want to, now.'

'I want to tell you a secret.'

Pushing his chair back from the dining table, Selest beckoned her, still tugging at her hand. Elena didn't have any judgement left, let alone a better one, so she let herself be drawn out of her seat and towards him.

'It might be easier if you were to come down to my level.' He patted his lap, and Elena sat down upon it without thinking twice. Only when Selest put one arm around her waist did she start to think better of it.

'It's only to hold you steady!' He took her hands in his, holding them lightly. 'Now, bend down and I'll tell you this secret.'

Elena did as she was told, then something reminded her that this was all wrong.

'You blew in my ear!'

'What's wrong? Don't you like it?' He was laughing again, and would not have let her go even if Elena had had the sense left to try and get up.

She looked at him narrowly. 'Was that the secret?'

'No, Elena. If I promise not to be silly again will you let me whisper to you properly?'

She was suspicious, and ducked away from him several times before he held her still enough to whisper.

'I'm not Henry, Elena...' he breathed softly 'but I did enjoy this morning. If you're honest with yourself, so did you.'

Elena sat still for a long time before realising that there was no more to the message. She leaned against his hands, but they no longer restrained her and she was free to sit up straight. Selest had sat back in his chair, evening shadows gathering about him like a welcoming cloak. He was watchful now, neither threatening nor light-hearted.

Ever since his arrival Elena had imagined this moment. At first it had been with fear, then curiosity. Now it was with longing, and she didn't know what to do.

'I—I disappointed Henry so often...and now I'm bound to disappoint you...'

He raised one hand and brushed her hair back as gently as though she were a child. 'Shh. No, you won't. That's the wine talking. Plenty more fish in the sea, you said. Remember? All this is up to you, Elena. If you're happy just to sit like this, then we'll go no further. It's all up to you.'

In the gathering dusk, Elena looked into his eyes. They were darkened with tenderness and she knew that she was nearly lost. The love she felt now for Selest was different from that Henry had commanded. Her feelings now were of pure love, not the affection of duty or habit.

'Emil——' she said at last. 'I—I think you ought to go away. Now. If you stay here I'll get too fond of you and——'

'And what?' he said softly in the half-light. 'We're both thinking the same way, Elena. I don't know if I shall have to leave tomorrow, the next day, or in a thousand years' time. It's your decision, Elena. Go up to bed, and leave me here. Stay, and we could go out for a walk, or simply sit here. It's your choice —but please, don't send me away from here before you've thought about it properly...'

'I've thought about it too much and for too long, that's the trouble.' Elena sighed and stood up, but she didn't release Selest's hand at once. 'Gulzun never told me that pleasure would bring so much pain.'

'It needn't.' His tone was low and clear in the silent room.

Without a word Elena bent and picked up the crutches that lay beside his chair. 'Now. Please? Before I lose my nerve as well as everything else...?'

This time it was Selest who hesitated. Taking the crutches from her, he stood up, uncomfortable for the first time with the thought of needing their support.

'You go on,' he said quietly. 'I'll follow in my own time.'

Elena drifted towards consciousness. Something heavy was laid across her—an arm...

She jumped awake violently, but strong hands restrained her.

'All right... It's all right, Elena—take a minute or two to wake up properly...'

His voice slipped through the quieting dark, one hand settling her hair.

'Oh, no! Oh, what am I going to do——?' She tried to pull away, but Selest held her fast.

'There's really nothing to be afraid of, Elena——'

'There is! I must get up, right now...' She was still muddled with sleep. 'Gulzun gave me something, but I forgot...'

He drew her back towards him and placed a tiny kiss behind her ear.

'Nothing happened, Elena. Don't you remember?'

She remembered feeling as warm and comfortable in his arms as she did now. More hazy recollections flooded back and began to fill her with hot shame. His caresses and kisses in the warm spring evening. The feel of his firm, eager body against hers. Gentle words that had made her feel so loved and cherished. Safe and secure. And sleepy...

'Elena? Have you gone back to sleep?'

He was stroking her hair again. Elena dragged herself awake. Then she became aware of the after-effects of too much wine on her head and moaned.

'Would you like me to go?'

There was silence in the dawn-cool bedroom. Elena thought of Henry's kind words, and her gritted teeth. She had loved Henry enough to endure it then, and with every moment that passed she loved Emil more. What was an instant of discomfort if it meant pleasing him?

Twisting in his arms, Elena nestled against him and shook her head.

'Don't go. Stay.'

It was like nothing that Elena had even dreamed about. His kisses and caresses never frightened, only coaxed and reassured. Gradually Elena too felt the tide of love that was drawing them ever closer.

The moment passed.

She was still smiling.

Emil set a necklace of kisses about her neck, the warm dampness of his hair brushing her face.

'And what would my lady like for breakfast?' he whispered, and Elena realised that dawn dimness had been replaced by strong shafts of morning sun. 'I'd offer to bring you breakfast in bed,' he continued, 'but juggling a tray and crutches up the stairs might be a bit tricky.'

'You aren't cross, then?'

Emil nuzzled her ear, tracing its contours with the tip of his tongue. 'I'm delighted. Why on earth should I be cross?'

'Henry always was.'

At once Elena was enveloped in another warm, lingering embrace.

'Well, you've got me now, and I find you absolutely exquisite.' He kissed her long and lovingly, then gave her a playful nip on the tip of her nose. 'Give me a head start and I'll have breakfast waiting out in the garden. That is, if the range hasn't gone out.'

He slipped from her arms and sat on the far side of the bed to pick up his crutches.

'That's it?'

His spine flexed as he turned to look at her over his shoulder. 'What else were you expecting?'

Elena didn't like to say. Sensing her distress, he reached for her hand and held it. That simple action made everything easier.

'I mean—you aren't cross? You aren't going to shout at me?'

'As I told you before, I'm not Henry.' Emil smiled at her. 'And I happen to think that there are more fitting places to shout and frighten than a lady's chamber.'

He tucked the sheets up around her, then pulled on his shirt and breeches. Mastering the crutches once more, he worked his way to the door.

Warm waves of sleep were lapping about Elena, but she still sensed that he had stopped. Opening her eyes, she saw him watching her.

Elena had seen that same expression in his eyes when he watched over Milo and Hamelin as they slept.

She felt safe.

# CHAPTER ELEVEN

WITH no Ascony in the house there was no hot water for washing in the bedroom. Elena had to pull on a robe and stumble downstairs.

Meeting up with her in the hallway, Selest adjusted the collar of her robe and arranged the thick luxuriance of her hair over it.

'That's better. Now, what time do you call this? I've been down here long enough to get the range going from cold!'

'I went back to sleep.' She brushed her fringe back with a sleepy gesture.

'If you *could* manage to stay awake, then there's fruit-bread and honey in the dining-room. No toast, I'm afraid. It'll be a long time before the fire is clear enough for that.'

She went towards the dining-room and he followed slowly.

'Elena? That wine really must have left your wits muddled. You haven't noticed.'

Hindsight made her spin round. 'You're not using the crutches!'

Selest limped up to her. She took his arm, expecting him to lean on her, but he didn't.

'I've been trying a few steps now and again. It's murder when I start off, but it gets easier.'

They reached the dining-room and he collapsed grate-fully on to a chair. It was still early enough to be chill outside, so he had set breakfast at the table. The garden doors were open, and fresh air set the curtains swaying slightly.

'When is Gulzun going to bring the children back?'

'Whenever you like.'

'And the staff? Are they really going to stay away?'

'Only for a day or two.'

Elena's eyes narrowed. He was pressing fruit-breadcrumbs together on his plate with one finger, and looking quite unconcerned.

'You enjoyed all this scheming, didn't you?'

He looked up and winked. 'I've told you before. You deserved a holiday. Don't you feel better already?'

Elena had to confess that she did. Sitting in a peaceful house, wriggling bare toes on sun-warm tiles, she felt abandoned to pleasure.

Faraway cries of fishermen were echoed by gulls flashing silver against solid blue above. Out in the garden little birds added courting sounds of their own.

She lay back, stretching in cat-like luxury. 'I am so *happy*.'

Selest paused in his crumb gathering, but did not look up. 'Don't forget what Gulzun said, mind. About letting me go.'

'Soon?'

'If I can walk, I can fight.' A trace of his old hostility surfaced. He pushed his plate away and began drumming his fingers on the table-top. 'I thought that we might go to the market today. If we go while it's early the other Franks will still be sleeping off last night's merrymaking.'

He had changed. In a moment he had regained most of his early Frankish arrogance. There was none of the tender sensitivity that he had shown only an hour before.

Elena stood up and went to get ready. What had she said that had made him change so abruptly? She could only wonder.

His ill humour did not last long. By the time that Elena had washed and dressed he was whistling happily about the hall as he waited.

With Frankish disregard for dignity Selest used low walls and high kerbs to rest on when his ankle grew tired. He had refused to bring his crutches, but as the day progressed his walking improved and the rests grew shorter.

They visited the quay again. A last boat was loading to ferry Crusaders across the Bosphorous, and they watched the Franks preparing to leave for the holding camp. Celebrations the night before had stunned the men into near silence, and there seemed no eagerness about them now.

'There will be other ships soon, when the next batch arrives,' Elena said reassuringly, but it seemed to have the opposite effect on Selest. He limped away in the direction of the palace, finding the cobblestones hard going. 'You're getting better all the time. Don't worry—you'll soon be fit enough to join them again, my lord.'

'What happened to "Emil"?'

He stopped, eyes searching her face. Elena took his arm for the walk to Gulzun's, but Selest was silent for most of the way.

Nothing Gulzun had to say could cheer him, either—only Milo and Hamelin were able to raise a smile. They dragged him off to see Gulzun's enormous marble and ivory bath. It was quite big enough for little boys to swim in, so it wasn't long before the sound of laughter and splashing was coming from the room along the hall.

'You're looking better,' Gulzun said slyly as the girls sipped rose-petal tisane together. 'Any particular reason?'

Elena shrugged, squirmed and tried to change the subject. 'I hear that another wave of Crusaders is expected any day, Gulzun. You'll be kept busy.'

Her friend frowned. 'Watch your step, Elena. If you intend letting Emil go, send him away now. You've seen what he's been like here today. If you want more fun, get rid of him before the next batch get here. If not——'

'What? Make him stay? How do you suppose I'd manage that?'

Leaning forward, the Turkish girl whispered slowly, 'If you want him, he's yours. Mark my words—you only have to say. I wish I could say the same about . . . well, you know.' Gulzun sighed. 'What with having Milo and Hamelin to stay...'

She went quiet and Elena did not press her. Eventually Gulzun began pleating the edge of her pale green veil and continued, 'I must admit, last night after they were asleep I got out the box of little Hussein's things. I spent hours going through it...'

Her fingers worked over the delicate material until it was a bundle of crumpled dampness. Elena did not know what to say. In her eagerness to diffuse the situation she picked on exactly the wrong subject.

'They say that Duke Godfrey will make himself King of Jerusalem before he's finished,' she murmured. 'If he gets there.'

Gulzun's eyes glistened. She gulped several times, but did not cry. 'Oh, he'll get there, Elena. But he won't ever be called King.' Her voice was full and tense. 'I've heard the others teasing him about it, but he maintains that there can only ever be one real King of Jerusalem...' She hung her head and trembled with the effort of resisting grief.

'Even though he's so remote, you really love him, don't you, Gulzun?'

'As much as Emil loves you.'

Elena laughed. Emil Selest could be as distant as a cold moon towards her. How could he love her when there was so little time?

The boys had begged to be left with Gulzun for another night. Elena was worried that Milo was missing Father Johann's little lessons, but Selest disagreed.

'He's learning far more from Hamelin,' he said as he sat with Elena in the firelight that evening. 'Book-learning can be picked up quickly enough later on. I managed.'

'You can read?' Elena was astonished.

'And reckon. And write my name.' He pretended offence at her surprise. 'There's nothing much to do when you're stuck in a verminous camp outside certain city walls for months on end. Some of the priests gave lessons to relieve the boredom. That's what they said—although I think it was just an excuse to shout and rap knuckles!'

'Eban and Ascony taught me,' Elena said, snuggling up closer in the warm fireglow. 'I often wonder what Henry would think if he knew.'

'Learning isn't for girls.' Selest hugged her closer and arranged her veil over her toes. 'The priests told us that their heads are too small. Too much learning is apt to give them headaches.'

'I don't get headaches, and Eban says I'm quite clever. For a Greek!' She laughed. 'He's only teasing, of course.'

She picked up a stick from the woodpile, charred it against the hearth before them and charcoaled small, neat letters on one hearthstone.

Selest was highly amused. 'What's that supposed to be?'

'My name, of course.' She looked puzzled, then traced the outline again with her stick. '"Elena Rethel".'

'No, my love! There's no "M"'s in that, yet you've put two. And a lot of your other letters are wrong, too. Here, let me show you.' He took the stick and wrote more words on the flagstone. 'Your name, and mine beneath.'

'I've seen Henry use those letters.' Elena thought for a moment. 'I know—perhaps Greek and French don't only sound different. Perhaps they have different letters, too.'

Selest pulled her back in his arms. 'You are silly!' He laughed. 'Imagine how long it would take to learn alphabets as well as languages for every country!'

He used the stick again to draw a heart shape enclosing both names.

'What does that mean?'

He kissed her, then laughed. 'It keeps them together, nice and neatly. In French or Greek.'

Tiring of the game, Elena yawned and settled herself even more comfortably in his arms.

'I'm tired.'

'It's been a long day.' He brushed her hair into order with his fingers then kissed the top of her head. 'I'd go to bed if I knew where it was to be tonight.'

She looked up into his dear face with its merry brown eyes. They were serious now, and Elena wondered whether Gulzun had been right.

'As I've always said, Elena. It's up to you. Your decision.'

The choice was between losing him quickly now, or facing real heartbreak later on. Sharp pain, or long drawn-out suffering.

In simple reply Elena lifted her face for the first of many kisses.

Their idyll could not last. Ascony and the Khars returned the next afternoon, startling Selest and Elena as they lay in each other's arms in the arbour. Elena leapt up at once, but Selest was reluctant to release her.

Ascony's face betrayed no emotion. A curt nod to Selest and a greeting to Elena gave nothing away. He answered her nervous questions about their trip with polite economy, and left Elena tortured with guilt.

To escape his good-mannered reserve she went to collect the children from Gulzun's, but returned to find Selest in even better humour than she had left him.

'Poor Ascony isn't very impressed with me at all. If looks could kill I would have been murdered long ago!'

'Has he been rude to you?' Elena began, but the kitchen door opened and Ascony swept out. At once the children rushed forward, eager to show off the toys that Gulzun had bought them.

Ascony gathered Milo into his arms and made a great fuss of him while glaring at Elena. When he had greeted the boys sufficiently he patted them off towards the kitchen and advanced towards Elena and Selest with measured tread.

'That poor little fatherless child,' he said with feeling, looking Selest up and down with naked scorn.

'Ascony,' Elena said with equal meaning, 'if you have anything to say to us, it might as well be out in the open.'

'I would speak to you alone, lady. We need not bother to inconvenience your—"lodger".'

Elena grasped her servant firmly by the arm and towed him into the second guest room. 'This won't take long, Emil,' she called back, shoving Ascony through the door and following him.

She was angry enough, but Ascony's fury prevented her from getting in the first words.

'Get rid of him, lady. Khar has heard him talking, and this Frank means nothing but trouble, as I have always warned.'

'*I* decide when my guests remain, and when they leave.' She folded her tunic about her neatly and sat down. 'What exactly has Khar heard?'

'He didn't mention it until we were on our way home, or I would never have left you, lady! Khar says that the infidel dog——'

One look from Elena stopped him in his tracks. Only when he had mastered his fury did she allow him to continue.

'The Frank has come here only to seek his fortune. Khar overheard him telling you that he is going to send for all his relatives to be parasites on our wealth. He has you ensnared, lady!'

'Ascony.' Elena folded her arms and tried not to let his erratic gestures put her off. 'Emil is my guest, and this story has gained nothing in the telling. Even if it were true, you have no right to make such accusations behind his back. Thank you for telling me, but try to be a little more tactful next time.'

'But you don't deny that he's wheedled his way into your affections, and other places——'

'Ascony!' Elena stood up, rage adding inches to her height as she sprang towards him. 'That is none of your business! And if I hear that you've been spreading any stories around the city I'll—I'll dismiss you!'

Both of them knew that losing Ascony was the last thing that Elena would want, but both kept up the pretense of righteous indignation to the end.

'It's the poor little fatherless mite that I feel sorry for,' Ascony muttered as he swept off to the door. 'No decent mother would ever farm such a baby out to—to a house of shame!'

'Ascony.'

He stopped and looked at her defiantly.

'Go and have a nice grumble to the Khars, then bring us some tcha. Emil and I will be out in the garden with Hamelin, and the poor little fatherless mite.'

The eunuch rewarded her with only the clack of his sandals on the tiles as he marched away.

The next few weeks were happier than any Elena had ever known before. Constant warnings of disaster from Ascony could not spoil the simple pleasures she now enjoyed.

Hamelin and Milo thrived. With plenty of good food and exercise they both grew. Hamelin filled out as quickly as Milo lost weight galloping around after him.

Ascony tried his hardest to maintain decency and order. On the first night of his return he set Milo to sleep in Elena's room while tucking Hamelin up in Selest's bed. He had reckoned without the boys becoming lonely. When Selest and Elena retired they found the boys both curled up together in Elena's bed.

After that Selest and Elena tried hard not to offend Ascony's morals, at least in the eunuch's sight.

'This is like being a kid again,' Selest said between puffs at the muslin drapes of Gulzun's spare room. 'Sneaking away from the family.'

Elena lifted her head and frowned at him. 'I don't know how you can be so casual about it. Lying in bed in the middle of a beautiful afternoon! It's the most sinful thing I've ever heard of.'

'I can't get up for the simple reason that you're lying on me, woman. You don't seem too eager to leap into action, either!'

He took a deep breath and tried to blow the fluttering muslin banners about them even higher. Elena's head rose and fell with his chest, but she neither moved nor spoke. He repeated the action several more times to tease her, then realised that it was no use. She was miles away with her thoughts.

'What's the matter?'

'Nothing.'

'"Nothing" doesn't make people sigh like that, Elena. Something's wrong.'

She pressed her cheek against the soft fur of his chest and hung on tighter.

'Elena?'

He touched her hair, arranging and rearranging the thick tresses across her back. She had started to wear it simply, in the Frankish fashion. To Selest's delight the glittering waves were also free from scented oils now.

'Gulzun said that the Crusaders who arrived yesterday are the last big batch,' she said slowly at last.

'Oh.'

He stopped playing with her hair and began blowing at the curtains again, but without enthusiasm.

'Once they've gone across to the holding camp it won't be many days before they move on. And that means you, too, Emil.'

He sighed, but said nothing. Their friendship contained many companionable silences, but this one was a pale shadow through which Elena could see only sadness and hopeless longing.

'When will you go? Tomorrow?'

'There's no such day,' Selest said at last. 'Tomorrow never comes.'

There was nothing unusual about the way in which that next day began. They all ate together at breakfast, which had become the custom. Hamelin and Milo giggled as usual, taking forever to eat their egged bread. Selest waited on Elena with impeccable manners, handing her orange juice, fruit-bread and cheese in turn without needing to be asked. Only when she had sufficient did he take food for himself, and then without the barbaric greed that had characterised the first days of their association.

Elena was impressed. Perhaps restraint and good manners would rub off on all the Franks if they stayed long enough in Constantinople.

When breakfast was finished there was the usual scramble for outdoor shoes, cloaks, cash, keys, and the lost toy that Milo could not leave home without. Finally everybody and everything tumbled out of the front door, but it was not a happy sight that met their eyes.

'Mummy! Look at that man!'

Out on the Mese lay a man, face down in the gutter and half covered only by a thin red and gold sheet. At once Elena gave Milo's hand to Selest.

'You run along nicely with Emil, Milo. I'll go and help the poor old gentleman.'

Selest's laughter held her back long enough for him to take hold of her hand.

'No need to play the Good Samaritan, my love. It's only Normandy.'

'Mummy! Mummy, look! He's drinking that muddy water!'

Milo and Hamelin howled with laughter as the creature Normandy hauled itself further into the gutter, lapping like a dog at the gutter fluid. One hand still restraining Elena, Selest knelt down beside Milo and put his arm about the child.

'That's what happens when you don't stick up for yourself, young Milo. Normandy is a waste of space. He lets other people walk all over him. He doesn't speak up according to his size, and so he gets pushed around by everybody. Now, you don't want to end up a loser like him, do you, Milo?'

Milo giggled and aimed a punch at Selest, who fielded it cheerfully.

'That's right. You remember Normandy's shame and you won't go far wrong.' The Crusader stood up and started off again, but Elena was reluctant. She pulled away as though to cross the street.

'I must just——'

'No.' He had taken a firm grip on her arm and was almost dragging her along the Mese.

'But he's ill!'

'Only with the sort of sickness that comes out of a bottle. He's a loser. Get mixed up with that wretched specimen and you'll never be free of him.'

Eyes flashing, Elena turned to Selest. She reached up and opened the brooch fastening his cloak, but he did not stop her.

'I'll take him this old cloak of Henry's. You surely could not deny a poor victim some decent covering?'

'If it's Normandy, yes.'

'Even if everything he has is gone?'

'It's not gone far. That's how his staff try and keep him off the alcohol. They take his clothes when he's asleep, thinking it will keep him in.' Selest shrugged, the lithe grace of his movements in contrast to the grovelling blob that was Normandy.

Elena followed Selest and the boys, but looked back several times until the unfortunate Normandy was lost to view.

They walked on sedately towards the shop. Hamelin and Milo were either a mile in front or a mile behind them, peeping through still-closed shutters into the sleeping shops behind. Elena gave them the key to run on ahead and unlock the shop door, and quick as coneys they were gone to do her bidding.

'I'm sure he could be persuaded to stay. If you put your mind to it,' Elena began hesitantly. In the end she knew that Selest was the one that she would have to convince if Hamelin was to stay.

Selest strolled on beside her, the early sunlight burnishing the auburn glints in his thick curly hair. He made no comment but instead gave her a half-mocking smile, knowing that she had more to say. They had reached the open shop door before she gave way under his look of amused anticipation.

'I wondered if Hamelin might like to start lodging with the apprentices today...just until...'

Milo and Hamelin were nowhere to be seen. Instead, muffled laughter and heavy thuds came from the apprentices' room overhead.

'Surely they might teach him rough ways, my love?'

'I think he is more likely to do the teaching in that respect, Emil.'

Remembering their earlier disagreements on the matter, Elena flushed shyly and went towards the counter. Selest did not follow her but instead leaned against the door-frame nonchalantly. Much to Ascony's disapproval Elena had given Selest the money-bags to carry, and he was fingering the two pouches hanging from his belt.

'These must contain more money than my whole family has ever seen in their lives.'

His words and the sight of him toying with the money-bags made Elena a little wary. She trusted him, but had known Ascony for a lot longer and usually respected the eunuch's judgement. In his eyes Selest was dangerous.

Elena threw back the lid of the cash box and looked at Selest steadfastly.

'Eban will need that money to open the shop,' she said quietly.

'And you don't think it's safe with me?'

'I never said that.'

'But that is what you meant.'

A silence fell heavily between them, lightened only by laughter from above.

This was the nearest that they had been to a disagreement for weeks. When Selest continued, his tone was soft but Elena felt uncertain.

'All this——' He waved one hand carelessly at the work-filled shop. 'It would make some man a fine living, don't you think?'

'We manage.'

'That isn't what I asked, Elena. And you know it.'

He walked forward, the floorboards barely whispering at his light tread. Close enough now for Elena to see the fine texture of his freshly shaved skin, he stopped.

'Very well, then. Perhaps I must speak plainer. Lady Elena Rethel, will you marry me?'

'No.'

The reply was sudden, instinctive, but it was Ascony speaking and not Elena herself. Selest drew back a little, the usual easy smile faltering.

'No more than I should have expected,' he said acidly.

Elena was thrown by the easy manner by which he took the rebuff, and almost offended. 'Don't you want to know my reasons?'

'Not particularly. The "reasons" that you would give would be all falsehoods, anyway.'

'Are you calling me a liar?'

He shrugged, untying the bags from his belt with deft fingers.

'A liar deceives others for his own ends. You deceive only yourself, madam, which is not quite such a crime.'

Elena thrust out her hand to take the money-bags from him, but he caught her wrist and moved quickly around the counter to be at her side.

'I've been trying to get you to start acting for yourself, Elena. Forget Ascony's jealousy and let me make you happy forever. Marry me. He'll soon get over it.'

'It's not Ascony——'

'It is, my love. He's filled your head with a lot of nonsense because he resents me.'

'It's Henry. I can't marry you because of Henry——'

She could not finish. Selest had pulled her into a rough embrace and was kissing her with a new, urgent passion. There was no resisting him. Cool and sweet, his mouth caressed hers while she was enclosed in the warmth of his embrace. Dizzy with rising passion, Elena lost all self-control. Despite her refusal she was kissing him, twining her fingers into the soft luxuriance of his hair to hold him closer. At this he broke away from her eager mouth to cover her throat and neck with kisses.

'I—I would marry you, Emil,' Elena said between kisses. 'I love you so much that I couldn't bear to lose you—now or ever.'

'Then say it. Agree. Worry about Ascony later, my love...'

Elena knew he was right. She returned his caresses eagerly.

'... when my family arrive he'll soon be won over by them...'

Selest had broken his own spell. Elena tried to push him away but his grip was certain.

'No!'

'What's the matter?' Selest was genuinely surprised. Tousled and lightly flushed with her attentions, he looked at her quizzically. She was still held tightly enough to feel the rapid excitement of his heart, but could not afford to let it influence her.

'Stop this at once. You'll have to go home. Eban will be here at any minute.'

'He'll be able to manage the children on his own, then. Come back with me. Now.'

He dived towards her neck again but Elena repelled him with more force. This time he took on an injured air.

'What is it, my love?'

'Don't! Ascony warned me what it would be like, and he was right! You've ensnared me!'

He put a finger to her lips. 'Ah, now hush. You're not exactly an unwilling partner. I didn't force you into any of this, did I? We're the best of friends, aren't we? And I felt you come alive again in my arms just then. Are you going to throw all that away because of what Ascony says? It's time that you had a bit of fun——'

'No! That's all it is to you, isn't it? Fun! You can't understand that people have feelings that run deeper than simple pleasure-seeking. What Ascony said was true! All you're interested in is setting up your family over here, and you're using me as the excuse! Leave me alone!'

'Elena! No!'

She thrust herself from his embrace and dashed to the foot of the staircase. A call to the apprentices resulted in frantic scrambling and laughter from the room above as they hurried to get ready for work.

Hot and tearful, Elena turned to order Selest off the premises.

There was no need. He had already left.

She dashed to the doorway. Despite a slight favouring of his left leg, long strides had already taken him almost to their turning.

If he had gone on, she would have forgotten all reason and run after him. As it was, Elena saw him turn into her street and felt a little reassured. He had gone home. This had been the first time they had been apart for weeks. Perhaps a couple of hours' separation might not be a bad thing.

As Elena turned to slip back into the shop the pathetic form of Normandy caught her attention. She had quite forgotten him, and without Selest to restrain her knew that she would have to offer him some sort of help. The morning air from the sea was chilly. He might die of exposure out in the road.

She went to the nearest drinking fountain and filled the bowl with clean water. Selest would not know, but all the same Elena was wary.

It took her some time to reach the figure lying in the gutter. Normandy made no movement, either when several townspeople stepped over him with murmurs of disgust or when Elena knelt beside him with a bowl of water.

'Here, my lord. A little clean water for your thirst.'

The figure twitched, stirred slightly then gave a heavy moan. He was face down, but Elena could see that his skin and hair had the dull, dry look of malnutrition. Scars of childhood beatings crazed his back, their faint silvery trails crossed here and there by the welts of more recent conflicts.

Elena placed the bowl beside his hand, which was curled into a loose fist. He gave another huge sigh. Without raising his head a hair's breadth more than was necessary, he moved slightly until his face rested on the edge of the bowl. Tipping it unsteadily with the movement of one hand, he gulped back a few mouthfuls, pouring more over himself and into the gutter than he took in.

At that moment a small dark figure emerged from a doorway close at hand. He dashed forward to Normandy and began tugging and heaving at the sluggish form as though it were a bag of turnips.

'Now come along, my lord. What are you doing out here? I don't know. We can't even get a decent night's rest without you wandering off now, can we?'

Normandy was dragged away, still clutching his red and gold standard. Elena was ignored, and picked up her bowl to go back to the shop. She wondered what possessed men like Normandy to take up travelling. If he was going to spend his time in a drunken stupor he might as well have stayed at home.

\*    \*    \*

The morning was not especially busy. Most of their business was with vintners and the palace, where glassware was ordered in quantity. Any trade done in the shop was usually small souvenirs sold to pilgrims. Filled now with a chaos of Crusaders, Constantinople was no longer a popular destination for honest visitors.

At lunchtime Elena suggested that Eban might like to take the orders round while she watched the shop. While Hamelin, Milo and the apprentices ate cheese and fruit in the upper room, Elena swept the pavement outside.

In the warm sun many people stopped to talk. They were all nervous of the Crusaders, with their brash arrogance, and wanted to know how Elena was faring with two of the newcomers under her roof. She was pleased to tell them that the reality was nowhere near as threatening as their image.

A flower seller had set up her pitchers of water around the drinking fountain and now lily, rose and jasmine made the marble steps bloom with their exotic beauty. Gulzun, at a loose end, strolled up and stopped for a snack.

As the shops about them closed for lunch, Elena, Gulzun and the flower seller were soon almost alone on the broad sweep of the Mese. Suddenly a movement caught Elena's eye. A small figure was hurrying along the marble way from the north. Dodging between pools of dark shadow and constantly turning to check for pursuers, the figure was immaculate in Crusading whites, but unnaturally nervous.

By this time the other girls were interested in his progress, too, and watching him with interest. With his quick, furtive glances the Frank soon noticed their scrutiny and dived into a side-street.

The girls waited. Sure enough, inquisitive as a rock mouse the small Crusader soon risked a peep out at his observers. Elena called across to him.

'There's no one about save us, my lord!'

'Shh!'

The hiss was almost silenced by distance, but energetically waving arms gave the frantic message. Elena started towards him but the girls giggled in disbelief.

'You're not going to have anything to do with him, are you?' Gulzun pulled a face.

'Why not?'

'Because that's Normandy, that's why not!'

Elena remembered the pathetic crumpled form in the gutter and hesitated. The flower seller gasped, and seemed more impressed with the Frank. She began telling Gulzun that he was reckoned to be a Good Bet.

In that split second Normandy sensed their sympathy and with one last look for pursuers marched smartly across the Mese towards them.

Gulzun groaned and turned away. Why, Elena couldn't imagine, for Normandy seemed quite recovered from that morning's collapse. His round face beamed, eyes merry with mischief and above all his manners were faultless. As he drew near to the girls he stopped, bowed low then advanced to take their hands in turn and brush each with a formal kiss.

'Good afternoon, dear ladies. My name is Robert Curthose, Duke of Normandy, and I wonder if you could possibly be called upon to aid this poor knight in his time of trouble.'

His Greek was passable, which was astonishing as he was the first Frank that the girls had heard even attempt their language. Gulzun was caught off guard and forgot to sneer, while Elena smiled and the flower seller giggled coquettishly. Elena took command of the situation.

'Of course, my lord. What is your wish?'

Normandy looked about him nervously and licked his lips. 'Wicked rascals mean me no good. I've been stuck inside for hours, and I just needed some exercise and entertaining company.'

'The raddle house is in the next street,' Gulzun cut in, but Normandy merely chuckled indulgently and winked at her.

'No, no, dear lady. You misunderstand. All I desire is pleasant company and most of all in this excellent climate a cooling drink. Out of the sight of my pursuers.'

Thin hair made his flush all the more apparent and Elena took pity on him.

'If you would like to come inside my shop, my lord, you can refresh yourself without fear of discovery for a while at least. Although I regret that as some of my staff are Mus——' She stopped, mindful of the Crusading Cross on his tunic. 'Engaged elsewhere, there may be little to drink that is to your taste.'

Eban would only allow lemonade in the workshop— hardly the thing for a seasoned drinker like Normandy.

Gulzun was horrified. 'You're not going in there alone with him?'

'Keep your hands on your holiday money.' The flower seller was more practical.

'You two can only ever think the worst of people,' Elena hissed. 'He's an old man. Look at him! And he has such beautiful manners.'

'Watch out, Elena. They say he's a real wolf in sheep's clothing...'

Normandy had stood aside in polite silence as the girls whispered together. He then gave Elena such a winning smile that her heart went out to him.

'Come along, my lord. Perhaps you might like to see some of our stock while you rest.'

Normandy leapt at the offer and Elena with equal enthusiasm, and immediately swept her off to the shadowy depths of the shop.

'I trust you have quite recovered from this morning's—er—indisposition, my lord?'

Normandy turned to her, his eyes wary. At length he murmured, 'A disturbance of the inner ear, the physicians say. My balance is often not what it might be.' He laughed, but it was a nervous sound.

At the shop doorway he stood aside for Elena to enter, bowing slightly as she did so. Once inside he stood in the centre of the shop, looking about rather uncertainly. While Elena went out to the back for a jug of fruit juice and two glasses she told him to look around. When she returned he had not moved a muscle.

'Don't want to break anything,' he muttered uncomfortably.

'You hardly seem the type to have come Crusading, my lord. Your fellows would be only too eager to come in and start breaking up the place if we let them!'

He accepted the glass of juice that she offered and swallowed it at one pass. Elena refilled his glass, which went the same way. The third draught must have touched the sides, for he stopped halfway and looked at it thoughtfully.

'Only fruit juice?'

'I'm afraid we have nothing else at the moment, my lord.'

'Pity.' He finished the glass and placed it back on its silver tray. 'Prefer the other stuff, really. Helps me to forget.'

'Forget what?'

'I can't remember!' He exploded in a fit of laughter, but soon stopped when he saw that Elena was merely uncomfortable.

'I'm sorry. I suppose that's why everybody hates me so much. They all tell me to take things seriously, but if you can't have a laugh when you're in my predicament, when can you?'

'You are in trouble, then, my lord?'

Normandy shrugged, his heavy features sagging and dull. 'I've been in trouble since the day I was born. Not quite the right sort of son for William the Conqueror to produce. The Normans are all so brilliant at religion and fighting.'

'And you aren't?'

He looked up at her, shocked. 'I'm the best! I forced myself on so that Father would notice me and be proud.

But it didn't work. He always preferred William and Henry, because they're better actors than I am.'

It was Elena's turn to laugh while Normandy looked uncomfortable.

'I would have thought that Normandy needed a duke, not an actor, my lord!'

'Everyone there acts. Franks are all the same. Nobody could ever be as boringly tough as they all pretend they are. It's put on to impress people.'

Elena thought of how embarrassed Selest always was when he was caught making a fuss of the children. And the shame he had felt when in pain.

'Are you quite sure they aren't what they seem?'

'Positive. Show me a Frank and I'll show you a quivering heap hiding behind a granite exterior. That's why they don't like me. I drink and dance and sing and whistle and love my children. I let the side down and show those stuffy Normans as they really are. I'm an embarrassment to them.'

Elena knew then that she had to get back and apologise to Selest. If Normandy was right, she knew now why Selest had been so eager to go, yet so put out when she talked of it. He had been trying to get her to make him stay. In the end he had been forced to cast off reserve and propose. Once again Elena had hurt him because she had not understood his feelings.

'My lord—I'm afraid I have suddenly realised that I have pressing business elsewhere.'

Now she was hurting poor, gentle Normandy. She could see from his face that he expected to be thrown out on the street.

'Sit in here for as long as you like, my lord. There's plenty more fruit juice in the jug. And if you should ever need any help... well, my house backs on to the city wall. The last building, overlooking the sea.'

Normandy was almost pathetically grateful. He shook her hand warmly all the way to the door, but soon dodged back into the shop and anonymity when she had left.

Gulzun was unimpressed with Elena's sympathy. She agreed to keep an eye on the shop and children until Eban returned, but only as long as she didn't have to have anything to do with Normandy. Elena agreed, then hurried back to the house.

It was very quiet as she slipped into the cool hall. Ascony emerged from the kitchen at her arrival, but when assured that there was no trouble went back to his housekeeping.

Elena found Selest in the dining-room, poring over a large drink. As she closed the door with a click he looked up, then almost as quickly transferred his attention back to the brimming cup on the table beside him.

'Trouble at work?' he enquired mildly after taking a long drink. Elena shrugged. A light breeze lifted one of the fine linen curtains. Outside in the sunlight, playing waters laughed in their black marble rills while the green shades of spring were already deepening to summer.

'Leave that. Come out into the garden.'

For a long time the only sound within the room was the tap of her sandals and sussuration of silks as Elena walked towards the garden doors. She did not look at Selest, but neither did she sense him looking at her. Reaching the threshold, she paused and looked back. He was staring at his glass, turning it between slow fingers.

'Emil?'

When he turned to Elena his eyes were hurt and suspicious.

'What would Ascony think? You alone in the garden with a scrounging ruffian?'

'He can think what he likes for once.'

Selest leaned back in his chair. After a moment he stood up and followed her out into the garden, but the act was performed more out of duty than anything else.

He walked beside her, the slight limp more noticeable now. When they sat down in the little arbour he lowered himself on to the seat with great care, one hand to his knee.

'Your leg still troubles you, then, my lord?'

Selest looked across at new growth bursting from the apricots, fan-trained against the garden wall.

'Not really. As it appears that I am to receive my marching orders I can't afford the luxury of a weakness. There's no room for wasters on our mission. The strong weed out the weakened. It's the way of things.'

Her pity began to evaporate. Selest was determined to be hard done by and make her suffer. Considering what she had steeled herself to say, his attitude was unnecessary.

'If you choose to go, then let it be your own decision, Emil. Not mine. My immediate concern is that...is that...' Her nerve was failing. She thought he might laugh, and nearly stopped altogether. Only the recollection of poor Normandy's words made her continue. 'Someone came into the shop today and made me realise that everyone has feelings, even if they conceal them through some foolish sense of honour. I was rude and thoughtless this morning, and I'm sorry.'

A bird began to sing from the old mulberry tree, a cascade of liquid notes rippling to earth. Selest leaned forward, elbows on his knees, and studied the clean pebbled path.

'Well, well. Here's a thing and no mistake. The fine lady offering her gracious apology. What a lucky fellow I must be.'

'Don't be bitter—Emil...' Without her thinking, Elena's hand went to his shoulder. At the last moment she read the pain in his eyes and did not touch him. Looking away, he picked up a handful of the small white pebbles. Pouring them from hand to hand with casual speed, he avoided her gaze.

'A professional soldier can't afford to make mistakes in sizing up a situation. It seems that I am not cut out to be a professional soldier, then.'

He threw one of the pebbles into the rill where it plopped out of sight with a hiccup of water. Elena knew she was losing him. When he stood up to go she could bear it no longer.

'It was my fault. I should have considered your proposal and not rejected you so cruelly. It was wrong of me to think only of preserving Henry's memory, of listening to Ascony... I should have thought of all the other things—companionship, the future, longing——'

She reached out to him again. There was no resistance, no turning away, so she took his hand and held it in both of hers.

He spoke slowly, without looking at her. 'You realise that I can't ask you again——'

An hour ago Elena would not have understood. She looked up now to see that he was almost showing embarrassment, fingering his belt nervously with his free hand.

'—after you've turned me down——'

Elena had to keep him. She knew now that she couldn't let him go, now or ever. To have any chance of happiness at all she must now risk enduring his earlier pain.

'Would you be willing to consider a proposal from me?'

High in the mulberry the bird continued to sing and was joined by a rival in sweet duet.

'Don't laugh at me, Elena.'

'I wouldn't, my love. Not about something like marriage. It's far too serious.'

Emil ran one hand through his hair in a gesture of desperation, looked about as though there might be spies hidden behind every plant, then said sullenly, 'Will you, then?'

'I was going to ask you, remember?'

'Yes or no?' he spat out at last, crucified with hot embarrassment.

'The answer is yes, my love.'

Even the birds paused in their song. At first Elena wondered whether Selest had heard her acceptance, for he said nothing. Then the shame and uncertainty left his expression and were replaced by a cautious wonder. He looked away quickly and collected his thoughts.

'We must discuss things. I fully intend to be master in my own household, but——' He paused and gave her a smile that was almost shy. 'I know that someone else has the same idea in mind. He's already suspicious of my motives.'

'Don't be hard on Ascony. He thinks he's doing the right thing, warning me off. He believes you'll want me to set your family up here.'

He put one finger on her lips to still all further comment.

'I know, my love. And I have thought of it, which is why Ascony must be in on our discussions. I want it to be out in the open. I would like a loan for them, not charity. They'll pay back everything as soon as possible, or face the proper consequences. If you don't feel able to commit yourself—and I won't press you—we can find someone who will.'

He took her in his arms and held her close. 'And I don't intend to be idle, either. As well as helping Father, I intend to get myself a job. If Eban has no room for an extra apprentice then I shall find somewhere that has.'

Elena smiled up at him. 'Oh, but there's no need, my love...'

'There's every need. I want to be useful, not a drain on your charity.'

'And how will you like sharing a dormitory with young ruffians half your age?'

She giggled and Selest kissed her with slow, thoughtful gentleness.

'Perhaps the boss will take pity on me. I've heard she has very loving ways. She wouldn't send an old cripple off to a lonely bed every night, would she?'

'That rather depends...' She dissolved into a giggling heap as Emil began to nibble her neck.

'You know me, Elena. I've been known to injure myself for the chance of sleeping in a decent bed.'

Elena returned his kisses with a new eagerness, but Selest was more practical.

'Haven't you got a job to go to? There isn't time for loafing around if you're going to keep me in the manner to which I would like to become accustomed. Go on, woman. Off to make an honest penny.'

'Must I?'

He disentangled her fingers from his hair and kissed the tip of her nose.

'Yes. I'll still be here when you come back. Ascony and the Khars can busy themselves cooking up a special dinner, then you can break the news to them later if they haven't already guessed,' he finished ruefully. Elena pulled away from him and shook out the creases from her filmy overdress.

'Much as I hate to leave, I suppose somebody has to earn our daily bread. Anyway, there might be someone still waiting for me back at the shop.'

'Who is it?' Emil grabbed her playfully. 'I'll have his teeth for souvenirs.'

'I shouldn't think he had many left. It's only the Duke of Normandy.'

He stopped teasing her and looked grave. 'I told you to have nothing to do with him, Elena.'

'He was hot and bothered, so I gave him lemonade and the chance of a sit-down. That's all.'

'Hmm.' Selest was unimpressed. 'I'll walk to the shop with you and send him on his way rejoicing.'

'He's all right, Emil! Besides, every minute he was expecting to be tracked down by the other Normans. They've probably caught up with him by now.'

Selest was thoughtful for a moment, then decided that he should display a little trust.

'All right, sweetheart. If you consider that there is no risk then I respect your judgement. But just be sure you don't give him any more encouragement. An inch is as good as five miles to that scoundrel.'

# CHAPTER TWELVE

ELENA promised, but it did not seem to be necessary. When she arrived back at the shop the duke was no-where to be seen. Gulzun told her that Normandy had been found by his brother-in-law and taken back into custody.

The afternoon was a little busier at the shop. Elena packed up orders while Eban served. It was all she could do to resist the temptation of telling Hamelin the news. She thought it might come better from Selest, and wanted Milo and Hamelin together to be the first to know. Hamelin could be offered the chance of lodging with his new friends the apprentices at the same time.

Elena was so full of plans. Happiness bubbled up through her like lively wine. In the end Eban suggested she should leave early and enjoy the rest of the day in sunshine, not cooped up inside.

There were no outstanding orders to be packed and the workshop was clean and tidy enough so Elena agreed. As a wild extravagance she bought herself two mixed bunches of flowers from the girl outside and let the boys carry them home.

Nothing could match Elena's delight now. She hurried back along the Mese as quickly as the boys could go. Even those few people who never normally spoke were touched by her happiness. One look at her delightful expression encouraged everyone she met to pass the time of day. Elena thought that there could truly be no end to her happiness.

Until she rounded the corner into her own lane. It seemed choked with horses, men, carts and banners. What on earth did it mean? A fire? An accident?

The boys ran on ahead and were engulfed in the crowd. No, it couldn't be too much of a disaster. There were no Pechenegs about, only Crusaders. Norman banners dipped and fluttered over the heads of the crowd like exotic blooms.

Normandy. Elena started to run. Selest had been right—what a fool she had been! To give the duke directions to her house, to offer help—now he had been run to ground in her house and the place was under siege.

It was difficult to force a way through the herd of great war-horses and their owners jostling up against her front door. A fat boy sneered at her truculently when she asked him to move them aside and offered no help. In the end Hamelin managed to squeeze through the crowd and flick the door-knocker twice with the very tips of his fingers.

There was the sound of something heavy being thrust against the door, and Ascony's voice.

'No more! No more, I say! Go away, heathens!'

'Ascony, it's us! Let us in!'

There was a pause, then the sound of great iron bolts being slid back. It must be serious, Elena thought. The door might be locked but it was never, ever bolted.

She picked Milo up and managed to wriggle her way to the front, but when Ascony did open the door the press of men and horses forced Elena and the children through the gap with such speed that she almost bowled him over. Almost but not quite—for the crowding inside the house was almost as bad as that outside. Men and horses seemed to be everywhere. The animals were being led through to the greenery of the quadrangle while their owners admired the décor with expressions ranging from pleasure to shifty greed. They were drinking too—at least some of the noise was shouts for more wine and applause as it was found.

Ascony was thin-lipped with rage. Beneath the dusky olive tint of his skin he was as pale as Elena had ever seen him.

'Lady,' he said at last, when a cheerful thump on the back from one of the party forced words from him. 'Do you not consider that I am now and have always been a worthy servant to you?'

'Of course, Ascony. But——'

'But nothing, lady. I will serve you and your guests, but I would have thought that I deserved to be fore-warned of this . . . this . . .'

Words failed him. Together they looked helplessly at the laughing, shouting, clapping, cheering waves of men that lapped about the once-clean walls and immaculate floor.

'Oh, Ascony . . .' Elena whispered. 'What are we going to do?'

Two things happened as though in answer to her question. Selest strode out of his bedroom, on to the landing above the sea of Crusaders. On the ground floor the duke had spotted his benefactress and was making a bee-line towards her.

'Dear lady! How very nice to meet you again! Come along and have a little drink with us. I must say you have a very nice place here. Such a shame our landlord decided he couldn't put up with us any more. Still, jolly lucky you offered to help out, wasn't it?'

Elena was swept into the throng by her noble guest. Above her Selest was glowering down on the throng and Elena felt almost hopeless. All she could do was hope that it was all a terrible nightmare, and she would wake up.

It was not a dream. If it had been, then the sudden and horrifying harangue that leapt from the upstairs landing would have frightened her awake.

Thunderstruck, the crowd was silenced for a moment. Everyone gaped up at Selest's sudden tirade of abuse, then they all started to gabble their horror at such insults.

'I—said—shut—up!'

Selest thumped his fist on the banister rail with every word. The Duke of Normandy, who had been gaping like a smacked trout, was the first to regain his composure. He struggled to the foot of the marble staircase, his standard-bearer in tow.

'I won't be spoken to like this. I'll have you know that I'm the rightful King of England!'

'And I'm master in this house.'

The duke was not to be outdone and called in his brother-in-law as reinforcement.

'Tell him, Etienne!'

The Count of Blois was horrified at being dragged into the matter. He twittered nervously and tried to dissolve into the background.

Selest silenced them both with a glare. 'It is approximately twenty minutes' march from here to the court of the Emperor Alexius. You will take your motley crew from here and march them double-time to the palace. Once you are on the Mese it is dead ahead, so that not even you could fail to miss it, Your Grace. I'm sure the Emperor will be only too pleased to entertain you all. At any rate I will certainly be delighted if Alexius gets you off my back! Well—best foot forward, my lord! Unless you are away from these premises within the next two minutes I shall——'

'You'll what?' sneered the Duke of Normandy, remembering who he was at last and stepping forward, sword drawn. He was lent courage by the press of his entourage with their cries of, 'We are on the Lord's side!'

'Don't, my lords! Please—calm down and discuss the matter reasonably...' Elena began weakly, but shrivelled under Selest's furious scrutiny.

'I should think that you've already said enough, Elena. Enough to handicap yourself with this parasite. As for you, Normandy, unless you go right now I shall call the Pechenegs and have you evicted bodily.'

The crowd shuffled back at this, leaving the duke alone on the first step of the stairs.

'I'm more than a match for any bunch of foreign rabble!' he spat through clenched teeth. When others sprang into action, Normandy talked. When others had the sense to keep their heads down, Normandy rushed ahead regardless.

'Your Grace,' Selest said with heavy sarcasm, 'you are welcome to stand and fight but I fear it will be on your own.'

Several members of the duke's party were already sidling towards the door.

'Ha! Bring on your heathen hordes! The worse the odds, the better I like it!'

Normandy's trouble was that he was always too busy being keen. He never saw danger until he actually tripped over it.

Selest's voice rang through the emptying hall. 'What do you think of your gentle knight now, Lady Elena?'

Elena pressed her face to a cool marble column and closed her eyes. About her the crowd was melting away like snow in summer.

'I think——' Elena began in a small voice. 'I think that Franks are all ungrateful, pig-ignorant wretches with not one of you any better than you should be——'

'Oh, now! Don't take on so!' At once Normandy threw down his sword and rushed to Elena's side. Hauling up a corner of his Crusading whites, he dabbed at the tears that would keep spilling down her face no matter how hard she tried to stop them.

'What did he want to go and upset you for? He's a nasty man. A very nasty man indeed.'

'Me?' Selest was incensed. His rage increased as Normandy led Elena to the stairs where they sat down together.

'There, there, dear lady.' Normandy's solicitations knew no bounds. One arm around Elena's shoulders, the other hand patting her knee, he cooed comfortingly. 'Don't cry. I've got my eye on a little girl in Italy. If it's God's will that I return from the Holy City safely I'll pick you up on the way back and you can be a lady-in-waiting for her. How's that?'

Beside himself, Selest stamped down the stairs. The effect was rather spoiled when he had to clamber past the duke, but indignation more than made up for that.

'Normandy! Take your hands off my woman!'

The duke gave a deep, long sigh and pursed his lips. Giving Elena a little shrugging chuckle and a last pat, he stood up, bowing to her graciously.

Pulling himself up to his full height proved more impressive than usual, as Normandy was standing on the first step of the stairs. His nose was almost on a level with Selest's chin.

'Apologise at once, sir. I won't have such language used in front of a lady.'

The last few hangers-on scampered out at the confrontation, dragging their goods and chattels with them. Ascony grabbed the children and hustled them out too, before trouble started in earnest.

Of the Normans only Peverel the standard-bearer remained, dipping a red and gold banner dangerously about his master's head as he searched for an elusive Byzantine flea.

'Well? I'm waiting for your apology, rogue!'

'Oh, for pity's sake don't fight! I wish you would all go away and just leave me alone!' Elena stood up and without looking at either man came down the last step and started off towards the kitchen.

'Apologies, dear lady! I was merely trying to defend your honour...'

'Thank you. But I think that your presence will be expected at the palace with your men, my lord. Perhaps it would be better if you were to leave.'

'Why, of course.' Normandy suddenly remembered his dignity. Chubby face wreathed in smiles, he inclined his head to Elena then, with a trace more amusement, to Selest. 'Indeed, lady. The Emperor will be expecting me. Can't start the party without good old Robert, can they?' With an extravagant gesture he poked his forefinger into Selest's shoulder. 'Pardon me!'

Selest was so surprised at the affront that he moved aside and let Normandy pass. Just then Peverel caught his little irritation and the simultaneous dip of the royal standard caught Duke Robert a resounding crack on the skull. The standard-bearer's reward was to have his ears soundly boxed.

'Peverel! Why don't you ever look at what you're doing?'

Peverel's apology was lost in a whimpering crescendo as the ill-matched pair finally made their way to the front door and sunlit street beyond.

Selest wasted no time in following Elena to the kitchen. She was alone, the Khars having slipped out into the hall to right the ruin left by the Crusaders. She kept her back to him, chopping vegetables with rapid, angry movements.

'There—I told you that Normandy was trouble, didn't I? Still, no matter. He's gone now. Although he'll be back,' Selest added lightly. Elena did not reply. When he approached and put his hand on her shoulder she turned away savagely and marched over to a row of pots hung beside the fire.

'Both Normandy and his standard-bearer have left their horses in the quadrangle,' Selest ventured, trying to lighten the ominous atmosphere with a laugh.

Snatching one of the pots from its hook, Elena stalked past him to ladle in water from the kitchen tank. Without speaking she hurled handfuls of chopped cabbage into the pot with much splashing. Selest followed close behind her as she took the pot to the cooking range. Thinking that she was upset only by the visitors, he tweaked the ends of her hair in fun.

It was a mistake. Dropping the pot on to the hob with a crash, Elena turned on him. Her dark eyes were blazing with an unfamiliar fury, her whole body was taut with rage.

'You are not the master of this house. I am.'

Selest made his second mistake. He tried to contain her rage with his good humour.

'Hardly the master. More of a mistress, I'd say—ow!'

Elena had struck out at him, a savage blow connecting with his arm.

'And I am not your "woman".'

'But I thought——'

'Then you thought wrong. Out of my way!'

She barged past him, heedless of his dismay.

'Elena! Elena, come here! It was only a turn of phrase—I didn't mean it. Don't be cross!'

His pleas were in vain. Elena stormed out of the kitchen and through the hall to the staircase. The Khars pretended nothing was happening and carried on with their cleaning, even though Selest went after her. He was loudly proclaiming his innocence while avoiding the stigma of an actual apology. By the time he reached the landing Elena was steaming out of his room with an armful of clothes. These she tipped over the banister, immediately returning for another load.

'Elena, what are you doing?'

'Isn't it obvious?' she said through lips drawn into a thin line of rage. Selest's shield was the next thing to go over the banisters, then, dusting her hands ostentatiously, Elena went back into the guest room.

When the sound of furniture being dragged about was the only thing that emerged Selest took his life in his hands and went inside.

'Er—what are you doing?'

'What does it look like?' Elena balanced on a chair and began to take down the damask curtains. 'I always like a good spring-clean after we've had guests.'

'Then you do want me to go?'

'It would seem like that, yes.'

Released from its hooks, the first curtain slithered to the ground. The second followed it, then Elena turned her attention to the bed. Ripping off the covers in a few frenzied movements, she then started to wrestle the pillows from their embroidered cases.

Selest did not suffer overmuch from pride, but he wasn't a man to cave in at the first sign of a problem. He stood his ground. This problem had one very vulnerable point, and Selest attacked by probing its soft underbelly.

'What's going to happen to poor Hamelin?'

'You can ask him yourself, since it would seem you'll be lodging with him at the workshop until the next flotilla leaves for the holding camp. If he's bent on the folly of following you into battle—well, that's his decision. But if you'll let him see sense and he wants to stay here and work, all well and good.'

A loud rattling at the door-knocker sent both Elena and Selest out on to the landing. It was Normandy and Peverel again.

'Pardon us, dear lady. And you, sir,' the duke added haughtily. 'We appear to have been a touch forgetful. Peverel—fetch our horses, and make it snappy.'

'Fetch the horses and make it snappy,' Peverel chanted to himself, an innocent grin illuminating his features. Shouldering the royal standard, he narrowly missed beheading his liege lord.

'Oh, give me that!' Normandy snatched up the banner and fetched Peverel a stinging blow with it. 'Can't you do anything right today?'

Forgetting her own irritation, Elena complained at the duke's treatment of his standard-bearer. Peverel soon put her right.

'We're the best of friends, the duke and I. He's taught me everything I know. Isn't that right, Duke?'

'It certainly is——' Normandy began, but was cut short by a tapping at the door. With perfect good manners the duke answered it.

It was Ascony. He had brought Milo home again, but explained that Hamelin was still back at the shop. Milo was uncertain of the visitors, but Elena's voice reassured the little lad and he edged past Normandy to stand in the hall.

He watched Peverel leading the horses out of the quadrangle with suspicion rather than surprise. Then he transferred his attention to first the royal standard then the Duke of Normandy himself.

The duke chuckled and patted Milo indulgently on the head. A dubious cast crossed the child's features.

'Milo, come here!' Elena fled down the stairs and gathered Milo up with a kiss.

She was grateful for the relative peace of the kitchen to calm her temper. Milo mixed and shaped parsley scones under her watchful eye then Elena cooked them while sending Milo to collect eggs from the larder. These she cracked into the frying-pan with as much vigour as she would have used on Selest's head.

When the eggs were cooked she gave Milo his tea then put up scones on a plate over boiling water, covering it with a second plate. Calling Ascony to watch over Milo, she rose and went quickly out of the room.

The duke and Peverel had gone. Selest stood before the pile of jumbled belongings beneath the landing. He had found his kitbag and was busy stuffing things into it anyhow. Without pausing or looking at him, Elena threw aside a comment as she marched up to her room, sandals nipping at the cold marble.

'There's supper set up for you in the kitchen. It won't keep.'

'Suitably laced with ground glass, I assume.'

Elena's sandals clicked even more rapidly as she went up the stairs and rustled along the landing. Something in her manner must have struck Selest as surely as a blow would have done. He threw down his kitbag with a clatter and strode after her. Taking the stairs three at a time, he caught at Elena's arm as she reached the threshold of her room. Snatching her back, he forced her to look up at him. Ignited by rage, his eyes were no longer merry but fiercely accusing.

'All right! Hamelin and I leave for the holding camp on the first available ship. Does that satisfy your foolish pride? To know that in a matter of weeks we could be tortured and killed and left for kite fodder by the Turks?'

'Now you're being childish.'

His anger unnerved her, especially as he must have read the first wicked thoughts that she now regretted with all her heart. It was one thing to imagine that he deserved all that was coming to him, but quite another to have those hasty thoughts put into words.

'Childish? The girl who lives in an ivory tower calls me childish? Let me tell you, not even this ivory tower will save you, so divorced from the world that you can't spot a scoundrel when you see him!'

'Oh, can't I?' Elena cried. 'Well, it might have taken me some time, my lord Selest, but I've certainly spotted what you are now!'

'All right, then, what am I? You tell me. Go on! Am I less than a man because I'm still alive and not living on here in a shrine of memories?'

'Shut up!'

'Is that it? I'm nothing to you now, but if I go off and sacrifice myself I can have a memorial here where my shade can share with Henry as we both feed off the nectar and ambrosia of your youth?'

'Shut up! Shut up!' Anguish lent Elena the strength of ten. She wrenched out from his grasp, threw herself into her room and, slamming the door, collapsed against it.

He did not try to follow her, to prolong the agony. Elena sobbed noisily, telling herself that she didn't care whether or not he heard. She cried for a long time—or at least she tried to. When abject grief had finally dragged her down to lie on the marble tiled floor, Elena admitted the truth to herself.

After the first horror of his death, few of her tears had been for Henry. They had all been shed through self-pity, not loss and longing. 'What am I going to do now?' tears. 'However am I going to pay off these debts?' tears. She hadn't even had the decency to weep for poor fatherless Milo. She had called on his father's name, certainly, but only in her rage at Milo's mischief. Elena saw now that her one preoccupation first, last and always had been with herself.

Dragging herself to her feet, she went to the washstand, her movements made awkward from the chill of the floor. After bathing away the remains of her makeup she straightened her hair, adjusted her gown and went out on to the landing.

The hall was deserted and silent. Looking over the banister rail, she saw that the heap of belongings below had disappeared. As she hesitated on the cool landing a breeze creaked open the front door, which had been left ajar.

He was gone.

Elena expected him back every moment. He hadn't eaten his tea. Surely he would be back for that?

He was not. His dinner, too, lay waiting until the water beneath it had boiled away and Mrs Khar slipped it quietly into the gutter-pail.

As dusk fell and the lamps were lit Elena went to sit in the dining-room. Looking out over the garden, she was constantly reminded of their first meeting. How her feelings for him had changed since then. And now time was slipping away from them like sand in a glass.

Half unnoticed, Milo crept in. With a smile Elena pulled him on to her lap, and for the first time in ages he was glad of the affection.

As the shadows grew deeper he took his finger out of his mouth and pushed his face against her neck.

'Mummy, why hasn't Hammy come back?'

There was no point in hiding what could already be the truth.

'He's going off to be a soldier, sweetheart.'

Milo chewed on his soggy finger for a while, then turned large, limpid eyes on his mother.

'Why?'

'He is a Frank, and that is how they spend their time. Playing rough boys' games.'

'Hammy wouldn't play soldiers with me. Ascony says it upsets him.' Milo sighed, then gave a truculent sneer. 'Hammy's silly.'

Elena shook him gently in reproof. 'Now! You get upset when I wash your hair, but I don't tease you about that, do I?'

'No, Mummy.'

'Then you shouldn't tease Hamelin.'

Not that you'll get the chance again, Elena thought, then patted Milo on the back.

'Come on, then, my little soldier. Let's march up the marble hill and do battle with the bedclothes.'

Milo was missing Selest as much as Elena was, and grizzled at having to go back to his mother's room.

Elena had plenty of time to think while Milo got ready for bed and said his prayers crossly. The argument with Selest might have brought Elena to her senses, but she still had a remnant of pride left. She would apologise, of course, but it wouldn't do to seem forward. No, let Selest stew in his own juice, just for tonight. Ascony had told her that there were no ships due to leave that day. He would still be in the city.

Elena wasn't going to go running back to him yet. She was sure to see him when she went to the shop the next morning.

Elena slept little and rose very early the next morning. Leaving Ascony in charge at home, she slipped out into the dawn-dusted streets.

Bakers were already piling hot, fragrant bread into baskets to mark out their pitches between the colonnade of the Mese. Elena stopped at the cleanest and chose a large sweet cake studded with almonds and rich with spices. A peace-offering.

As the baker wrapped her purchase Gulzun came tumbling into the shop breathless with excitement and bangles jingling.

'Just coming to fetch you—wherever have you been? Come on! Everyone's down at the docks already...'

A crawling fear began to work its way over Elena.

'Normandy and Blois can't be leaving already—they've only just got here...'

'No, silly. Oh, but have I got things to tell you about Normandy. He's certainly opened my eyes, that's for sure! Now I know why all the women go stupid over him——'

She rolled her eyes at the memory but Elena brought her back to the present with a jolt.

'What's happening at the docks?'

Gulzun clung to her arm as Elena told the baker to keep the change.

'Well, even though Normandy and Blois are supposed to be the very last group, the Emperor's getting a bit touchy in case more hordes descend. He's put on a few extra boats for loiterers left over from the previous gangs. When I saw Emil and Hamelin going down to the quay as I was leaving Normandy's party, of course, I asked them where you were.'

'What did they say?'

'Emil said that Henry doesn't let you out on your own.'

Elena had been feeling apprehension and fear. Now she only felt indignant.

'Oh, he did, did he? Well, as from now all that is changing. I'm my own woman and neither Emil Selest nor anyone else will be able to say otherwise. Come on.'

Elena marched to the shop, ready to donate her peace-offering cake to the workers before going off to give Emil another piece of her mind. She had another shock in store. The workshop was very nearly deserted.

'Where is everybody?'

Eban stood as she entered, brushing wood shavings from his apron. He looked uncomfortable and worried.

'Down at the docks, lady. I—I hope you don't mind, but I let them go seeing as how the little lad was so upset——'

Gulzun clucked in sympathy and Elena placed the spice cake on the counter.

'Poor Hamelin. He didn't want to go, did he?'

'Indeed no, lady. He cried all night and looked like a little ghost this morning, he did.'

'I can't let him be taken.' Elena clenched her fists. 'Emil's got no right to torture Hamelin just to get back at me.'

Gulzun grinned. 'I knew there must be something. Had a row and now he's gone off in a huff to spite you?'

'Something like that,' Elena muttered, then, leaving the cake with Eban, hurried off towards the dock. It was all Gulzun could do to keep up with her.

People were already scurrying and swarming down to the quay. The sight of ships ready to leave drew them like a magnet, especially when it was the brave boys going off to fight for the Holy Cause. It mattered little to the Byzantines that only hours earlier their 'brave boys' might have been breaking up taverns, brawling in the streets and chasing all the women. Last night they had been cursed nuisances. This morning they were heroes to a man.

Men from the imperial guard stood in a cordon around a snaking shuffle of men queuing for the narrow gangplank to embark. The watching crowd was good-natured enough and needed no forceful restraint. They were happy enough to accept money or valuables from Crusaders suddenly struck by remorse at their previous bad behaviour.

Many were so eager to make amends that the line of Crusaders frequently came to a standstill while apologies were made. For their part the Byzantines were equally eager to make amends, but on a more spiritual basis. Forests of arms thrust out money and tokens to be taken as offerings to the Holy City.

If all the tokens did actually get laid in front of the altar, Gulzun said, giggling, no one would be able to get into the church.

Everyone except Elena was joyous with noise. She seemed the only one untouched by the party atmosphere.

'Look—there they are!' Gulzun jabbed Elena in the ribs and pointed through the waving arms in front of them.

Selest and Hamelin were within five yards of the gangplank. Once there the log-jam of bodies would make certain that there could be no turning back.

Hamelin was nearest to them. Beside the hale and hearty form of Selest and the other towering Franks he looked even smaller and younger than ever. Selest bent to jolly him along with a laugh but Hamelin took little notice of his surroundings. Head down, he was staring at his feet. Elena was sure that she saw his shoulders heave as though he was trying not to give way to tears again. That and the thought that Selest might be off to his death thinking that she did not care nearly broke Elena's heart.

'Let me through! I must get to them!' Elena plunged into the crowd, fighting against the torrent of people. Ahead of her the queue moved on, leaving a space in front of Hamelin. There were only two more yards to go before they reached the gangplank.

A dog yelped as Elena accidentally trod on it in her urgency. She could not get through the crush. Several people deliberately barred her way, not understanding her frenzy, and despite her tearful pleas there was no way through to the queue. Jammed in securely between a fat, perspiring eunuch and a brood of young children, all Elena could do was shout.

Her voice was one of thousands, all as insistent and urgent. Only when she was nearly hoarse did Selest turn and scan the crowds on their side of the queue. All pride gone, Elena leapt up and down, waving frantically. He was looking straight towards her. He must see her! He must!

Selest turnéd away and was lost to sight. Another two steps now and he would be on the gangplank and out of reach, perhaps forever. There was nothing more that she could do.

'Come on. I'll take you home.'

Somehow Gulzun had managed to fight her way to Elena's side and slipped her arm about her friend.

'They'll be all right, you'll see. What is it—nothing but a cock's stride from here to Jerusalem? Then they'll be back, quick as a flash.'

With one last look back Elena tried to pick out the tall, proud figure of Selest, but it was impossible. The crowd was too thick, the cause too hopeless. She had seen the last of poor Hamelin, for certain, and as for Selest . . . How could she ever explain how she really felt now? She had seen her last hope of happiness slip away.

The streets were practically deserted. Chickens shuffled about, scratching up clouds of dust in the search for scraps. A dog lifted its head as Gulzun and Elena passed, its heavy chain clanking in the silence.

'I suppose—I'd better go and check on the shop,' Elena said quickly. She had been unable to disguise the tremble in her voice and Gulzun looked at her.

'He said he would be back,' the Turkish girl said firmly. 'And you were the one who turned him away, remember? Don't start piping your eye now, after what you've done to him.'

Elena gulped and spoke with artificial brightness. 'I was worried about Milo at first. To keep him safe and secure I would have denounced Roland himself. Then——'

Gulzun laughed and linked arms with her friend. 'Then you'll just have to be patient and wait for them to come back, won't you?'

'But it's so dangerous—I've heard such stories...'

'Pooh! What makes Emil so special that the Seljuk single him out of that great multitude? No, don't answer that!'

Gulzun laughed again, but they continued their journey in silence. Passing through patchworks of light and shade dappling the warrens of streets, they walked slowly back to the shop.

The staff were all standing about inside. Considering that they had all been so fond of Hamelin, Elena was immediately suspicious to find them back so quickly. Their expressions of astonished pleasure as the two girls entered the shop also put her on her guard.

'Why aren't you all still down at the docks?'

Everyone muttered at once until Joshua emerged as spokesman.

'We thought it best to hurry back quickly, madam, knowing that you were so eager to get the current orders out——'

'Don't give me that.' Elena strolled about the shop, pausing at a packing case here, a pile of woodshavings there. Every eye in the place was upon her.

Lifting a finely formed water jug from its nest of shavings, Elena flicked it idly with her finger. The ringing tone echoed through the workshop.

'Now that Hamelin's gone I suppose you'll want another youngster to take his place, Eban.'

'Might be an idea, lady,' Eban muttered, staring at the floor.

'Is that what all this is about? Making out that you've got far too much work on? You want a pay rise, is that it?'

A chorus of denial met this. Elena happened at this point to turn her steps towards the large wooden counter. Immediately three young apprentices materialised in front of it, and Elena knew she had been right to be suspicious.

'You've got something hidden under the counter.' Her eyes narrowed and she scrutinised Eban. He withered. 'It isn't a private job, using my materials and time, is it?'

'Of course not!' The chorus was genuine enough. Eban had been stung into recovery and the rest of the staff muttered at the very suggestion.

'Let me see what you've got behind the counter, then.'

No one moved. Only when Elena strode forward did the apprentices slink aside and let her pass. Their expressions convinced Elena that whatever they had hidden would warrant a life sentence at the very least.

Elena bent down, took one look beneath the counter then beckoned for Gulzun to join her.

'I can explain, lady. It was my idea...'

Elena laughed Joshua's plea aside. Hamelin was curled up in a ball on a shelf beneath the counter, eyes squeezed shut.

'Oh, poor little chap. It seems a pity to disturb him when he's fast asleep. And when we've got gingerbread for tea, too——'

Hamelin's eyes shot open and he grinned. Elena offered him her hand and with her help he clambered out of his hiding-place.

'We saw how upset he was down at the docks, lady,' Joshua said apologetically. 'Poor little lad was breaking his heart. We couldn't let him go. As soon as my lord Selest turned his back for a minute we enticed him away.'

'What did you intend doing? Hiding him in the loft and feeding him on scraps?'

Suddenly Hamelin let out a wail and dived back under the counter. He was just in time. Selest dashed into the shop, pale and breathless.

'I've lost him! Elena—you've got to get your people to help look...he could be anywhere!'

Torn between the relief of knowing that Hamelin was really safe and the pain of seeing Selest again, Elena had to steel herself to speak again.

'After our last meeting, my lord, I would have thought you would be offering apologies, not orders.'

'That child could be lying dead or injured somewhere!'

'And instead you want us to find him so that he can lie dead or injured on some foreign battlefield?'

Selest marched towards the door. 'You won't help, then. Fine. You're content to deprive him of the chance of making something of his wretched life. Instead of glory you want him left behind to beg in the streets——'

'Oh, now you know that isn't true!'

'He starved before, when he was on his own. This time it will be all down to you.'

He stamped out and on to the Mese. Standing in the middle of the highway, hands on hips, he looked first one way, then the other.

'Now's your chance,' Gulzun whispered in Elena's ear. 'Go out and make it up between you.'

'I don't know if I can.' Elena played for time.

'Another five minutes and you'll have lost him again. He'll be down to the quay and gone who knows where.'

'Er...' Elena dithered, but someone else had already leapt into action. Hamelin darted from his hiding-place and out on to the Mese. He stopped dead a few feet behind Selest and waited for his friend to turn around.

All the staff crowded to the doorway to watch. After seeing Selest give Hamelin a hug of genuine rapture, they waited while the boy chattered away busily for some time. The two Franks were some way from the shop, so the conversation details were lost to their audience.

Finally the apprentices could stand it no longer. They tumbled out of the shop and begged that their little friend be allowed to stay.

Selest seemed almost overwhelmed by the reception. His hopeless gaze searched out Elena and he beckoned to her.

'My lady? If I could speak to you for a moment?' Every ear strained at his words. 'In private.'

Meekly Elena followed him out to the other side of the Mese, where they wouldn't be disturbed. Hamelin had disappeared beneath his friends, and a cheer told Elena that Hamelin at least would be staying in the city.

'I don't think that this is going to be easy for either of us,' Selest said in a low voice. 'I—I spoke hastily yesterday. I'm sorry, Elena.'

Elena felt warmth creeping up to her face. 'That's all right.'

'No, it isn't. It will never happen again.'

'W-what did Hamelin say to you?' she cut in quickly, hardly daring to read hope in his words.

'He suggested that you might have something to say to *me*.'

Elena floundered about for an age. She seemed unable to find the right words, or indeed any words at all.

'I'm glad you're going to look after him, Elena. The boy needs a mother.'

There was still nothing that Elena could say. She wanted to burst out that Hamelin needed a father too, but that wouldn't have conveyed all that she felt.

'Mind you,' Selest continued, drawing lines in the dust with the toe of his boot, 'you'll have to be careful that those two boys don't grow up too soft. You do tend to be a bit over-protective, Elena. Boys ought to be able to take care of themselves. It might be better if you were to find yourself a husband to be a father to them.'

There was a long pause. Elena watched the patterns that he was drawing and thought she recognised the shape.

'He'd have to be firm, but fair,' Selest continued. 'A steady sort, but young enough to understand the little rascals. And if he was well travelled, strikingly handsome, modest with it and had a full set of newly acquired table manners—well, do you have anyone in mind for the post, lady?'

Elena was quiet for so long that at last Selest slipped his arm about her waist and drew her to him. There was an excited mutter from the direction of the shop, but she did not hear it.

'This is evidently not the time for jokes, Elena. More direct action is called for, so I'll make things easier for you. Will you marry me?'

A roar from away down at the quay announced that the last ship had set off across the Bosphorous.

'What about the Crusade?'

'Blow that.' In a deft movement he ripped the red cross from his shoulder, then kissed her with long, lingering sweetness. 'There. Has that made up your mind?'

Oblivious to the applause from her shop, Elena looked up into his steady brown eyes. A mischievous grin was playing about his lips.

'There will be a lot to discuss,' she pretended to frown, 'breaking the news to Ascony, sending for your family, telling mine...perhaps another kiss would help me make up my mind, lord?'

A little breeze gambolled up the Mese from the sea, tugging at a cloak here, fine linen there. No one paid it any attention. Tired of being ignored, the breeze picked up a little red cross from the road and bowled it far away in a flurrying, flickering dance.

The other exciting

## MASQUERADE
### *Historical*

**available this month is:**

# DEEP WATERS
## *Victoria Aldridge*

Trapped in a small enclave of Swedish whalers on the northern tip of New Zealand, by the death of her adoptive parents, Jara Perrault knew it was only a matter of time before she was drawn into an unsavoury life.

The providential arrival of Captain Kit Montgomery, looking for a crew to sail to Macao in China, gave Jara her chance. Persuading Kit to take her on board as the cook was reasonably easy. Discovering the crew were violent convicts was something else – only Kit's protection could save her.

But Kit harboured secrets, and their destination proved a revelation in more ways than Jara expected!

**Look out for the two intriguing**

## MASQUERADE *Historical*

**Romances coming next month**

# DEAR REBEL

## Mary Nichols

Like many men in his position, Lord Carthorne was more concerned to protect his property, the lovely manor of Waterlea in the Fens of East Anglia, than to take sides in the escalating war between Charles I and his Parliament.

So he had no hesitation about using the childhood betrothal between his daughter Alys and Cromwell's captain, Sir Garret Hartswood, to get out of trouble. This was an enormous shock to Alys, who had forgotten the betrothal, and was a fervent Cavalier to boot! There seemed to be no escape from Garret's relentless intention to honour the agreement . . .

# NOBLE BUCCANEER

## Yvonne Purves

*Debtor's prison – or marriage to a stranger!*

Elena Worth agreed to marry Anthony Drew, an East India trader living in Malaysia. But on arrival, after a long and arduous journey, she discovered Anthony was dead – and that he had willed her to Dutchman Lord Stephan Van Coen!

Trapped on Lord Stephan's island, Elena was horrified to learn that everyone there was involved with piracy – but even with every course of action seemingly blocked, Elena refused to admit defeat . . .

**Available in November**

# TWO
## HISTORICAL
## ROMANCES

Masquerade historical romanc
bring the past alive with splendo
excitement and romance. We w
send you a cuddly teddy bear a
a special MYSTERY GIFT. Then,
you choose, you can go on to enjo
more exciting Masquerades every tv
months, for just £1.75 each! Se
the coupon below at once to – Read
Service, FREEPOST, PO Box 23
Croydon, Surrey CR9 9EL.

# &

# TWO
## FREE GIFTS!

- - - - - - - - - **NO STAMP REQUIRED** - - - - - - ⟶

**Yes!** Please rush me my 2 Free Masquerade Romances and 2 Free Gifts!
Please also reserve me a Reader Service Subscription. If I decide to
subscribe, I can look forward to receiving 4 Masquerade Romances every tw
months for just £7.00, delivered direct to my door. Post and packing is free,
and there's a free Newsletter. If I choose not to subscribe I shall write to yo
within 10 days - I can keep the books and gifts whatever I decide. I can
cancel or suspend my subscription at any time. I am over 18.

Mrs/Miss/Ms/Mr _____ EP93

Address _____

_____ Postcode _____

Signature _____

# *Experience the thrill of 2 Masquerade Historical Romances Absolutely Free!*

*Experience the passions of bygone days
in 2 gripping Masquerade Romances - absolutely free!
Enjoy these tales of tempestuous love from
the illustrious past.
Then, if you wish, look forward to a regular supply of
Masquerade, delivered to your door!
Turn the page for details of 2 extra FREE gifts,
and how to apply.*

# An irresistible offer for you

Here at Reader Service we would love you to become a regular reader of Masquerade. And to welcome you, we'd like you to have two books, a cuddly teddy and a MYSTERY GIFT - ABSOLUTELY FREE and without obligation.

Then, every two months you could look forward to receiving 4 more brand-new Masquerade Romances for just £1.75 each, delivered to your door, postage and packing is free. Plus our free newsletter featuring competitions, author news, special offers offering some great prizes, and lots more!

This invitation comes with no strings attached. You can cancel or suspend your subscription at any time, and still keep your free books and gifts.

Its so easy. Send no money now. Simply fill in the coupon below at once and post it to - Reader Service, FREEPOST, PO Box 236, Croydon, Surrey CR9 9EL.

## NO STAMP REQUIRED

Yes! Please rush me my 2 Free Masquerade Romances and 2 Free Gifts! Please also reserve me a Reader Service Subscription. If I decide to subscribe, I can look forward to receiving 4 brand new Masquerade Romances every two months for just £7.00, delivered direct to my door. Post and packing is free, and there's a free Newsletter. If I choose not to subscribe I shall write to you within 10 days - I can keep the books and gifts whatever I decide. I can cancel or suspend my subscription at any time. I am over 18.

Mrs/Miss/Ms/Mr _____ EP94

Address _____

_____

_____ Postcode _____

Signature _____

mps MAILING PREFERENCE